Tribalism

Truth Between the Lies

Printed in the United States of America

First edition *2014*
ISBN No. **0-9744423-3-X Paperback**

ebook **ISBN No.** 9781458193391

SouthernGirl Publishing

Tribalism

Truth Between the Lies

Clarence Mason Weaver

Chapter One
Face to face with reality!

BANG!

Jordan fell to the ground, he realized that he had been shot. The weeds and dead grass of the field were coarse against his skin, but the warm blood soaking his clothes and hair was actually comforting; he had not felt warmth in so long. He mustered enough strength to roll over onto his back. With eyes wide open, Jordan saw his mother flailing about frantically, running towards him, and he could hear her screaming, "They shot my boy! They shot Jordan!" His mother's face began to get cloudy, and as his vision faded, he could hear his girlfriend Iris calling out to him. But things slowly got quieter until he could not really hear anything at all. Jordan was dying in this open field called "The Pass", and there was nothing that he or anyone else could do about it. His fourteen short years of life flashed before him. As he drifted away, his heartbeat became louder and louder in his ears; it raced like a horse in full gallop. Various decisions he made all week, all his life, had set him on this journey. Choices had produced unseen results. Jordan was coming face to face with his reality. How did he get here? He remembered now; it all started last Friday.

FRIDAY JUNE 8, 2007

"Pass the blunt, Jay-Low." Jordan reached out from the couch to his tall, wiry framed older friend Jay-Low who stood by the old television, inhaling as if it was his last breath. They were downstairs in the basement of Jay-Low's home, and his grandmother was upstairs in her room. Jordan could barely make out Jay-Low's silhouette in the dimly lit, grungy basement, and the gray haze of weed smoke did not make it any easier. Once upon a time this basement was a warm and inviting place, well decorated and full of character. After Jay-Low began to hang out there, everything seemed to just deteriorate; soon it was nothing more than an ugly, dirty, unkempt incubator for trouble. There was a cooler in the corner for beer and an old coffee table in front of the couch that served as an ashtray and a resting place for their feet. A dimly lit room with no telephone and only a bare light bulb hanging from the ceiling was enough for these guys. The basement was their hangout. It was a place where they could gather with their friends and not be bothered.

Jordan, Jay-Low and the other members of the drug ring were taking a little relaxation before they hit the corner. Jordan was a typical gangster, drug dealer, tough guy. He ran with the bad crowd and liked it.

Jordan thought he was hard. He considered that a compliment and a high achievement. Living in a rough neighborhood full of thugs and thieves, having a reputation was very important. Being only 14 years old and already a gang leader gave him status and a good deal of respect in the neighborhood.

He dropped out of school because of disciplinary problems. Jordan could not stand adults telling him what to do and getting nothing out of it. So, he got a job; robbing people and selling dope. Jordan had no problem hurting someone if it was part of the job; however, his main objective was to move the drugs. It was easy, profitable, and only required a little violence. Despite his fierce determination to do the wrong thing, Jordan had people around him who tried very hard to keep him out of trouble. His mother, uncle, and even the family preacher did and said all they knew how to, but Jordan did not listen because they did not understand. Jordan expected to spend most of his life in prison - and that was alright with him.

They divided the cocaine and marijuana before heading out to their corner to sell. As Jordan took a hit on the blunt, he observed the table in front of him. The otherwise regal, oak finish coffee table was full of cocaine, tiny plastic baggies, crack pipes, and thousands of dollars in cash. There was also a 45-caliber pistol and a clip. Jordan took a long toke on the blunt before he reached out and grabbed a roll of twenty-dollar bills from off of the table. There was over a thousand dollars in that roll, and it was only one of many. "Man, I wish this was all my money!" Jordan exclaimed, holding the roll up to the light. "Yeah? Well everyone thinks it's your money already." Jay-low growled back as he took the money out of Jordan's hands and tossed it back on the table.

"Ever since you got your punk behind caught last month and showed your behind on the evening news, everyone thinks you're getting paid out here. They saw the cops pull you off the corner and empty your pockets of all my money. The stupid news bragged about you having three thousand dollars in your pocket. They want all those lazy behind people watching to think you're making all that money on the block." Jay-Low was obviously angry about the incident, but Jordan was so busy reminiscing, he did not even realize it.

Jordan thought back to that night that the cops showed up. Cop cars pulled up to the corner in marked and unmarked cars with dogs and guns out. Jordan and the others began to run; he made it to field called 'The Pass' and ran into the darkness. He knew the field offered a way to freedom. He thought getting to the creek would confuse the dogs so that he could escape to the other side.

Jordan, running as fast as he could through the trees and brush, had only his knowledge of the field to his advantage. He had to hurry before they let the dogs loose. He could not get caught; just a little bit further and he could escape the noose they were waiting to slip around his neck. As his heart beat faster and faster, he tried to think of his next step. Was that rock just around the corner? Did the path meet the creek around here? He was running in pitch-black night to get away from the police, but they were closing in on him. He could hear their footsteps getting closer and closer. He could feel the vibrations from their steps pounding on the dirt path behind him. "Stop! Stop!" They shouted. "Stop or we will turn the dogs loose!"

That was Jordan's fear; he could not outrun or out hide the dogs. He had to get to the creek before they let the dogs loose and before the helicopters arrived. If he could get to the other side, he could blend in with the people walking down the street and even take cover in one of the businesses. But these guys were so fast; how could they be catching him? He was younger and stronger, and they had all of that equipment around their hips. How could they be catching up with him?

Jordan was running full speed in a complete panic when one of the officers leaped onto his back and brought him down in a cloud of dust. "You're under arrest!" the officer said, as the others soon joined in and piled onto his back. "Place your hands behind your back and stop struggling." As Jordan tried to comply, he worried about the police dogs that were straining at their leashes trying to get to him.

His heart was pounding and sweat was rolling down his face. He was caught; they had him. He was going to be a prisoner. They would take away his freedom and treat him any way they wanted. He was no longer the strong; he was weak. They took Jordan back to the streets where they had started the chase. The camera crews were out and the helicopters were flying around. Jordan was placed face first into the hood of a police car. His pockets were emptied and hundreds of dollars fell onto the ground.

Jordan leaned back to take another hit and smiled. "Yeah, three thousand dollars in my pocket, but we still have to buy more and pay off each other. Man, by the time we get more product and prepare it, we have only a few dollars for ourselves. We make more money just taking if off the punks on the street. At least then, we get to keep it all instead of working for the supplier. If I made all of that money, you think I would still be living with my mom in that Cracker Jack house? Man, I would be living downtown in a nice condo, partying every night with a house full of women." As the smoke floated up into the air, Jordan began to think aloud. "There has to be a better way for us to make this money. We're the ones taking all of the risk, going to jail, and getting shot at, while the supplier is living where we want to live, and has no risk. Why can't we be him? What's stopping us from getting others to sell for us so we can sit back and collect the money?"

Jay-Low, as the oldest and the unofficial leader of the group, understood Jordan's question; but also understood the answer. He had been in jail, and knew he would go back for a long time if caught again. That is why he did not go out on the corner to sell. He sent the younger members out like Jordan because they were juveniles and would not get hard time if caught. He understood the problem Jordan was bringing up. His crew was getting older and needed more money to keep them interested. They had only a few options; expand their territory, change their product line, or branch out into other activities.

Expanding into others' territory would invite a gang war, and changing products to include prostitution or pills meant finding new suppliers and trusting new people. Branching out into other activities like robbing, burglary, or even extortion would bring all sorts of problems. There was no thought about opening a real business. Legitimate business people were the prey for people like Jay-Low. The gang would never even think about opening a nightclub or store. That is where you went to spend and take money, not make money.

To the younger gang bangers, Jay-Low was an apt leader, although physically he was awkwardly tall, lanky, and weakly. His hair was short and soft, and he sported a fresh scar across his forehead delivered by Jordan's uncle, Thomas. Jay-Low was a high school drop out who was intelligent, but lacked ambition. He believed everything should benefit him. Jay-Low was very self-centered and had an ego the size of Texas. He thought he was smarter than anyone else around, and has little patience for anyone who disagreed with that assessment. Jay-Low believed a life of crime to be the only option available to him, and he intended to use it to the fullest benefit for himself and only himself. While he enjoyed the company of Jordan and the others, he had no real loyalty to them or anyone else.

He had been arrested and secretively tried to turn on Jordan and the others. He did not have anything the District Attorney wanted, but was willing to give up his associates if it meant a benefit to him. Jay-Low wanted the best in life, but did not expect to have to work for it.

Both Jay-Low and Jordan spent time in jail over the drug case. Jordan was taken to juvenile hall and booked. They took away his clothes and examined him in ways he never wanted to talk about again. Then they made him shower with other men and put on ugly clothes. All the time they had Jordan chained up like some dog. He only spent a few days there awaiting trial, but the total lack of freedom really got to him.

Juvenile detention had television that others controlled, food that others controlled, and a bed and roof over his head that others controlled. Jordan had dropped out of school because he had trouble with authority just to end up in a place with total authority over him. Juvenile hall was not a hard place to be, it just provided you with absolutely no control over your life. What Jordan feared most in life was the loss of control. To have others exercising power over him was the greatest humiliation he could imagine. He really did not want to go back, but also did not want to stop gang banging. He thought, 'there must be a smarter way to avoid one and keep the other.' However, until he figured it out, he decided to keep on gang banging with Jay-Low, taking the risk.

Jay-Low needed money, but never thought about actually getting a job. He did not understand the eagerness of some men his age who were actively seeking employment. A job to Jay-Low was a surrender of his dignity and pride to slave for someone else. Working was an attempt by the system to keep people so busy with their daily chores they would not see how much the system was abusing them. Employment was a sign of weakness. So were the concepts of taking care of a woman, educating his children and protecting his community. Jay-Low hung around with other guys who thought the same way he did, and they all had established this notion that employment was negative. It was more desirable to his circle to hustle than to have a job. If you rode down his street between six and seven o'clock in the morning you would see two things: you would see women at the bus stop heading to work and men on the corner hustling for money.

This separation of labor in impoverished communities causes both sexes to resent each other and the divide continues to grow. Men think the working woman considers herself better than her non-working man. She resents taking care of him and wishes he would help her and join in the work force with her. He takes her money and eats her food, but tries to disregard her work efforts. He claims to be looking for work occasionally, but no one will hire him. He has all of the excuses; a criminal record, no skills or experience, and a lack of education. He then justifies his criminal activity, lack of credit, and lack of retirement and health plans with a magical force called 'They'. 'They' will not let a Black man get ahead, 'they' will not let you start a business, and of course, 'they' will not give you a loan or credit cards. If one listened to Jay-Low long enough, one would easily understand why he gave more credit to 'they' than to himself.

Jay-Low was a nineteen-year-old high school drop out with no job experience and a criminal record. He had to justify his beliefs because that was all he would ever have in life. He was a hustler! He would hustle women for a place to stay, men for his prostitutes, addicts for their fixes, and other gang members like Jordan to sell for him. He knew he would spend more time in jail and would eventually hurt someone or be killed by someone. He saw his old high school friends that had moved on. Some had gone to college and were working on their careers; others had gone into the work place to deal with the society. And then some were like him and Jordan, conscientiously turning down the system and putting up walls they did not know would work against them.

These old classmates were clear evidence that Jay-Low's belief systems were not accurate, but he refused to consider any other alternatives. He had had friends who sat in class with him, got the same bad grades, and never studied but still decided that they needed to get into college. They started with junior college and were moving on to four-year colleges. It was hard for them to make such huge turnarounds, but they were succeeding. Of course, Jay-Low thought they were "sellouts" because those guys did not hang out on the corner with him. They were always busy studying or going to class. What a bunch of losers they were turning out to be.

Right as Jay-Low was about to respond to the youngster's question, his grandmother opened the door at the top of the stairs and called down, "Jay, I'm going to the store and then to the doctor's. I need you to come here and lock up the house." She contemptuously fanned the pale gray smoke from her face as she spoke. Her frustration with Jay-low and his friends was not a secret, but she had given up on controlling his activities. She did not like the young men in her basement at all hours of the day and night, but she knew it would cause trouble if she tried to stop them. As long as they did not bring their mess upstairs and kept quiet downstairs, she could tolerate it. Granny was a good church going woman, but the block she lived on was rough and violent, and the only people on the streets were people like her grandson. She knew her home would never be broken into with these young men downstairs, but she also knew that she could be a target of gang attacks from rival members. She feared for her grandson; he had been arrested before, and she spent most of her savings to get him a lawyer. Now she was so poor she could not move, own a car, or have any comforts. Her grandson's criminal case had caused the entire family to fall deeper into debt. Everyone was hurt except Jay-Low.

Jay-Low made a lot of money selling his dope, but never offered to pay his grandmother back for his attorney fees. He didn't pay rent or any of the other bills around the house, either. Because Jay-Low was a criminal, he did not have any form of identification, so he couldn't get a credit card, driver's license or a loan. He depended on relatives like Granny to take him places and buy things he needed. He had handicapped his adulthood by not participating in society. Granny knew that, but could not help him. She just wanted him to leave, even if it meant him going back to jail.

Granny's real name was Brynda. She may have been a grandmother, but at age fifty-seven, she was still a good looking woman. Brynda never married, but her tall, slender physique and flawless, dewy skin always captured the attention of men. Everything about her was smooth; even her short, silky hair bounced in rhythm when she walked. Brynda paced about all day, singing to herself. She didn't sing because she was talented, but as a way of escape. She loved life, but life had not loved her back. In her youth, Brynda had goals for herself; she wanted an education and a career. But she had a baby girl when she was eighteen and did not go to college. Her daughter died of a drug overdose when Jay-Low was three years old and Brynda took him in. There were few men in her circle, and most were undesirable. Church was just a place for the old women to gather, friends were people to borrow money from, and hope was a long lost companion.

She would not spend another dime getting him out of jail. She could not have any friends over because of his unruly behavior, no decent man would talk to her, she frequently found herself up all night worrying, and things were only getting worse. The neighborhood had gone down so much that no one from the outside would buy a home there, so she could not move. The insurance rates were so high that even though the house was paid for, she still could barely make the payments. Brynda was basically a prisoner in her own home.

Jay-Low sucked his teeth and sighed at her request. He wished his grandmother would leave him alone. She was always embarrassing him in front of the guys. She knew all of them since they were little, so she tried to act like their mother sometimes. "Okay, I'll come up in a minute. We're busy," he barked back. His grandmother's patience was wearing thin. "You're not that busy; put down the dope and come lock my doors! I also need you to walk me to the bus stop on Elm Street. It's too late to catch the bus on the corner, so I have to walk the six blocks to Elm Street and I do not like walking alone. Let's go!" Brynda shouted back, and she expected her word to be final…for once.

"What?" Jay-Low protested. "Woman I don't have time to walk you six blocks and back. Why don't you just cut through 'The Pass' right over to Elm Street? It is the fastest way out of here." Brynda knew that walking through 'The

Pass' was faster, but also it was rough. There were the overgrown weeds and the not-so-friendly people you were likely to meet going that way. But it would cut off 20 minutes for those wanting to escape the neighborhood in a hurry. Jay-low was right; if she needed to get out fast, 'The Pass' was the route everyone used.

"Okay Jay-Low, you're right, The Pass is faster. But you and your little friends are going to have to walk with me. I am not going into those fields this time of day by myself. So get your behinds up and let's go," his grandmother replied, hoping he would just come on. Jay-low started to argue with her but he knew it was not worth it. They all were going that way anyway to scout out something. He had a plan to raise more money, and had to get over on Elm Street anyway. So, they could walk with Brynda through The Pass. Jay-Low was even hoping that he could use this to get out of doing something else later. He figured he should get some extra credit for protecting his grandmother.

The neighborhood had seen better days! It wasn't the kind of neighborhood you take a leisurely stroll in; not anymore. Bordered by major streets and the freeway, it was well contained. There were no jobs there; most of the businesses had left the area due to high crime and taxes. Banks had moved out, and major grocery stores could not overcome the "crime tax." Businesses wanted to operate in the neighborhood; there was money there. The people were not unemployed; they had money. Most of the homes were owner occupied, but it was their wayward children who caused the cost of doing business to escalate.

Many people thought that the higher prices were the results of racism but even the Black-owned businesses had higher prices. Break-ins and shoplifting caused the business insurance rates to be astronomically high. So, the price of doing business had caused most to move out of the area. That also meant that you could not do banking or shopping in the neighborhood. Since most of the working people caught the bus, they had to do their shopping on buses then walk home through The Pass. However, the young thugs and other lost children spent time drinking, doing drugs, having sex, fighting, and just about everything else they could think up in that field, making it a dreaded travel option for folks just trying to get home. Anything that the neighborhood kids could not do at home or in plain sight for fear of getting caught, they did in The Pass. This kind of delinquent activity confirmed for business owners why only those businesses that exploit such people should operate in such an environment. Yes; the neighborhood had seen much better days.

The neighborhood youth were not all to blame, though. They had no real park, no baseball field, and no social or recreational hangout. So, they hung out on corners and each other's homes. At night, all you heard were the sirens and helicopters intermingled with the blaring of music from cars rolling down the street. Most of the streets were wide and paved, but they all had potholes and major cracks in them. It seemed the only city services available were the ambulance and police.

"Alright, alright granny, give us a minute and we will be right up." She knew what that meant. They needed time to pack up their dope and their money. She closed the door as a way of denying what was going on downstairs and waited in the living room.

After she closed the door, Jay-Low made an announcement to the 'crew'. There were just two others there in the room; Jordan, the youngster, and Randy-Boy, their eleven-year-old follower.

"Hey, listen up guys; I got and idea on how to make some money. We need to have a larger crew with guys like Randy-Boy here. He's young, eager and hungry. We need to front them the dope and let them take over our corners so we can expand. I think we should go out to the suburbs and colleges and give these young rich white boys a taste of this stuff." Randy-Boy was excited about being a role model for the gang expansion. He thought it was cool to have other guys his age he could mentor. But Jordan had second thoughts.

"How do we get money for the extra cocaine?" Jordan asked. "Most of the money we make goes back to the supplier. How do we front products to others with no money?"

"Well," Jay-Low said with his hands on his chin, "We gotta find a way to get the money." His lips slowly curled into a devious smile. "How about a little crime spree?" He picked up the gun on the table and held it in his hands. "Let's just go take the money from someone. All over town, you have suckers placing their money in businesses with customers spending their money. They're all waiting for us to come by and relieve them of it. Let's pick one of these suckers and raise the money for our expansion."

"Who are we gonna hit?" Jordan asked, growing excited. He always resented the local businessmen raising their prices, not wanting Jordan and his friends in their businesses, driving nice cars and looking down on them. Jordan wanted to pay them back and help himself at the same time. "That's a good idea - LET'S GO GET THIS MONEY!"

Located at the end of the Jay-Low's block was the field known in the neighborhood as "The Pass." It was a sparsely wooded, overgrown area with paths leading to the nearly dried up brook. The muddy little creek was once beautiful and clean, but as the neighborhood surrounding the field was developed, it was cut off and contaminated with waste. Littered with beer cans and food wrappers, the field was an eyesore in the community. There was even an abandoned couch and some other thrown away furniture that the neighborhood kids used to lounge and loiter. That one small slice of nature in the hood that should have been preserved had become a local dump for the hopeless and the shameless. The only sign of real life that was left in that field was the big oak tree in the center. The grand, majestic oak was obviously very old, and despite the death and destruction around it, the tree continued to thrive. It almost seemed like the tree lived on in spite of everything to prove some kind of point. Growing in the center of an abandoned, unkempt field was a solid beacon of hope, remembering the former times and preserving the memories. When people who have moved away from the hood came back, they always looked to see if the great oak tree was still there; it was a gateway to the past.

Set back from the main streets with no streetlights, The Pass primarily used as a short cut to the local small business district while it was light out. On the adjacent street were the liquor store, gas station, hair salon, barbershop, library, and dry cleaners. The Pass also connected the block with the frontage road along the freeway.

Jay-Low's crew gathered up their merchandise, money and the gun and left the basement. They met Brynda upstairs and started out the door. Brynda was both comfortable and nervous with her escorts. These young men were friends of her grandson, and all of them knew her since they were born. They had a reputation in the community that would keep most people from approaching them. She felt safe with them except for one thing; they had enemies. Some people did not like or respect her grandson and his friends. There had been problems with others before, and that always worried her. As they all walked down the street, she noticed that Jordan had on a large jacket, even though it was summertime. She knew why, but did not want to ask about the drugs he was carrying or the gun she knew her grandson had.

The four of them walked around the corner and approached the open field and series of vacant lots along the old creek bed that everyone called, 'The Pass'. The creek was only a small stream now, but old timers said it used to be a very deep running body of water. Because of the water that drained into it, no one had ever bothered to develop plot of land. Developers had built freeways, streets, homes, and businesses all around it, but The Pass remained as it had been for years. The entrance to The Pass was through a grassy field. Past the overgrown foliage and scattered trees there was a wide pathway leading to the creek. The creek was shallow now, allowing crossings in most places over the stepping stones. Once you get over the creek there was another open field bordered by Elm Street. The entire path was only a five-minute walk, which everyone took to avoid going around the neighborhood the long way. Once you got to Elm Street, you had the freeway exit, stores and businesses, and a short walk to the school. All of the children knew about The Pass, and all of them used it for many reasons.

As they walked along, Brynda made a comment about stopping by the liquor store to cash her check and pick up a few things. Jay-Low surprised her by offering to go in for her. Despite her suspicions about her grandson motives, Brynda was glad that she didn't have to go into the store. Brynda hated having to frequent the dirty, smoky neighborhood establishment; the weather beaten cinderblock building was a hub where all of the local hoodlums and criminals could convene. 'A pinnacle of the ghetto", she called it. Brynda knew that something might be up, but she agreed to let Jay-Low cash her check anyway. Jay-Low didn't offer to cash the check out of the kindness of his heart; he wanted to cash it for her because he had an idea.

The liquor store was the neighborhood bank. Because of all the crime and the lack of services in the community, there were no banks to cash checks. Since the store sold goods to the people, it had become the depository of checks for the few people with jobs or income. It was also the place you could depend upon for late night shopping. Picking up baby diapers, a beer, or a midnight snack was the benefit of this store. Located right next to The Pass, it was the first business you came to as you exited the field. As Jay-Low, Jordan and Randy-Boy approached the liquor store, Jordan got an idea of why Jay-Low wanted to cash his grandmother's check.

As they walked out of the trees from the creek, the crew followed Jay-Low across the field leading to the back of the store. "Hey man." Jordan whispered to Jay-Low. "We're gonna hit the store aren't we? That's why you want to go and cash Brynda's check; you're casing the place." As they walked along Jay-Low let Brynda get ahead of them and nudged Randy-boy to walk with her. He wanted to talk to Jordan about his plans.

"Hey man, check it out. That place keeps a lot of money for the sucker's payday loans. They don't have any security, and the owners are scared of everybody. Let's check it out and hit them next Friday night. I bet they keep a few thousand dollars on hand for the payday crowd." When they got to the store, Brynda went to the counter to see the owner. Mr. Chan and his wife opened this store ten years before, and had kept it open despite the number of times they had been robbed. It was the only place where Brynda could get checks cashed or a line of credit. She did not like the high prices, but she understood why they charged so much. Frequent robberies raised insurance costs.

Chronic shoplifting raised the selling price of merchandise. The demand for late evening and early morning hours required extra employee time, and the slow hours did not pay for themselves. The owner worked very hard, and his wife and daughter helped as much as they could. They loved the neighborhood, and most of the customers appreciated their efforts.

Brynda wanted only a few items, but Jay-low wanted information. He noticed that there were no cameras and that the owner was not armed. He could have had a gun behind the counter so they would have to catch him away from the register. Jay-Low started to plot out the heist in his mind. Jordan would pull off the robbery, and Randy-boy would look out at the front door while he would stay near the field to keep an eye for the police coming down Elm. They had a plan to escape; split up and meet at Jay-Low's. The best time would be next Friday, the fifteenth. Payday, welfare check day, and military payday meant a lot of checks to cash, which meant plenty of cash on hand. It was all planned; they would have enough money to buy a large amount of cocaine and marijuana to front new drug dealers in the area. Soon they would have people working for them and they could relax and become real players.

So it was set. They would rob the store that next Friday, the fifteenth. They just had to set the time, the escape plan, and the rendezvous point. They already had the gun, and agreed that Jordan was the triggerman. Jordan had robbed before. He was good at it and he enjoyed it. Since he was a child, Jordan had snatched purses, broke into homes, and stolen cars. He drew power from the look of horror grown men gave him when he stuck a knife to their backs and demanded their wallets. He thought it was fun to scare women and take money from children. Jordan was perfect for this job. He was young, aggressive and would not be afraid to do it.

They had one week. It was going to be the biggest robbery the group had ever attempted. It was going to free them from the never-ending cycle of buying dope, selling dope, and then buying more dope. They could finally get free and pay their way into the real game. It was a chance for the gang to become major players in the neighborhood.

When Jordan got home that night, his mother knew that he was up to something. He had that contrived look of calm that was designed to mask mischief and excitement. Since his behavior took a turn for the worse a few years ago, Lynette had learned to recognize that look; she saw it too often. Jordan was turning out to be more and more like his father, and Lynette was losing hope and patience.

As Jordan stomped through the house, half drunk after a night of hanging out, Lynette looked upon her son with a steady gaze, a stare that Jordan knew very well. Whenever Jordan's mother became frustrated with him, she would give him this look. Her body language may have suggested that she was angry, but her eyes confessed a great love for her son. However, her love was mingled with a certain pain that caused Jordan to feel ashamed whenever she looked at him that way.

"Mama, why you keep lookin' at me like that," Jordan asked. "You always lookin' at me like that. I don't like that, ma. You gotta lighten up or cheer up or something. Don't be lookin' at me like you're disgusted with me!"

With a great sigh, Lynette shook her head and answered her wayward son, "Jordan, I'm not disgusted. I'm concerned about you. You are just so much like your daddy, it hurts to-"

Jordan cut her off mid-sentence with a sharp reply, "Don't compare me to that bastard! He run off and left. I may not be doing what you want me to do, but at least I'm still here! You just like the rest of 'em, ma. You think a black man ain't nothing, and every man that does something you don't like reminds you of my daddy. I don't even know that cat for real, and here you are making us twins. Let me get up out of here before I do something I regret."

As Jordan stormed out of the house and into the streets that consumed him, Lynette burst into tears. For the first time she let go and wept for her son's father. Ford had abandoned them years ago, but his presence was still haunting Lynette through her son. The fact that Jordan was becoming more and more like his father as he got older was a cause of stress and pain for Lynette, but also a reminder of lost love and lost hope. That's why when she looked at him the way she did, her gaze revealed conflicting emotions. Love for the fruit of her womb and the love of her life, and sorrow for the way they both rejected her love at every turn. She went to her room and fell on her bed, tears rolling down her face, and began to dream of Ford. Her life with him was a nightmare he had given to her, despite the dream she was trying to give to him.

Lynette closed her eyes and saw Ford as a young man, big, black, and strong. He was about 6'2 and 250 lbs., muscle-bound with a dark, chocolate brown complexion. Although his skin was thick and leathery from hard living and excessive drinking, it was still smooth to her touch. When he was sober and in a good mood, Ford was good company, making Lynette laugh and smile as he joked and flirted with her. He never stopped flirting with her; he was always able to bring out her femininity with his deep, velvet voice and his big, wide smile. With full lips he professed his undying affection for Lynette, although he never said he loved her. But his eyes confessed his love, or so Lynette thought. At the time she didn't understand who and what Ford really was inside. To Lynette, his hard, scowling face, tired eyes, and clenched jaw were just a mask and a defense mechanism designed to protect the sensitive, caring man that was hiding inside, waiting for a chance to be free. She was the only one who had this kind of hope for Ford; he rewarded her faithful adoration by resenting her for wanting and expecting him to become greater than what he was.

As she drifted off into a deep sleep, Lynette saw Ford's big smile. His full brown lips were usually pursed and frowning, but when he was happy, he smiled as wide as the horizon, his large white teeth unveiled like a winter sunrise. When Ford smiled, as rare as that was, he revealed his true self; a man who was rejected by society but who had the potential to be happy, free, and productive if he could just build his confidence and maintain his dignity. Ford's smile also drew attention to his soft, wavy hair. His large, dark exterior was so hard that his soft black hair was a contradiction to his face. However, when Ford smiled, it all seemed to come together and make sense. He was a whole man, powerful, but at peace in his soul. What Lynette would come to understand as time passed was that this vision of Ford was a fantasy; the man she knew he could be had never even been born inside him. Instead, Ford was a raging sea of conflicting emotions; he desired peace but he was hardened under the foot of the society that conditioned him to be no more than a workhorse and a stud.

His kind words were not love; they were only seduction. His embrace wasn't a promise to be faithful, but a gateway to the sex he craved for his own comfort and validation. Ford was a taker and a liar; his smile was the only thing honest about him. Deep down inside Lynette knew this, but she thought his smile was proof that he could change. To see a man so hardened show even a little warmth and kindness was enough to inspire a woman to cultivate that side of him and try to touch his heart and procure his affection at any cost. His smile was so rare that it became a prize, and finding that smile became an endless pursuit for Lynette. His smile so captivated her that she endured the pain of his degradation and the insanity of his mood swings in the hopes that when the storm was over she would be able to make him repent of his evil and offer her a sacrifice of joy to ease her pain. The most basic shows of affection became priceless jewels. She wanted to prove that he was a man and not a beast. She wanted to prove it to him; she wanted to prove it to the world. Her man, the black man, was not a savage brute or a soulless slave – the black man was human. If she could just love him enough, he would realize his humanity and return her love. Then, once and for all, the black man could take his rightful place as the leader of the successful black family. He could gain strength from the love of his family to fight against the forces that held them all under the weight of the mentalities that enslaved them. Lynette made it her mission to love her man to freedom.

She was hoping love would be enough to save her son, because that's all she had.

Saturday June 9, 2007

Jordan's mother Lynette asked him if he heard the news about "Little Boy." He was Jordan's friend since kindergarten, and he had been shot in a drive by the night before.

"No! Really? When? Where? Jordan asked.

14

"On the corner of Elm and Roberts, last night around midnight. He's dead Jordan. He didn't make it." Lynette watched Jordan closely. She wanted to gauge his reaction to the death of his friend. It could have been Jordan on that corner the night before. Lynette had been trying to get Jordan to see the empty life he was leading and where it was going to take him. Little Boy used to come over and watch cartoons on Saturday mornings. They learned to ride bikes together, and now he was dead.

"Dead? Shot?" Jordan could not believe it. He fell back on their dingy beige living room couch, disoriented from disbelief. His best boyhood friend had been killed. They had just spoken two days earlier. He ran with the same crowd as Jordan and sold dope in the neighborhood. Actually, his set controlled a very good corner. The major Avenue that ran across town through the neighborhood and it brought in a lot of outside traffic. It would be the perfect place to launch their new venture. Jordan knew it would cause a little problem with Little Boy's set, but they needed his corner.

Jordan was used to hearing about shootings. He could remember seeing a man shot down once. It was over nothing, just a silly argument outside a bar. Dude was disrespected and tried to defend his honor, but the other guy had a gun. No honor in being shot up or beaten down. The argument was over a parking space. Jordan remembered one of the guys involved was a quiet man named Henry. He remembered how Henry simply didn't deserve that. All that time being quiet and respectful for nothing; he still got blasted in the end.

There was not a lot of time to mourn his friend and there was nothing he could do about it. Business was business, and he needed that corner. Little Boy was dead and that was that. As he was making his plans for the corner, there was a knock on the door. It was Pastor Obedi, the preacher. He was coming to pick up Lynette for choir rehearsal. At least that was the story. Jordan suspected more was going on with them. He noticed that his mother spent a little more time preparing herself when Pastor is picking her up. He also noticed how she got in just a little later on those nights. Lynette was a beautiful woman, and men were always hitting on her, but Jordan did not like the idea of her dating. After all, he was the man of the house and did not have time for some dude to try to "raise" him or "save" him just to impress his mother. If a brother's game was so weak that he needed to play on the woman's kids, he had no game and Jordan had no respect for him.

Jordan was pretty good at getting rid of any men hanging around his mother. Jordan and his friends could be very intimidating, and it just was not worth the drama for most men. But even Jordan had to admit, Pastor Obedi was not easy. He basically ignored Jordan and his friends and acted like he was supposed to be there. He was not afraid of the gang, and even confronted them.

Pastor Obedi headed a men's group called "Block Busters" and they were really gave the thugs a hard time. These do-gooders were running around at night trying to pull hookers off the streets and trying to pull drug dealers into line. Jordan and his friends had met these guys on the streets. They were always in their faces with their signs and bibles. Although the "Block Busters" were very "non-confrontational", their presence was still bad for business. How many men would pick up a hooker if his church deacon was there protesting? And now here was the head of this group coming to pick up his mother. He just didn't understand; Jordan could have easily put a bullet in him if he did not stop messing with his money. What would make a man come out at night unarmed to confront gang members on their own turf? Secretly, Jordan understood this man; at least he was not like the other weak punks his mother drug home.

"Hey, Preacher Man; moms is in the back. She'll be right out." Jordan had no respect for the Reverend Obedi. He thought his church was just a hustle for poor, pathetic people looking for an escape from reality. That is exactly what he was doing on the corner; selling to poor, pathetic people looking for an escape from reality. As far as he was concerned, the reverend was just a player like everyone else in the hood. He had all the fools giving him their money on Sunday and all they get was a song and a story. In fact, the only difference between the Reverend and himself was that on Sunday you got a song for your money. All he saw at church were old women and children. Most of the men stayed home and allowed the women to attend church.

"Greetings Jordan; I am sorry to hear about your friend. He was a fine young man." Pastor Obedi was hoping for a chance to have a conversation with Jordan. His mother had asked him to speak to him about his recent activities. Being arrested and on probation was serious, and Jordan may very well have been facing his last opportunity to turn his life around.

Jordan looked at the reverend and thought how phony he was. He was not feeling bad about his friend; he did not even know Little Boy. But there may have been some information Jordan could get from the reverend. Even though Jordan was planning to take over Little Boy's corner, there still was the question of revenge and who to go after. Little Boy was not part of Jordan's set, but he was part of the gang. Maybe this old preacher knew who the police were looking for and Jordan could find them first. Jordan was thinking it might be the same dudes who shot up his home and scared his mother and siblings. Those punks were really going to pay if Jordan confirmed that it had been them.

"Hey Rev, do you know what happened to Little Boy?" Jordan inquired, hoping the pastor would take the time to speak about the shooting.

"No, Jordan; the police just do not know what happened. No one saw anything and no one heard anything. He was approached by a car last night, probably thinking it was a customer. They shot from the passenger's window, and then drove off."

"What kind of car was it?" Jordan knew some of their enemies and would have probably recognized the car.

"No one seems to know." The preacher's answer told Jordan that no one was talking. There had to have been witnesses, but everyone was scared. That meant they knew who it was and he needed to find out from the streets.

"Jordan, how have you been doing?" The reverend was taking the opening to continue the conversation. "Have you been keeping yourself out of trouble?"

"Reverend, please! I have been surviving. I have been taking care of my business the same way you have been taking care of yours. I am just a player like you; I have been playing my game, and you have been playing yours. How is your game doing, anyway?" Jordan sneered at the reverend, mistakenly thinking that he had outwitted him.

"I know Jordan; you think all life is a game. Maybe you are right; I do not know. But either you play the game or the game plays you. Right now, the game is playing you. You are the one on probation, a high school drop out, and risking your life. I may very well be a hustler but if I am, my hustle gets me home safe and I am not worrying about the police. I may be playing a game, but the game is playing you. So do not call yourself a player; you are just being played." The reverend also came from these streets, so he knew what language to use to get to Jordan. He only wanted to get him thinking because that was the key to figuring out his world.

"Listen, Jordan," Reverend Obedi continued, "I want you to think about something: if you want to sell dope, you are going to do time. I know you are tough and can do the time. How long do you have now, three years probation? You are broke and only working for the big pusher. I have a better idea for a real hustler. Go to Pharmacy school for those three years and sell dope in the store. Same game, but you will be protected by the police instead of chased by them. You will be in the game instead of letting the game be in you. That is what a real man would do, but you go ahead and be tough...and I will be smart."

Jordan looked at him like he was crazy. "Three years of school? Man you are out of your mind; I'm not going to school." What Jordan was thinking about how hard school was for him. Learning and reading was hard. But he did remember some of his classmates. Some had gone on to high school. Some had plans of becoming doctors and athletes. But Jordan already had a job; selling dope. He did not need a degree, just a corner and a supplier. He and his set had a plan for next Friday. They would expand their business. He did not need school; he needed cash.

He remembered some of the guys that were in school with Jay-Low. He called them "sell outs"; those guys who leave the hood and try to make it in the White man's world. He remembers those guys, trying to get into college. Why? No one would give you a job with your gang tattoos and police record. He remembered this one guy in Jay-Low's class named Charles, who grew up with Jay-Low. Charles even ran with the gang for a while, but thought he found a better way.

Jordan saw these people all the time, leaving the hood for college or good jobs, and then changing. They began to buy homes in the suburbs, driving Volvos, and ignoring where they came from. Why didn't these guys give something back to the community? These self-righteous idiots were trying to look down their noses at people like him. Trying to help people "escape" the hood only harms the hood. When the educated and ambitious ones leave and never come back, whom does that leave...victims and victimizers? Jordan was not going to be a victim, and he was not going to leave.

Before Jordan could respond to the Reverend, Lynette came out and they left. When the preacher got to the door, he paused. "Hey Jordan, your friend's funeral is next Saturday at the church. Can you make it?"

"Of course, I will make it. There is nothing that would keep me from my friend's funeral. I'll be there Saturday." Jordan did not like funerals, but it was important that he attend.

The preacher was standing at the door holding it open for Lynette. He kept his eyes on Jordan and asked, "What about the wake on Friday? Friday around eight o'clock p.m., the family will gather at seven. Are you busy?"

"Friday? Rev, I got some important business to take care of Friday. I will show respect for my friend at his funeral, but I don't think I can make it for the wake."

"Come on, Reverend." Lynette said impatiently. What could be so important that he would not make his friends wake? That was a shameful act, and she did not want to spoil the rest of her evening trying to figure it out. She just wanted to go.

Jordan's ears were still ringing with the pastor's words as he got ready to leave. He had to meet with Jay-Low to plan how to get Little-Boy's corner. Hmmmm, Jordan the pharmacy guy? What a laugh.

Reverend Obedi helped Lynette into his car and walked around to the drivers' side. He looked over at Lynette who was fastening her seat belt and said, "You look lovely tonight, and I like that blue dress." He said while smiling deeply and looking into her eyes. "Thank you," Lynette cooed shyly. She knew he liked that blue dress; that is why she wore it. Pastor Obedi was a single man and she was a single woman; why not try to get his attention. She knew that he liked her and could tell he wanted to talk to her. But she also understood that it would be inappropriate for him to make any unprofessional or presumptuous move on her. After all, he was the pastor and she was in the choir. So Lynette knew she had to give the reverend a few signals to let him know he should try a little harder.

"You know Reverend, I did not have time to have dinner tonight. I was so hurried trying to get the children fed and getting myself dressed for rehearsal. Do you think you could drop by one of the fast food restaurants after rehearsal so I can pick up a bite?" Now if that did not give him a hint, he was asleep.

"No! No! Sister Lynette, that will not do. I truly appreciate your schedule and the time you give your family. It is a sacrifice for you to help with the choir, and the least I could do is get you a good meal occasionally. Why don't we stop by Mr. A's Steak House after rehearsal and get you a proper meal?" he replied. Lynette began to protest that it was too expensive and too much bother. But her protest fell to silence when the reverend placed his hands over her hands with a gentle pet of reassurance. "It is not only my pleasure Sis. Lynette; it would also be an honor. I have wanted to spend a little quality time with you for a while now but did not know if it was appropriate. I have a lot of respect for you, but you are also a very charming woman, and I like being in your company. Therefore, if I cannot take you to dinner and spend sometime with you, I will be sitting down for my usual TV dinner tonight. Come on sister, save me from myself."

Boy, Lynette really liked this guy. She wondered how long it would be before Jordan ran him away. She guessed it would take a lot longer than the rest. Reverend Obedi was not a man easily intimidated. His men's group met every Friday night at the church for prayer. After dark, they stopped praying and went out into the streets. They spent all evening witnessing to the street people and offering help. Their mission had challenged some of the tough streets in the hood. She felt safe and protected with this man.

Later that evening, after choir rehearsal, the reverend and Lynette sat down for dinner. It was her first real date in three years, and she felt so good relaxing. After they ordered and had a glass of wine, Reverend Obedi asked her a question. "How has a woman of your character managed to stay single for so long?"

Lynette was too old and too tired to play pretty. "In a word… Jordan! Jordan takes up all of my time, my affection and my life. He worries me to death and I cannot sleep. Pastor, I find myself jumping in fear every time a car slows down in front of my house. Every time he leaves, I am both relieved and terrified of what may happen. Sometimes, I just do not know how I will go on." Lynette folded her hands on her lap and hung her head. She figured he would make polite conversation and end the evening early. Who would want to deal with her and her children and all the drama of a gangbanging son?

Reverend Obedi looked at her across the table. She was a beautiful, talented, gentle woman. Her intelligence and charm made her stand out from other women. The Reverend had been single too long, and he was looking for a wife. He understood her dilemma, but also understood what he was getting into. He figured Jordan was not that bad, and Lynette was really that good.

"Listen lady, you have enough to worry about in your life to start worrying about me. I am a grown man and capable of taking care of myself. I know you have a few problems with your son and it is a tough road to plow, but let me worry about that, not you. You have spent all of your life worrying about your brother or your sons. Maybe it is about time you allowed a man to worry about you."

Lynette just stared at him as he continued speaking. "It has got to be tough for you to live in a day when men do not respect women. I do not know if it is women's liberation or the single women rising men on their own. It does not matter to me; what matters is that you do not have anyone in your life you can depend upon. I want to be that person, if you will let me."

Lynette was speechless but curious. "What are you talking about, Reverend?"

"Call me Charles tonight. What I am saying is you need not worry about your son; he is going to be alright. I know you cannot see it now, but that boy is looking for something and he is thinking about something. You cannot look without finding, and you cannot think and remain a slave. I have a feeling that Jordan will be facing his manhood pretty soon, and I am trying to give him something to consider. Lynette, every man must face his reality before he can face himself. Jordan has not been able to face it yet. I can tell by watching him that he is really looking for a way out of where he is. He has just lost his best friend, and it will make him think further. Sometimes dramatic experiences in life will make us reconsider our own lives. I think Jordan is about to face his reality. The boy is going to be alright; let's worry about finishing this great steak."

Lynette batted her eyes softly, smiled, and continued to eat. It was the best steak she had ever eaten, and now she was relaxed enough to actually enjoy it. Every few seconds she caught herself looking up and glancing towards Reverend Obedi. Could he be the one? She knew her son needed someone to lead him out of slavery into freedom. Jordan needed someone to show him the way. Could this man be the one to reach out and point towards freedom? She sat quietly, buried deep in her own thoughts.

CHAPTER TWO
IT'S NOT PERSONAL, IT'S JUST PERSONAL!

Sunday June 10, 2007

Jordan and his crew decided to get tattoos. They wanted a way to set themselves apart from the other people in the community. Uncle Thomas tried to talk Jordan out of tattooing his body. But why? Uncle Thomas had plenty of tats himself, many representing his past gangster life. Now that he was older and no longer gang banging, he wanted to stop Jordan from marking himself. But what Uncle Thomas really wanted Jordan to realize was the way law enforcement used tattoos and graffiti to keep track of Jordan and his fellow gang bangers.

As Jordan walked into the busy tattoo parlor, he thought about his last conversation with his uncle. He told his uncle Thomas that he had decided to get the initials "RS" to symbolize the "Roberts Section" of town and his gang territory. Uncle Thomas also had "RS" tattooed on his arm, and other members of the gang did, too. Sure, it was a way police could identify them, but you really could not tell one RS member from another just by the tattoos. "RS" gave clout and respect. It also brought fear to the other punks trying to come into the Robert Street gang territory.

Uncle Thomas told Jordan that tattooing gang signs on your body was a police tag. It was not a claim on your own life, but a way for someone else to have a claim on your life. They were self-inflicted wounds for a lifetime of identification and a lifetime of affiliation in exchange for what seemed to be only a short period of discomfort just so you could stand out in the crowd. Uncle Thomas thought tattooing oneself was like the Old West use of branding to mark cattle. It was the same as tagging the neighborhood. Not working to own a business, but willing to mark it as your own. Tagging and tattooing identified which plantation you belonged to, not which community you belonged to. It was just adding to Master's control. Police keep track of and control of gang members by following the tagging and tattooing in the neighborhood.

But Jordan noticed the other people in the crowded tattoo parlor. Sitting along the poster covered walls were White teenage girls, Chinese males, sailors of varying races, and the tattoo artist was Vietnamese. It was not just a Black gang thing; it was something everyone did. Body marking had been going on for a long time, and it did not start with gang membership. Uncle Thomas was out of date on this.

Jordan really did understand what Uncle Thomas was saying, however, because he could see some hints of it in the real world. Jordan was not foolish; he knew the cops kept the prostitutes and junkies on the block as spies on him. He knew they took pictures of gang members' tattoos and of gang tagging to keep track of the gang's communications. Even though they tried to change names and disregard identification cards, they still knew the police could find them whenever they wanted because of the trails they left in the community. In spite of all of this, however, Jordan had to represent. He had to represent his people and his hood. Nothing else mattered.

As Jordan sat and waited to get RS tattooed on his arm, his cell phone buzzed. It was his girlfriend, Iris. This was the third call he had received from her today. He had not returned her calls because he was planning his escape from the hood. He was trying to get this business expansion off the ground, and did not have time to entertain her. That's all girls wanted; your attention. Why didn't she just wait for him to call back? He got the messages she left and understood the weekend was here. She probably wanted to go to some lame party or shopping.

Jordan liked Iris a lot, and really thought they would be together for life. But if he gave her the time she wanted, it would really put a drag on his game. He knew she was beautiful and others desired her, and it made him proud to be seen with her. However, she would not want him broke, so he had to sacrifice time with her for time with his crew. Plus Jay-Low and the crew had more in common with Jordan than Iris. Iris did not smoke dope, play video games, sell crack, or deal with the police. She was his girlfriend and he cared about her very much, but having fun and living his life did not always include her. But he decided to answer the phone this time. Maybe she would stop bothering him.

"Yeah, baby; what's up?" Jordan was with his friends, and he was not going to show any affection to Iris, only control.

"Hey baby; you busy?" Iris was not going to wait for the answer. She knew he was busy hanging with his hoodlum friends. She really worried about Jordan. He was smart with no ambition, he was strong but only wanted to hang around weak people, and he loved her but could not show it. But Iris had something really important to talk with him about, and she could not even get five minutes of his time. However, she had no problem getting his time or attention when he wanted something from her.

"Well, I know you're busy, but I need to talk to you." She continued without waiting for him to respond. "I'm at your house; your mother and I are talking. When will you get here?"

"Hey baby, you and mom just hang out; I'll be there later on. Jay-Low and I have some business to take care of. I'll be late getting home, so why don't we get together Friday night?" Jordan figured that after the job he would have a little money in his pocket. All she wanted was to go shopping and by some clothes. He figured that was why she had been calling so much. Friday was freedom day for him; his plan of escape would work. He could just sit around and wait to get off probation. Then he could travel and really expand his business. Jordan knew Jay-Low could not be trusted for the long run. But Jordan already knew enough about the business to run it on his own. He had already determined that if or when Jay-Low went back to prison he would take over the set and the drug business. He did not need Jay-Low, and the more he hung around him, the less he trusted him.

"I'm sitting in the tattoo chair; why can't we just talk now?" Jordan asked, trying to get the conversation out of the way.

"No, I will wait; there is something I need to talk to you about, but not over the phone. I'll catch up with you on Friday, but maybe before that evening. I have to meet your mother and go cash my check and we're going shopping. Can I catch up with you that afternoon when I get off work?" Iris was pushing Jordan, and she knew he did not like that. But she was his girlfriend and figured she should be more important to him that his no good friends. All he wanted to do was hang out with his friends.

'Okay, Iris! I'll be around the hood. Catch up with me." Jordan was not going to give her a place and a time to meet. Not on Friday; not this Friday. He would be preoccupied with the plans. This was for her and his mother as well as himself. He would always take care of his mother and Iris, but she had to get off his back now and let him get back to business.

Iris hung up the phone and turned to Lynette in the kitchen. Lynette looked at her, smirking. "Let me guess; he has no time for you?" Iris' eyes fell to the worn kitchen floor. Although the yellow and white vinyl tiling was faded and peeling, she could still see some of the little flowers on the tile by her left foot. Iris focused on those tiny flowers so that there wouldn't be enough room in her mind for disappointment. She quickly looked up, and regained her composure. After all, the smells of soul food saturating the small kitchen were too comforting to be denied. Soul food was about love and comfort, even in the midst of pain. Even Lynette's new augmented, health conscious soul food recipes were about love. Although the curtains were dingy, the stove was ancient, and the breakfast table was a little wobbly, this kitchen had a lot of love in it. Iris felt that love from Jordan's mother Lynette, and that gave her hope.

Lynette liked Iris a lot, but did not understand why she hung out with her son. Jordan mistreated her and disrespected her. He insisted that she wear revealing clothes and never gave her any attention.

Lynette and Iris got along fairly well; after all, Lynette was still very young herself and both loved Jordan. Lynette would often pick her up on Fridays to help her cash her check. Iris only worked a few hours a week, but at least she had a job. Being only fourteen, she did not have credit, and even the liquor store would not cash her check without Lynette's help.

Iris liked talking with Lynette because she had seen a lot. It was different from talking with her own family; they still thought of her as a child. Lynette would explain things to her and let her talk. She wished there was more time to sit and just talk with her. Most of the time that she was over to Lynette's house Jordan was there also. Jordan commands all of the attention in a room.

But next Friday Lynette had agreed to take her shopping for summer clothes. After they cashed their checks, they would walk a few blocks and shop at the discount stores along the street. Iris was really looking forward to this talk with Lynette; she had something to talk about.

Lynette wanted to talk to Iris, too. She thought they were having sex and hoped Jordan was using protection. Of course, protection with a fourteen year old was asking a lot. The last thing she needed was another baby to take care of, and that is just what would happen.

Iris smiled back at Jordan's mother. "No, mama; he is busy. We're going to meet Friday right after work. I will still have time to get with you to go shopping. Are you still going to show me those shoes at Harry's?"

"Sure, sweetie." Lynette assured her they would be meeting up as soon as she got off work and back to the hood. "What do you need to talk with Jordan about? Is there something I could help you with?"

"No, mama; just stuff. Nothing important." Iris replied softly, obviously hiding something.

"Well sweetie, you know I will always be here for you. If you need anything, just give me a call." Lynette really did like this sweet young lady. She just hoped that Jordan would see Iris for who she really was.

"I appreciate it, Miss Lynette." said the thankful young girl. She decided to open up a little more. "You know, there are some things I am confused about. Can you tell me how the welfare system works? I was thinking about trying to move out of my mother's house and become independent. Mom said since I have a job and have not been in trouble, I should be able to go down to the court and get emancipated. I know how to do that, but I don't know how to get on welfare."

"Welfare?" Lynette was shocked. "Girl you don't need no welfare. All welfare will do is keep you where you are. You don't see me on welfare do you? With three kids, I certainly could get it. But I wanted to work and show my children how to succeed. I know I only have a low paying job, but hoped it would show my children that you get what you work for. I don't know how the emancipating program works, but I don't think you can get that on welfare. It's a program for teenagers to get out from under control of their parents. It is for working young people whose parents have some drug or criminal problem, and the child wishes to work and take care of him or herself without having an adult taking guardianship over them. But welfare? I can't tell you a lot about that. What particular question do you have?"

Iris was surprised that a woman living in their community had such strong feelings about welfare. "Well, Miss Lynette, I was just looking for general information. I heard that the welfare department takes care of health, shelter, and food expenses so we can get on our feet. If I had someone doing that for me, I could leave my mother's house with all those problems and kick back on my own." Iris had another need for the information, but did not want to share it with Jordan's mother.

"I used to live on welfare when I was a little girl. Uncle Thomas was in the system, and it was not something I felt safe with. First off, the housing was always low income, never high income. The food was cattle food! You only received enough assistance to buy cheap food. What do you think happens when you feed your kids cheap food? They become mildly or severely malnourished. When you're grown, you will not have any experience in getting along outside the system. So, you will not know about checking accounts, getting loans, taking care of your home or the important of savings.

"I think we should try to get you a better job and prepare you for college. That would give you a better chance to get along in this world. If you are really having problems with your mother, maybe we can get you in a home or with another relative." Lynette did not want Iris to feel like she was receiving a lecture, but she did feel strongly enough about the issue that she was willing to go the extra mile to keep Iris from chaining herself to the destructive cycle of poverty and ignorance she was headed toward.

Iris had another, more pressing question, but she did not want to bring up right now. She would seek her answers elsewhere. Would the welfare system help a young girl get on her own feet if she really had to leave the home? Lynette was right about one thing, however. Those people she knew on welfare seemed to be suffering from an unhealthy diet, and they really did seem to have less ambition. But she needed help from somebody. If not Jordan, then maybe the government.

The system may have been designed to help poor people, but the mental and physical help it provided guaranteed that you would be dependent on the system and not on yourself.

That afternoon, when Jordan got home, his mother tried to have a conversation with him. She was not trying anything heavy, just a mother-son talk; a simple, quiet conversation with him. Jordan loved his mother and was frustrated with the problems they were having lately. He was growing into a man and life was really strange for him. He recognized she was trying to have a nice conversation with him so he tried to find a topic they both could talk about and have fun. Since they were in the kitchen, he figured that he could connect with her by talking about food.

Jordan's mother loved to cook, but the kitchen was for more than cooking. Ever since the drive-by shooting, the kitchen had become the family room. There was the little 19 inch television sitting on the counter among the newspapers, cups, and bowls. The kitchen table was covered with a plastic table cloth that was old and faded. The table top had a green vase in the middle with dried flowers and no water. Jordan's mother kept a dictionary on the table to encourage her children to read and to help them with their homework.

Everyone used the kitchen table as the meeting area and the family sat around it to watch television and play board games. The back door led to the back yard and the gate out to the front of the house. Everyone came and left through the kitchen. The old floors were so dilapidated that there was a visible path worn into the vinyl tile that seemed to charter every step taken.

It was a comforting sound when mom was cooking, pots and pans being used, water run. Cooking time, however, was also singing time. The old boom box radio was always turned to the urban station and the latest songs filled the air. Lynette loved to sing and to cook; her escape came when she could do both. The kitchen seemed to be a place of comfort. It was one of the few places Jordan and his mother could talk with less stress and get a little understanding. It was a safe place especially after the shooting. If Lynette had not been cooking and the children sitting there talking with her, they may have been struck by the bullets. The living room couch and the living room television were hit by gun fire. The front door and windows had bullet holes in them. That night Uncle Thomas boarded up the windows from the inside and barricaded the front door. Now the family had only one way in or out of the house. Lynette did not sleep as well and she had stopped singing.

"Hey mama, are you going to have your barbeque party again this Forth of July?" Jordan asked anxiously. "I can't wait to taste your chitterlings and ham hocks. Will Mrs. Emma bring her potato salad and cornbread? I really enjoy that barbeque; man, you can eat all day and sleep all night. You've got to make the pickled pig's feet and the crackling that I really like. Are we going to have the barbeque this year?"

"Yes and no Jordan." His mother had decided to make some changes this year, and she was sure Jordan would not appreciate all of them. "Yes, we will be having the barbeque for the Fourth of July, but we are changing the menu a little. Because Uncle Thomas has been diagnosed with diabetes, we are not serving a lot of the normal foods. There will be ham, ribs, and pork chops along with the sausages and chicken. But we are cutting down on the sauces and the other parts of the pig."

"What?" Jordan said, "No pig ears, pig tails or hog head cheese? What kind of party will that be? Everyone likes that. And no sauce with the food? Come on woman, you got to be kidding." Jordan was really playing with his mom; he did not like all of those foods himself. He found it a little troubling to clean the pig crap out of the guts and then boil them and eat them. Why put hot sauce on them, all you tasted was the hot sauce. May as well put hot sauce on rubber bands and eat that. But he was a little curious as to why his mother was changing the diet.

"So mama, you turning into a Black Muslim on us?" Jordan asked playfully.

"No, Jordan; we will still have the pig on the Fourth, but we will be living high on the hog, not low. My grandmother told me that eating the throwaways was necessary for her mother because it was all they had. They knew it was Master's garbage, but it was the only meat they could get. So her mother had to find a way to create taste in the garbage so her children would eat. She fried the crackling, boiled the guts, and added strong sauces and spices to hide the odor and the taste. It was bad, but not as bad as watching her children starve. Well, that food became part of a normal diet for Black children. Of course, Master would only slaughter a pig on holidays, so the garbage was only available on holidays. The slaves got used to looking for it on Christmas, New Years, and the Fourth of July when Master would kill the pig.

"So, Jordan, we raise our children to eat that way. They made it a tradition to eat that way, and their children made it a culture. Now we think it is normal to eat the guts and skin of pigs because your ancestors had to. Well, now son, we don't have to but we have acquired a diet that has made us both strong and weak."

"What do you mean mama; I am not weak, I am a strong Black man, and you are not weak, either."

"Jordan, you are right son; at fourteen you are very strong. You will get even stronger as you grow into adulthood. There is no one as strong as an eighteen-year-old Black man is. You guys dominate boxing, running, football, baseball and just about every athletic contest you like. But by age sixty-nine, that strong Black man has diabetes, heart disease, and will die of a stroke before he turns seventy.

"And that Black woman? You are right about her, too, son. There is no more beautiful woman than an eighteen-year-old Black lady. But by age thirty she is overweight and out of breath. There is something we are doing that is destroying us. Some Black doctors have begun to question our lifestyle and our customs. Why are we so strong, yet so weak a few years later? The first thing we are going to have to do is stop eating what Master has given us. Master has never had our best interest at heart. If Master gave it to you, it must be dangerous for you. So we are going to change our diet to a healthy one. Uncle Thomas is getting older, and I can see things now. So, I am changing our diet in order to help you develop better habits. Don't worry son; you will learn to enjoy my food. You always have."

Monday June 11, 2007

On Monday's and Friday's, Jordan met with his probation officer, Mr. Douglass, in his office. Officer Douglass was always on Jordan's case. Being on probation made you part of the system; Jordan wished he had just done his time. Three years probation meant mandatory appointments, going back to school, and not hanging out with the friends he had grown up knowing. Officer Douglass had grown up in the neighborhood also, he should have known how important friendship was, and he should have understood that Jordan would not stop seeing his friends. This probation stuff was just designed to keep Jordan in trouble and connected to the court system.

Jordan even felt like the probation office itself was designed to mess with his head. Everything was so stuffy and neat all of the time; nowhere to kick back, put your feet up, and relax. From the drab gray carpet to the small, boxy office that he was forced to report to, nothing about that place was inviting at all. The chair he had to sit in was uncomfortable, and the walls were pale and bare, except for Officer Douglass' degrees, certificates, awards, and pictures. What were those supposed to do, encourage him to go out and achieve something? All they did was confirm that Officer Douglass didn't know anything about what was really going on out here. One thing that they did do right, Jordan thought, was make you not want to spend too much time there.

The probation officer told Jordan to take off his hat or turn it around. "Why?" he retorted. The defiant Jordan knew the hat turned around backwards or to the side of his head aggravated adults and punks like him. It made him look crazy, and that is what he wanted. People leave you alone when you look crazy.

Officer Douglass looked at Jordan and sighed. "You look like a victim, Jordan. You look like you have no future, no hope, and no responsibility. You look like you are just making money for this criminal system and not for yourself. You look like you are being used to keep the schools weak and the taxes high. You look like the enemy, and I don't like my enemy to look that way. So either take it off, or turn it around." He did not want to play with Jordan; his Job was to dominate and regulate Jordan's behavior. He was the only person Jordan listened to because he had the power of the state behind him. Officer Douglass knew he could not change Jordan's mind, but he would change his behavior.

"Yeah, okay man, have it your way. I'll take off the hat!" Jordan knew he could not win this battle. Douglass was a warrior and he was in his territory. Jordan always thought of the police as fellow gang members. He knew them on a personal level and considered them barely on the other side of the law. He had seen cops do things illegal with drug money, prostitution, and other illegal activities. They patrolled the streets like gang members, and would claim certain areas as their own. Those areas were the business districts and certain neighborhoods where wealthy people and politicians lived. So he took off his hat and exposed the bandana he wore underneath it. Jordan knew that there were places he could not wear his hat in the style he wanted, so he wore the bandana to keep his colors up.

"Take that rag off, too!" the probation officer shouted. "You look like some school girl trying to keep her style together."

Jordan started to protest, but before he could finish his sentence, Officer Douglass reached over, snatched the bandana off his head, and threw it on the table in front of Jordan. "Now let me tell you something, Jordan," he snapped, not giving Jordan a chance to speak, "Be a thug, but not here. Be tough, but not here. Be frightening, but not here. Here Jordan, you will be obedient, polite, and respectable because here, Jordan, I have the power....ALL OF IT! You have none. Do not talk back, do not give me that look, and always answer with respect in your voice. I know you think you're grown, but I really am grown; you are not. This is my house, and I will not tolerate anything from you except full respect and cooperation. Now do we understand each other?"

"Yes, sir" Jordan murmured. He may have had to show respect, but did not have to have it.

"Jordan, if you knew the reason black men wear their hats that way you would stop." Officer Douglass continued. "It's not a sign of manhood, but of slavery. You are too stupid to understand the original reasons why we had to wear bandanas on our heads. Now we don't need to, but you thugs still cling on to the past because you have no future. Sad."

"Look, Officer Douglass," Jordan responded, "You are always preaching that ancient stuff about how it was back in slavery days. Man, this is not slavery days. I wear my clothes and hats the way I do because it is the style, and I have style. It's just the way we do it in the hood."

"Oh, it's the way you do it?" he mockingly replied. Officer Douglass had heard it all before from these young men. If it was new to them, it was new to the world. "Come here, Jordan; let me show your know it all behind something about style." Officer Douglass pulled out an old book on Black History. "Come take a look at these pictures, Jordan."

Jordan did not want to play this game. He was aware of all the nonsense about Black History. This was June, and all of the idiots were screaming about the celebration of Juneteenth and Black History. But taking up Officer Douglass's time to look at a magazine or Black History book was much better than being lectured about his activities. Jordan walked over to the desk where he was sitting and took the book out of his hands. He sat down in the chair in front of the desk and looked at the photos and pictures.

"What do you see, Jordan?" asked Officer Douglass.

"Some country negroes out in their fields," Jordan answered back.

"What kind of fool are you, Jordan? They are slaves, not country negroes, and they are in Master's fields, not their own. Take a look at their clothes, Jordan; how are they dressed?

Jordan still did not get it. "They look like hand-me-downs!" he exclaimed. Jordan was being honest. The slaves in the pictures had baggy pants and shirts way too big for them. Sure, he saw what Officer Douglass wanted him to see, but he was not going to let him know it. He noticed the hats and caps of the slaves were crooked on their heads very similar to the 'styles' of today. Jordan knew if he did not acknowledge seeing the style, Officer Douglass would think he was playing him.

"Yeah, they're trying to style with their hats on backwards and sideways, but they still look lame." Jordan tried to appease him, but all he did was make him angrier.

"You fool; they're wearing their hats like that to keep the sun out of their eyes. They have been working in the fields in a straight line. When the sun moved, they could not change their positions, so they had to change the positions of the hat brims on their heads. What you are calling a style today was a pronouncement of their position in life. A free black person would not wear his hat that way or his clothes. It was a sign that someone else owned you. Now young man, look at that photo and look at you. Do you see yourself in that old photograph? Can you make yourself out in the fields there? Is that your past or your future Jordan? Do you intend to be on this plantation forever? Master still wants you to be his field slave."

"No!" immediately spilled out of Jordan's mouth. He almost shouted, but remembered to be respectful. "I don't see myself in this picture, and this is not my future. I'm going to make it, and make it big." Jordan had been called a lot of things in his fourteen years, but never had he been called a slave. What on earth did Officer Douglass mean? He looked at the pictures more closely. There was one with a gang of slaves standing by a barn. He noticed one or two did not have shirts on. Some had marks on their bodies that he could not make out. They look like brands from a branding iron. Marks on their bodies. Jordan thought that must have been painful. He could not make out what the branding was, only that they were two letters. He closed the book and tossed it back on Officer Douglass' desk.

"Can I go now?" Jordan wanted to know.

"Yes Jordan, the door is open; walk through it." Officer Douglass said as he motioned to the office door. "I will see you next Friday."

Next Friday Jordan had plans, and they did not include visiting with his probation officer. Next Friday Jordan expected to finally make if out of the area. By next Friday, Jordan had planned to be free.

He was already downtown, so Jordan thought about going to the library and pick up Iris. She should be getting off work in a few minutes, and it would give him time to hear what she had been worrying about. It was probably something simple like what color dress to wear or whether or not he liked her new hairdo.

The more Jordan that thought about picking her up, the more he did not like the idea. The main reason was meeting up with her supervisor, Gilmore Jr., son of the Chief Librarian and all around jerk. He did not like this guy, and he knew the jerk was after his woman. Lusting after Iris was not the problem he had with Gilmore Jr., however. It was not even that he was White. It was his White attitude. The air about him said he thought he was superior.

Jordan remembered that the last time he picked up Iris, he and Gilmore Jr. had words. Iris did not like him coming on her job because Jordan's temper could have gotten her fired.

Jordan remembered a conversation he had with Gilmore Jr. one day at the Library. While he was waiting for Iris to pack up and punch out, Gilmore Jr. came into the office. They stared at each other for a second. These two guys did not like each other, and there was no secret about it.

"What are you looking at, man?" Jordan growled, trying to intimidate Gilmore Jr. He did not like the way the uppity supervisor was staring at him. Gilmore Jr. was a tall, lanky White boy from the South. He had moved into the area four years ago when his father was transferred from Mississippi. He had no real problems with Black people, but did have a problem with gangsters. And Jordan was a gangster.

Gilmore Jr. really liked Iris and could not understand what she saw in this thug. He could have treated her so much better than Jordan could. He was determined to have her one day. One day!

"I'm looking at nothing! That's what. You must be waiting on Iris, because I know you are not here for a book. She will be out in a minute; have a seat and try to stay out of trouble," Gilmore Jr. replied. He began to walk off, but heard Jordan murmur something under his voice.

"What, you think you're better than me?" Jordan said, responding to the condescending remarks and looks he had been getting from Gilmore Jr. "What? You got a question for me?" Gilmore Jr. shot back.

"Why do you White folks think you are superior to us? It seems like you are always making an effort to point out to Blacks that we are your slaves and we're supposed to work for you. You seem to be trying to convince yourself you are superior…maybe you have doubts?"

"No, boy; you misunderstand." Gilmore Jr. responded. "We don't have to convince ourselves that you are inferior; we only have to convince you. Once we convince you, you will convince your children. If we fail to convince you, you will raise your children to work against my children, not for them.

"You see Jordan, it's not personal; it's just personal. It's not that White people hate Black people; it's that we love White people. If we can get Black people to work in our fields and help us take care of our families, then we will do it. It is not personal; it is personal. I do not care any thing about your family. I care about my family." Jordan just sat in his chair, completely stunned as Gilmore Jr. continued.

"Slavery was never about hatred; it was about power. Who will work for my children? That was the question. We tried serfdom in Europe; it did not work. We tried Indians in America; it did not work. We tried indentured servants; it did not work. So we tried importing Africans, and that worked, so we kept it.

"It is not our responsibility to create freedom or opportunity for you. That is your job. We are not going to educate your children. You should take care of your own children. But if you allow us to tax you, and you send your children to our schools to learn the lessons we set up for them, then we will train your kids to work for our kids. Because it is not personal, it's just personal.

"You see Jordan, I do not know if you really are dumb or if you just act like it. But if you think every time you have a problem, White folks are the cause, that is dumb. If you also believe that every problem you have requires action from White people or the government or some body else, then that is really dumb. And Jordan, if you think I control your plight in life then I will control it. But it is not because I hate you, I do not give any emotions for you. But if you volunteer to serve me, I will allow you to. But it will not be personal; it will just be personal.

Tuesday, June 12, 2007

The next day after Jordan meeting with Officer Douglass, Jordan's uncle visited the probation officer. Uncle Thomas wanted to check up on his nephew's progress and offer his help to Officer Douglass. They knew each other from the old neighborhood, but did not really like each other. It was a long story, beginning with how Uncle Thomas and Officer Douglass hung around two different cliques in school. While Uncle Thomas was the thug, Officer Douglass always looked for the opportunities in life. Officer Douglass wanted to go to college and wanted a career.

When Uncle Thomas finally saw the light and turned his life around, Officer Douglass was his chief critic. He did not want to give this ex-gang banger any credit or respect. He was suspicious of Uncle Thomas from the beginning and had not changed his mind. But this day both men agreed to meet to discuss Jordan. Jordan was the interest of both men because they both saw themselves in him.

"How are we going to keep this kid out of trouble?" Officer Douglass wanted to know. "He seems determined to go to jail. No school, no hope. Selling drugs and no telling what else."

"How do we keep them all out of trouble?" Uncle Thomas asked in response. It was easy to focus on one child, but he knew there was a fundamental reason so many Black men embrace such self-destructive behavior. "They look at us not as role models, but as sell outs to 'the cause'. Yeah, the cause which has brought death and depression to the community. Why would they want to continue seeking a culture that has ended up in death for their friends? Why can't they see the future?"

Uncle Thomas reflected; "Well I know one thing; they're definitely not working hard. There is no reward for hard work. It's almost impossible to free yourself by working harder. Producing more makes you only more valuable to Master. We should have dialogue to explain the lack of work efforts in the Black community. Hard work is a negative element of sorts. It's considered "showing off" and trying to act White. Hard work is replaced with "working hard at getting something for nothing." Slaves who picked more cotton not only raised the quota on others, but also increased the work on those picking the seeds out of the cotton and those packing the cotton for market. Hard work was not deemed a positive trait for slaves."

Officer Douglass agreed, "They have a patriotic acceptance of criminal activities. Jordan doesn't think he's a part of society, so he feels his part is taking every advantage he can get. Trying to get away with something for nothing is the goal. Feels he has no other choice. The skill of criminal activity becomes the legends of the community. Pimps and hustlers are the heroes, while accountants and teachers are the victims. It is believed that prostitutes, pole dancers, and drug dealers make more money and live more exciting lives than any other occupation."

Uncle Thomas was beginning to see how much he had in common with the probation officer. "Hmmm, they are rejecting the American Culture. The Black man is always looking for his own culture. The Black man will make up things to celebrate as cultural. He will not believe in the American Culture if he thinks it enslaved him. On the plantation and during the slave trade, they looked to Voodoo and other magical control over their environment. In the present, we have the constant change of our names (Negro, Colored, Afro-American, Black, and African American) in an attempt to develop a separate identity in America. We have different celebrations an holidays, like Kwanzaa, and a special diet for New Years Day, for example."

Now Officer Douglass recognized that Uncle Thomas really did see it. Maybe; but maybe he was still playing. "Why does he specialize in entertainment, the Black man I mean? It was the only way he could prove his athletic ability without producing more for Master or competing with Master. He knew that showing off his strength by dancing and showing off his intelligence by joking provided him a safe way to express his humanity. It was against the law for Black people to show intelligence, so "stop acting smart" was a common warning. We still find the women at the discount department store on Saturday morning calling to their children by saying, come here boy, and stop acting smart. Acting smart is a sin in the Black community. Being smart was reserved for White people. As a matter of fact, showing intelligent behavior was called 'acting smart'."

Uncle Thomas was beginning to understand. "Then there are superstitions or willingness to accept fake gods: Since he has no power he looks for ways to control his environment. Gambling, voodoo, superstition, astrology; anything to do with chance over planning and studying. Everything Jordan does or has done in the past reflects around 'possibilities and probabilities.' Sure, it is possible to win the lottery, so you play five dollars a week on it. However, it is not probable that you will win, so you don't play your entire paycheck on it. If you believe in the power of luck, chance, or superstition, you would lean more towards acting on possibilities rather than probabilities. You can look at neighborhoods, families, or individuals and clearly tell who acts on possibilities or probabilities. SAD!"

They looked at each other for the first time without any contempt. Uncle Thomas stood up to leave. "Officer Douglass, I got a lot of work to do. Let me know if I can be of any help to you."

Wednesday, June 13, 2007

The gang was sitting around Jordan's house that afternoon. Lynette was not there, so they could have a moment of peace and quiet. They had to make final plans for Friday and did not need to be around Brynda at Jay-Low's house. They were sitting around smoking weed and watching television, going over the plans. They had the time of day figured out and where to split up. Jay-Low had the gun and gave it to Jordan to keep at his house. Jordan put it under his bed. He still thought under the bed was a safe place to hide things. He used to hide his report cards from Lynette under the bed. He still thought like a fourteen year old, even if he had a gun.

Jordan was a little nervous about the job. He had robbed individuals before, but this would be his first business. This was a little more dangerous because businesses sometimes fought back. It was not like robbing someone in their homes or cars. You probably will not fight over your wallet, but something you have put your whole life into may cause you to fight back. Jordan wanted to ease the tension by talking to Jay-Low. It crossed Jordan's mind that his sister had begun to hide things under her bed the same way he hid important things. Jordan did not realize that his sister knew Jordan hid his most important things under his bed, and that she often searched out of curiosity. What would she have found that day if she checked?

As they sat talking, Jay-Low asked Jordan about his girlfriend. "Hey how is that fine girl of yours Iris doing? She still sweating you to stop banging?"

"Yeah, she still trying. I haven't seen her in a few days. I've been busy, and she places a lot of grief on a brother." Jordan did not feel comfortable speaking about Iris to these guys. He knew they would hook up with her if they could get away with it.

Jay-Low said, "You know what the problem is Jordan? You only got one girl and that allows her to have too much power. You should be playing these women; then you could manage them better. But you got to make sure they know you're in control. I got babies all over the state. And women in every major city and at least five babies." The youngest of the group, Randy Boy, wanted to hear more about the babies Jay-Low had. Jay-low began to brag about his children to the youngsters. Jordan had a question for Jay-Low. It was a question based upon the life Jordan had lead without his father bringing him up.

"Hey, Jay-Low? Do you feel good about not being in your children's lives? You do not feed them, clothe them or even help with their homework." Jay-Low looked up at Jordan and laughed. "Well I got them here and that's all I'm going to do. Making babies is what a hustler do, not taking care of a brat. I've made plenty of babies because I'm a real man."

Jordan disagreed; having grown up without a father, seeing his friends make babies and then abandon them got under his skin. Jordan's relationship with his father was poor at best. He knew his dad as "Forty," a nickname he acquired because malt liquor was his favorite drink, and it came in 40 oz. bottles. It was also a play on his name, Ford. This was actually short for Oxford; his mother wanted him to be someone special when he grew up, and she gave him the most distinguished, special name she knew. Oxford. However, more impressed with muscle cars and drag racing than high society, Oxford shortened his name to Ford when asked who he was. He was ashamed that his mother gave him such a white name; that could get you killed out the streets. He couldn't appear to be weak or a sellout; that was a death sentence. Ford had to be tough to survive, and the toughness of his father was what Jordan remembered most about him.

Ford was in and out of Jordan's life when he was a small boy, and he left for good by the time Jordan was nine years old. His father never paid him much attention; he didn't know what to do with Jordan, so he didn't do much of anything. Ford himself had no father, so he had no example to follow and his heart didn't have enough love in it to make up the difference. Jordan remembered his father staring at him every now and then with what appeared to be an emotionless gaze. He was too young to understand that it was an attempt to connect with his offspring, to feel something for the boy. Part of him wanted to be a better father to Jordan and a better companion for Lynette, but it wasn't in him. Ford was a tramp, a vagabond, and a fugitive in his own world, running from the responsibility he had been taught to avoid. Sometimes when he was drunk, before he got angry, Ford would sit Jordan on his knee and ramble on, spewing nonsense about how Jordan had to be a player when he grew up and how the game would take care of him if he took care of the game. He also told him to find a good woman like his mother. Minutes later Jordan would hear his father yelling at this 'good woman', and then rushing out into the streets where he felt he belonged. Ford didn't have a real home, and despite how Lynette offered him one, he couldn't find it in himself to commit to her. To settle down and be the man Lynette wanted him to be would defy his very nature. Ford wasn't a husband or a father; he was a stud.

He did have some natural compassion and affection for his son and Lynette, but he was a predator who had been bred to breed. Ford had kids all over town, and he didn't take care of any of them. He had no relationship with any of his children and no devotion to any of their mothers. His idea of intimacy was sexual conquest. A woman was a possession to be had or a means to an end. However, his predatory nature was not malicious; it was just self serving. Being reduced to a stud by the hopeless culture of poverty and ignorance in which he was raised caused him to embrace his role as a breeder and turn it from a mark of shame and insufficiency to a badge of honor. The shame of fathering children he could not adequately care for would have destroyed his pride and his mind if he didn't convince himself and others that it was a sign of power and sexual prowess. The strength of his loins compensated for his powerlessness to provide and protect and his weakness against the forces that would prevent him from being the man God created him to be. He used the strength he did have to run, and Jordan never forgave him for that.

"So you mean real men don't take care of their babies, they allow other real men to do it?"

Jay-Low was quick to answer; he was not going to take any responsibility for those women and the babies they made. "Jordan, women will always try to use babies to tie a brother up. You just try to get some sex, and they're trying to make a baby. Then they expect you to spend the rest of your life working your butt off to take care of them. Every time they get mad at you, they throw the baby in up in your face and demand you jump through hoops to be a real man. Hey, what does a female know about being a real man; how long have they been a man? The only real men out there are brothers that can take care of their business. It's hard enough being a man without a broad demanding you be her provider. All women are good for is sex and 'what-nots'; what-nots include cleaning, cooking, and keeping the kids quiet while the game is on."

Jay-low was on a roll and he continued. "You know Jordan, women ain't nothing! What else can a woman do for a man but have good times with him? What else are they good for? Do we want to be around them to go shopping with them? Can they shoot basketball, play video games, or rob some punk? Good times Jordan, that's all they're good for. Now a real player like me can use a woman for many needs, but she is only made for having fun with."

Jordan asked Jay-low if he beat women or took money from them. He remembered his father fighting with his mom and how money was always missing. Taking money from these punks in the streets is one thing; it took courage and strength to rob another man. But to take money from a woman, especially your own woman seemed a little weak to Jordan. It just seemed like a man should be able to be strong without the need to prove it to his woman.

"No, I don't have to beat them; I'm a lover, not a fighter. I have five babies all over town and I am only nineteen years old. That's manhood in the hood! I been making babies since I was fourteen, man I can run some wenches! See, Jordan, I got game and I tell you man, you gotta have more than one wench. Having only one allows her to run you because you need her to be nice to you. But if you have more than one and your main girl gets out of line or in one of her moods, you still got your other honeys to take up the slack."

Jay-Low's grandstanding began to irritate Jordan. "Jay-Low, man! Quit messing around! You know as well as I do that you did not get those wenches pregnant on purpose; you just didn't know how not to. I don't know who ran a game on whom. They wanted babies and you gave them up. Your game only works on weak-minded wenches that will give it up to some crazy man like you. So you only see weak women and then have babies by weak women and your babies are around the other weak men that they have in their lives and will grow up to be weak themselves, and you say this proves you are a strong man? Man, the only person benefiting from your little tricks are the welfare caseworkers. You are just making new cases for those clowns to manage. You are providing more boys for juvenile hall and more girls for Section 8 housing. You are not pimping them, the system is pimping you. So while the judge, bailiffs, warden and police may see full employment from your children, you get no benefit. Your sons don't even know you, your daughter resents you, and the women you think you dominate just use you like you are a prize stud bull. Now you are my boy and all that, but don't tell me about manhood of the hood. I like my girl, and as a matter of fact, punk, you like her too. So the only reason you want me to have other girls is so you can have my girl. Now you are my homeboy Jay-Low, but you need to back up off my woman and while we are talking about it, you need to tone up your language about her, too. We cool, man?"

"Yeah homey, we cool. I didn't mean to disrespect you." Jay-Low said the words, but was thinking what a sweet honey Jordan's woman was and how much he would like to add her to his stable. This young punk Jordan did not know what he had and probably could not take care of her anyway. He would watch what he said around him but continue to watch her also.

Jordan did not want to say anything because he did not want the guys to think he was weak. But what Jay-Low was saying did not make any sense. He knows Jay-Low and understands the pain he went through as a young man without his father. He remembers how frustrating Jay-Low would get when his father did not show up for promised visits. Jordan could remember his own life without a father. Seeing other kids in the park play catch with their fathers really did hurt. He understood the anguish of a girl getting pregnant on purpose. And he witnessed all the court ordered child support on a brother without a job. But to think it was okay not to want to take care of your child did not make sense to him.

Thursday June 14, 2007

Jordan was hanging out alone, running errands for his mother when he stopped next door to the liquor store to visit the barbershop. The barbershop was where all of the wise men of the community gathered to play cards, checkers, watch television, and philosophize on life. It was a place for all the men to come together; old, young, working, and unemployed would congregate. It did not matter if you were the high school drop out or the college graduate; you still needed a haircut. Even if you lived in the suburbs, you could not find a Black barber out there, and Black hair required a Black barbershop.

As he walked in, some of the old guys playing checkers in the corner called out to him. Jordan spoke and smiled to acknowledge their greetings. It was customary to greet the elder statesmen of the barbershop. Over on the other wall was the line of chairs for those waiting their turn to be serviced. Jordan took his seat after pulling a number for the tag. Two television sets hung from the ceiling; one carried the news and the other carried sports. Whatever story came on; there were discussion about it. Whether it was about the political commentary on the news or the local basketball team, everybody had a comment and everybody would share it.

The barbershop was loud and active until a woman brought her son in to get a haircut. All of the talking quieted down until the woman left. The barbershop was not a place for women; it was the man's domain and they liked it that way. But the barbershop was also a place for the community to stay in touch; people left bulletins of upcoming events, lost dogs, and job postings. The barbershop sold local neighborhood products like Aunt Emma's pies and Mr. Bernard's incense. The televisions had the volume turned down and the captions were on because the barbershop always had music; loud music was always playing.

As Jordan took a seat, he noticed the young man setting next to him. This guy was about his age, but he dressed funny; the type of dress that would get you beat down in his neighborhood. "You don't leave around here, do you dog?" Jordan asked.

"Live around here?" The young man seemed annoyed at the question. "Do you mean in the state of Maryland? Or do you mean this county, city, or neighborhood? If you mean do I live next door to you or on your block, no I do not live here. And by the way, I'm not your dog, either."

"Yeah, DOG! I knew you weren't from around here with that polo shirt on and those Stacey Adams on your feet. You could probably buy some good

Nike's with what those cost." Jordan was trying to tease this guy because he did not like him.

"So?" The young man asked. "Oh I see; there is a certain style for the neighborhood. Some committee got together to determine which color rag you were going to place in your back pocket, and which DOG as going to be beaten down because they were on the wrong corner wearing the wrong tennis shoes. Do you hear yourself talking? You criticize me because I choose to have my own style. What's wrong with you?"

"Hey, punk! You think you better than me?" Jordan barked as he stood up over the guy. He was not going to take this from this punk, especially on his block."

"Hey you, don't get tough with me! You don't have your boys with you today, so you aren't that threatening. I have no problem dealing with you, so back the heck off me!" he replied, unafraid. The young man obviously came to this neighborhood prepared to deal with people like Jordan. "And since you asked, yes I think I am better than you at some things, as you're better than me at some things. I bet I cannot sell dope as well as you, or do a drive by. But can you get into college? I do not know who is better as a human; I just know I have my own style. I did not criticize you, but you attacked me. I did not call you a dog; you called yourself that. Sounds like you may not respect yourself...DOG!"

"You know what?" Jordan said while looking at the owner of the barbershop. He knew the men here would not let things get out of hand. "You are too stupid to understand what "Dog" is in the hood. It is like saying hello; it's a greeting, fool."

"Well, you be that dog." The young man was finished talking to Jordan, but had to make one last comment. "The only way you can be a 'dog' is for your woman to be a wench. Somebody may be playing a game on you, my friend. Whoever has you thinking you are a dog is your enemy. Not me. And remember, they shoot bad dogs." With that, the young man got up and left the barbershop. Some men in the shop praised what the young man was saying. Others thought he was arrogant and looked down on the hood. The conversations went on and on until another game came on television or news items hit the stations. Jordan was still angry, but he also thought about what the young man said. If he was a dog, then....

Friday, June 15, 2007

This was the day! It was going to be the day of freedom! Jordan sat on the bed before getting up. He was reflecting on his life and how much he wanted it to change. Jordan grew up tough in the streets of Dorchester County, Maryland. He was tough and everyone knew it. His fourteen years had provided plenty of reasons to be angry. He did not think it was so bad. He had friends and he was popular. They were the wrong kind of friends and the wrong kind of popularity. Jordan was a gang banger and enjoyed it. He did not buy into the notion that life made him a criminal; he believed that criminals made him a life. He enjoyed being a criminal.

Jordan thought it was fun to stand around with his friends and take what he wanted. He thought of himself as a warrior, not a criminal. He was protecting his neighborhood from others just like him, and would fight to do so. While he was involved in many types of criminal activities, he considered himself a drug dealer. It was his job to move crack for the gang, and he was good at it.

The business side of drug dealing did not interest him. He did not want to become a major mover of drugs; he had seen what that led to. Jordan just wanted to have money for a good car, great clothes, and the crib to pull it all together. He just could not think of another way to do that without becoming a major drug dealer. He did not want a job; jobs were for losers. A job was for those punks that could not make it in the hood.

Jordan felt that he had lived with his mother Lynette for too long and wanted to move out, but he needed money for that. Lynette was twenty-eight years old, never married, and had two other children; she needed her space too. Jordan was trying to be rational about it but he just wanted to leave. Jordan was the oldest and the wildest. His mother constantly argued with him on his late hours and the company he was keeping. He had been in trouble with the police since he was eleven years old. He skipped school so much and got into so much trouble that he finally dropped out.

Lynette worked hard all day. She took two buses to get home on the two-hour commute. How could she watch Jordan all of the time? Jordan's gang friends watched over him much more than his mother. As soon as she got home from work she had to prepare for dinner, and that's what Lynette did on this day as well, as usual.

The home they shared was typical for the neighborhood. Tiny rooms, old furniture, no air, and very little heat. Jordan stayed in the room with his eleven-year-old brother, Tyrone. His six-year-old sister called 'Sis' stayed with Lynette in her room.

The house had bars over the windows and was surrounded by a chain-link fence. Inside, Lynette had placed plywood over the windows. She thought it would give her some protection if Jordan's enemies shot at the house again as they did last month. They had moved the television to the kitchen and no one spent a lot of time in the living room anymore.

Lynette had tried to turn her life around. Her brother, Thomas and she had it pretty tough growing up. Their mother died and left them with just each other. Thomas got involved in some serious things before he turned it around. She was no better than he was with drugs, drinking and plenty of men in her life. This made it hard to discipline Jordan and he knew it. She did the same things and he saw her do them. All she wanted to do was work and come home safely. It would have been nice if Jordan had fed his brother and sister, but that would have been asking too much. She would have been satisfied if he did not have his hoodlum friends in the house while she was gone.

She did go to church and had a few friends. The pastor of the church was helpful with advice, and even helped her get the job she had. Reverend Obedi tried to talk to Jordan, but Jordan wanted nothing to do with a preacher. "All they want is your money and to take a way your fun." he would say. "If God worked for them, why are they all broke? I got more money than the preacher; he should be selling on the corner with me." He was only kidding but his drug selling was causing problems. Jordan was already on probation for possession and he was promised jail time the next time.

Lynette's brother Thomas had tried to be a parent in Jordan's life, but his history on the block made Jordan more of a target than anything else. Therefore, Jordan got to visit with his uncle whenever he could, but the principal male bonding was done with his juvenile friends.

Lynette wanted to move but could not. She wished she could have lived closer to her job, but the rent was too high. If she got married, it would make life easier financially, but who would want an argument with a fourteen year old, smart mouthed kid everyday? Jordan saw to it that no real man would be bothered with her. Most of the weak men she dated only wanted a place to put their feet up and get a meal. They were not good role models for her children, and most were afraid of Jordan and his friends. However, Lynette was very good looking, so she gained attention from lots of men. Her tall, brazen physique, deep eyes, and silky, mid-length bobbed hair were enough to captivate any man; but her apparent unhappiness always attracted the wrong kind of man.

Friends described Lynette as very caring. However, she was completely overwhelmed with worry over Jordan and her other children. She felt trapped in her own home, and could see no way out. She had ambitions, but could not see a way to fulfill them. She wanted to be married, or even have a boyfriend, but that was out of the question. The only kinds of men who would be around her just wanted sex and could only make babies. No good man would tolerant her son or his friends.

There was one man in her life, however, that she knew she could count on no matter what. Lynette loved her brother Thomas, and truly appreciated his support and protection. She knew he had not married because he had to take care of her, and she felt guilty about that. She tried to get a good job to relieve the pressure on Thomas, but could not seem to get on her feet.

There had been a recent drive-by shooting of her home. The windows were shot out, and bullets were embedded in the walls. Everyone was alright, but now they all spent their time in the back rooms of the home. The front of the house was boarded up because Lynette could not afford to replace the shot out windows.

Lynette had two other children to worry about and they needed her right now. Dinner had to be put on the stove, and she had to get ready for work the next day. Jordan had to take care of himself tonight. She had no time to argue; after dinner, she had to run out and cash her check at the store if she wanted to be back in before dark.

CHAPTER THREE
LIFE OR LIFESTYLE

As Lynette returned home from work, Jordan met her at the front door. "What's up, mama?" They both instantly tightened up because of all of the tension between them. Did he go to see his probation officer today? Would she make a big thing over him not coming home last night? He was dreading the barrage of questions awaiting him.

If you asked Jordan, he would have said that he loved his mama. No one had better say anything about her, and he was still looking for the dudes that shot up the house and scared her. He loved her, but did not respect her. None of the love and protection she gave him could overcome the fact that she was just a woman. She had no power except what she could beg up from a decent man or manipulate from the weak ones. Men like him did not take mess from a woman. Women were there to provide for the man; get me out of jail or fix me some food. They were good for a lot of things, but they were not deserving of respect.

Mama was cool, though, and she did try to help with good advice, but what advice could she give a player? She had never played; she had just been played. Jordan had seen all of the weak men hanging around with his mother. More scared of him and his friends than anyone on the block. If he could not respect the man, he could not respect the woman with the man; that included mama.

As Jordan walked passed her toward the door, she asked about his probation officer, but Jordan just ignored her. He learned years ago that mama had no real power. What was she going to do, call the police on him? Hardly, he knew that the courts would place him in foster care or juvenile homes, but the bill for his stay would be sent to his mother.

If she called the police on him, her reward would be a $30 per day bill for his foster care cost. It would be free if she stopped working and lost the house. However, as long as she worked everyday and kept paying for a home, the state felt she could also pay for his care.

Jordan knew that as long as he did not attack her personally, he could get away with most things. Mama was not going to report the cocaine in his bedroom nor the gun under his bed. She was nearly broke, and 'the man' has placed him in charge of the household. If she reported him, it would cost her money.

So, Jordan just kept walking down the street, ignoring his mother's voice. He ignored it until she said something that stopped him in his tracks. "Your uncle Thomas is coming over Sunday; he asked if you were going to be here." Jordan turned around and stared back at his mother. He looked at her for a long time before saying anything. "Did you call him?" He wanted to know why his uncle was coming. Uncle Thomas was one person in the family Jordan did not play around with. He was nice and all that, but the dude did not play. He was serious and he was deadly. He used to be a serious gang banger in his day, and his gang name still warranted attention in the neighborhood.

"I did not call him, he called me. He's coming by to visit with me and wanted to know if you will be around. What should I tell him?" One thing Jordan knew about this Original Gangster, if he wanted to see you, it was best to be around. "Okay, I'll be here; but I got to get going now. Later." He turned and continued walking away.

Sunday with Uncle Thomas. Even his friends do not want to be around him then. Uncle Thomas use to go by the gang name "No Good One" because there was just no good in him. He did not care; not about you, or himself. He had a serious reputation for pimping, drugs, car theft, and rumors of murder for hire. He had friends in high places, and was the elder statesman of the block. Most of the guys he hung out with were dead or in jail. Uncle Thomas survived, and for that, he had Jordan's respect.

Jordan wanted to be like his uncle one day, except for one thing. His uncle gave up gang banging a long time ago. Not only had he gone straight, he became one of those gang counselor experts you see on television. You know, the guys telling you what they did was wrong and not to do it. He was making some legitimate money telling his story and giving out advice. As far as Jordan was concerned, doing twenty years of crime and then going straight was profitable. He was just working on his twenty years of crime first.

Even though Uncle Thomas had gone straight, he was still a no nonsense kind of guy. Gang bangers were always trying to get a reputation by standing up to him. It usually was a terrible mistake for the youngster. Thomas was tall and muscular with thick, wavy, graying hair and gray eyes. Time and the streets had aged him beyond his years; however, his spirit was still strong and powerful. Although he was on the right side of the law now, he was still fiercely intimidating. He would sometimes stand too close for your comfort because you never knew which mood he would be in and you did not want to make a mistake.

Thomas possessed a somber, lordly presence. Associates describe him as 'cold'. Like most warriors, he was quiet until you needed a warrior. His spirit had seen a lot, and he wished to rest from his past activities. As a gang member, he was violent and unemotional; as an anti-gang counselor, he was stern and uncompromising. His knowledge of the gang lifestyle gave him fire to keep going. He deeply wanted to change the mindset, of the gangs and the community but has very little patience with the politicians and city leaders.

Thomas was worried about Jordan and Lynette. He believed Jordan was heading in the same direction he went in as a young man. But the difference was that Thomas was forced into gang activity to protect his sister Lynette. He was trying to keep the household together. When the situation changed, he took advantage of it. When schools opened up for Black folks, he attended. When jobs opened up for Black folks, he went to work. He fought for the right to compete in this country, and he took advantage of those rights when they were won.

Jordan had the rights Uncle Thomas had fought for, but failed to take advantage of them. When people in the neighborhood started making money, Jordan and his friends began to sell dope and rob them. When people started building their own homes, it was Jordan that broke into them. It seems like Jordan as working to keep Black folks where Uncle Thomas had fought to leave. Uncle Thomas was determined to get this message into Jordan.

In many ways, Uncle Thomas had never stopped being the warrior. He could only be a gang member, so that was all he knew. When his sister and her babies were safe and had other opportunities, he only knew gang banging. So he learned a new system. He had never been married but considered Lynette and her children his family.

Jordan remembered last year when his friend Jay-Low confronted Uncle Thomas over his name. Uncle Thomas has insisted for years that no one call him by his gang name any longer. "That guy does not live here anymore." he would say. Well, Jay-Low called him by his old gang name one day. He was just trying to impress a girl standing nearby. Uncle Thomas walked up to Jay-Low and asked him if he was talking to him. Before Jay-Low could give his smart answer, Uncle Thomas had grabbed him by the neck and shoved his head backwards through a car window.

As Jay-Low was dangling out of the car, Uncle Thomas walked away saying, "If you don't want 'No Good One', don't call 'No Good One'." That was just how Thomas was; he did not play and you had better not play with him either. Jordan was going to be there Sunday just to hang out with him.

However, it was not out of fear of Uncle Thomas. Jordan had a lot of respect for this man. He was wise in the way Jordan needed wisdom. Even the cops showed some respect for him. Nobody loved him, and most did not fear him. However, everyone that knew him respected him. Jordan liked that, and was looking forward to speaking with him.

Jordan recalled a particular conversation he had with his uncle one day outside on his mother's porch. Uncle Thomas was really getting on Jordan's case for disrespecting women. He had just gotten off the phone with his girlfriend, and Uncle Thomas had heard him.

"Jordan, I really do understand why you treat women the way you do. You do not believe you can gain her respect. You are accepting the Master's opinion of her and of you. The man does not want you to have any respect for Black women. If you did, you would fight to protect her. That means you would fight him to protect her. So he has always tried to get you and her into a battle. That way, you will allow him to raise your children to work for him, and he will provide for your woman. She will be more loyal to him than she will be to you. Look at Lynette; she is more loyal to her job than her pastor. She does not even have a man in her life, but you do not respect her any more than you do your girl."

Jordan did respect his mother, so he thought. "I will hurt any fool that mess with her, Uncle Thomas. But she does not respect me. She thinks I am still a little boy and she treats me that way. If she showed respect for me, I would show respect for her."

"That is what the man wants you to think. If you were a respectful young man, it would not matter if a woman respected you. You would still be a man before her. She will not worship you, but your mother does respect you. But Jordan, as big as you are and as tough as you want to be, you are still a child. If you were not a child, you would be taking care of her instead of her taking care of you. That is the test of manhood. She does not have time to disrespect you; she is too busy trying to keep this home for you; she tries to work and feed her kids. Give her respect for that and try to help."

Jordan looked at Uncle Thomas with confusion. "Let me ask you something Uncle Thomas. Did you have respect for women when you were pimping them? How about when you sold drugs to them or beat up their husbands? Did you call it respecting the Black woman when you snatched their purses on payday or broke into their homes while they were at work?"

Thomas got frustrated with his smart-mouthed nephew. "Instead of listening you're always trying to throw something back, just like Old Forty." He regretted bringing up his sister's ex as soon as the words came out of his mouth.

Hearing his uncle mention "Old Forty" made Jordan's blood run hot. Jordan hated his father intensely, harboring bitterness on behalf of himself and his mother who was forced to raise him alone. When he realized his father was gone for good, it pushed Jordan over the edge. He was a decent kid before; he had behavior issues, but he was also sweet and he protective of a mother he adored. However, when Ford walked out the door and kept walking, his exodus conceived a bitterness in Jordan that would transform his personality and his perspective. Jordan didn't understand the pressure his father was under or the rejection he faced from mainstream society. Jordan didn't know the pain of inadequacy that caused his father to drink every time he had a chance. Jordan didn't understand these things and he didn't care. All he knew was that his father wasn't there. They didn't play catch, they didn't go fishing. His father never taught him how to be anything but mean, moody, and macho. Jordan embraced the hardness and emotional detachment he inherited from his father Ford, but he resented the one who passed down this warped legacy.

The only good thing that came from his father was the resolve to never abandon his own children. However, Jordan's loyalties left his mother just like his father did. He became so consumed with resentment for his father that in anger he began to mistreat the one parent who was faithful. Jordan loved his mother, but he learned how to treat her from the father who had abandoned him.

"Yeah, I guess so, huh? That's where I get my respect for females; by watching my uncle and my no good daddy."

Uncle Thomas understood where he was coming from. Always looking for a reason to justify how he was. "Well, Jordan, of course if you were that real man you are talking about, it would not matter what I did or what your father did. Be your own man. If you are learning from me, learn from the older, wiser me, not the younger, foolish one. I don't pimp women today! I don't steal from them or beat up their husbands today. I may have learned something about myself and about manhood. If you want to learn from me, learn from the man here today. But I understand it is our history. Black men and Black women have always had this problem between them. But the bottom line is, Jordan, you are being played. You do not have a woman; the man has your woman.

"The Black man cannot face this fact; he would lose his mind if he accepted that fact. The White man controls the women in your life and it makes you crazy. She does not belong to him. She gets her benefits from Master. She gets the education and so the Black man thinks she looks down on him. He cannot protect her so he loses his ego unless he ridicules her. Only free men respect their women. It was common knowledge on the plantation that you should marry a woman living on another plantation. That way, you would not have to witness her being abused by Master. The Black man had to ignore the abuse of his wife and children, so he replaced his natural protective role with neglect. You don't understand why you are the way you are, I do, and I hope you will learn about it the easy way not the hard way. Just keep your respect for your mother around me, okay?"

Jordan remembered their last conversation. He wanted to know if the neighborhood had changed much since back in the day. Uncle Thomas explained that everything had changed and nothing had changed. The streets still smelled of exhaust fumes, weed and cigarette smoke, and general pollution. City buses and cars of all kinds ran from morning until night, creating a rhythm of hustle and bustle. The young warriors on the corners were a part of that rhythm, hustling and moving whatever was your drug of choice, ready to fight and die to protect their set reputation or territory. Thomas took a deep breath and remembered his younger years. While the styles and individuals in the hood had changed over time, the spirit of destruction was still there. "You guys still think you are fighting for the hoods don't you? You still think that the color means everything. The man has you so beaten down that all you can hold on to is the color of the rag hanging out of your pocket. You call it your block but is really belongs to the cops. When they show up, you don't fight; you leave. A real soldier would fight for his community. You guys do not fight because you do not even have a community. It is just your colors against their colors and we both are ensuring poverty for our own communities. Look around this neighborhood. All you see is poverty. The "Bugs" over on the other set did not bring poverty to this block. We brought poverty to the block."

Jordan asked how he had added poverty to the block. "They have you so concerned with the color and image of the gang that you can't see what you're doing. With the drive by shootings, you encourage the trafficking of drugs you sell on your own corner. You are driving out jobs, business and services. Taxes go up because of the increase in police service, and property value goes down because no one wants to live around you if they do not have to. So, the poorer you get, the richer the managers get. When I found that out, I decided to get into the game myself. I gave up the life because it was not life, it was death."

"Yeah, but everyone knows your rep; you got the rep first." Uncle Thomas got a little impatient with Jordan. "Boy! You refuse to get it. I did not care then and I do not care now who likes me, fears me, or respects me. I didn't do anything trying to gain respect. My reputation came from me taking care of your mother and myself. We only had each other, and I had to take care of her. I was angry and frustrated by my failure to do so, and had to blame someone for my own failures. I could not blame myself, because that would mean I was weak. I could not blame the gangs, because that would mean I was wrong.

"Therefore, I blamed the mysterious thing called 'the man"; he was the blame for all of my problems, and he was also the solution. Since I blamed "the man', I could justify anger and criminal activities because "the man" had taken everything else from me. So we think we are brave but we really are afraid? We think we are tough but we are really weak?"

Jordan began to think. "I understand; is that why we change the meaning of our words? We call good 'bad'; we're just trying to change our view of the world, I guess. Just trying to change the ideal of the plantation we live on. How do we stop the guilt and the fear?"

Jordan had to admit it was a fascinating conversation, and he was looking forward to hearing more about this conversion. After all, Uncle Thomas had found something that pulled him right out of the gangs into a legitimate income.

"But aren't all those anti-gang folks just sellouts? All they seem to want is to surrender to the man and stop being themselves. Isn't that the real problem?" Jordan asked. "You think they are sellouts? Why? Just because they have moved on with their lives, they have sold out? Just because they have gone on a different path, they have disrespected you? Why are they sellouts? What do they have of yours that they could sell?"

Jordan looked at Uncle Thomas to see if he was joking. Everyone knew if you did not dress a certain way or believe in certain things, you were a sellout. "Those people that left the hood didn't stay true to the hood; they sold out their true Blackness for the White man's dream. They try to be accepted in the White man's world, but he is never going to accept them."

Uncle Thomas took a seat and leaned back; this was going to take some time. He rubbed his head in frustration; something he did when he needed to refocus and calm down. Jordan was just a boy, and Thomas had to remember that he needed guidance, especially with Fordy not being there to raise his son. "Boy, let me tell you about real manhood. Real men, Black or White, are not worrying about whether another man will accept them. It does not matter to a real man if another man wants him to live where he lives or not. If a man tells another man that he should believe, dress, and live a certain way or he is not Black enough, that man is a weak man. How can you tell someone that he cannot live across town? You are trying to control that man. It is you putting restrictions on his movement, not the White man Jordan; you are trying to control another man's life."

"What would be more important Jordan, keeping your mind on where you are going or remembering where you came from? You were not always on the corner selling dope, but it was something you thought about, planned, and went after. You forgot about riding your bike and playing basketball. You forgot about school and your little brother. Good or bad, Jordan, you have become what you've thought about. All I am saying is that if you only think about where you came from, you will never act on where you want to go. So I would say to you son, not to forget where you are going. So what do you want for Jordan in the future?"

"What future? I don't have a future. All I'll be doing is selling dope until some one puts a bullet in me or the cops put me away." Jordan took a seat next to Uncle Thomas to listen. Uncle Thomas placed his arm behind Jordan and continued. "That is what we call a cliché Jordan. It is an often used phrase but does not mean anything. Look around you son. Learn from the actions of the older people. Why don't you see very many old gang bangers? You may think they are all dead or in jail, but you have one sitting right here next to you. I am not dead or in jail, but I am old. I have learned something Jordan, and it is what I am trying to pass on to you. I wasted a lot of years learning these lessons, and wanted to give them to you before I die."

Jordan looked at his Uncle and knew there was something he was trying to say. "You mean you are trying to give something back to the community? That's why you are speaking to me?"

"No, Jordan, I am not trying to give something back to the community; that's another cliché, I do not owe the community anything. I am trying to give something to you. You are my family; you are my nephew. You should be trying to give something back to your mother, not the community. She is the one working her behind off taking care of you. She is the one going downtown to bail you out. It is not the community that has given you life; give something back to the ones who have loved and protected you."

"You mean my crew? My homeboys? Yeah, I will give my life for them." Uncle Thomas simply got up and walked away. When he got to the door, he turned around and looked at Jordan. "One day, son. One day you will understand. Just remember my words; you will see what the community offers and what your family offers. The community is always some organization run by people. The community is controlled by that same man you do not trust. He sets up organizations that only beg for better treatment on the plantation, never demanding freedom from the plantation. I cannot follow a person or group who simply wants to make my life easier on the plantation. I don't care for low-income housing, only high income housing, and I will never get that from them. I don't want a minimum wage increase; I want a maximum wage. I can only get that if I leave the plantation. When I am hungry, I don't seek a hand out cheese program; it will only help those distributing the cheese. I like steak Jordan, but I cannot get it from a program.

"I don't want to change this place; I want to forget it. I want to transform it; then I truly intend to forget where I came from. If that makes a sellout then let me get my check, because I will certainly sell out my plans to escape only to those wishing to go."

"Those organizations mostly do not know you and certainly do not care about you. But you are being encouraged to care and give something to them. Just remember what I have said Jordan, and when the time is right these words will give you comfort." Uncle Thomas closed the door behind him and left the house.

Jordan would not let it go. He got up and followed him out of the door. He had more questions for him, and since Uncle Thomas appeared to be in a good mood, why not ask them now? "Uncle Thomas, seriously man, what happened to you? People say you were the biggest banger around; what happened? They say you had wenches all up Roberts street and dope sales on every corner. Then you walked away. You turned your back on people and walked away. Something happened to you Uncle Thomas, and I just want to know what it was."

"Jordan, I simply began to think. I just looked around my world and saw it for what it was, not what I wanted it to be. What does every man want out of life? He wants to be protected, honored, and at peace. No real man wants to fight, but he will. He will fight for protection, honor, and peace. I was selling dope and pimping women in hopes to find honor, but was always looking for the better way. Well, one day I found the way, son."

"I noticed that the storeowners I robbed had better cars and better homes than I did. They worked hard all day and went home in peace. I worked hard all day and went home in fear. Fear of cops, fear of the owners, and most of all fear of people just like me. I thought the storeowners and johns were weak and I was strong. But I began to think, if they are so weak why do they have all of this money I want to take from them? If they are weak, why don't I, the stronger one, do what they are doing? Wouldn't I make more money than they did? If I was stronger, why were my home and bank account smaller and I could never rest?

"It was crystal clear if I just could just stop hating myself and look. The answer was right in front of me. I could gain more of what I wanted out of life and gain it faster if I went into business and made my money legitimately. So, you are right Jordan, I left where I was to go where I needed to be. I went into business for myself and I left all those pimps and drug dealers. They were not going where I was going, so how could we stay in touch?

"This is why I spend so much time talking to you. I have been where you are, and I know what is around the curve, son. I'm not trying to control your life; I can barely control my own life. I'm just trying to pass on some information from around the curve. Jordan, you cannot think and stay a dog. Think and be free!

There was one thing that struck him about the conversation with Uncle Thomas. He did all that he did for Lynette, his sister and Jordan's mother. Therefore, here was a gang banger that called every woman he knew a wench or a whore, but sacrificed his life, and apparently the lives of others, for this woman. The same woman that Jordan disrespected openly. Uncle Thomas probably did not like that. He made a mental note to treat his mother a little better, especially when Uncle Thomas was around. That was funny; Uncle Thomas had told him, "You will respect women when you respect the men around those women."

Jordan remembered the silence. Uncle Thomas had actually made him think. Then he spoke again. "They have us acting like a herd of sheep. Have you ever seen how a herd of sheep reacts to everything around it? The sheep is an animal motivated by fear. Fear; not love, not family, not loyalty, but fear of dying, or being hungry, or abandoned. The sheep spends all day long wondering if the sheepherder will take care of him. If the sheepherder does not respond to the sheep's needs, the sheep does not rebel; the sheep makes noise. Master will respond and gives more comfort to the sheep if it makes enough noise."

"Why do you compare us to sheep?" Jordan wondered, "I'm not a sheep, I'm not afraid. I will kill anyone that messes with me. People respect me and fear me; that does not sound like a sheep to me. I don't keep folks on any master's plantation. What do you mean? I do not even know Master. I just take care of my homeboys and they take care of me. We keep control over the hood so the other gangs will not take over our territory."

"You are correct, you do not sound like a sheep; but you do sound like a sheep dog." Thomas explained. "The sheep dog is trained to keep the sheep on the master's field, to direct the sheep where Master wants them to go. Some are sheep, some are goats, and some are the sheep dogs. However, all fear Master, and all work for him.

"You are simply keeping crime high on Master's plantation. You call it keeping control over your streets; young man you don't have any streets. You run the minute Master shows up in his police cars. Your job is to spread fear on the plantation so the slaves will look to Master for protection from you. You are the slave breeder making babies for Master to raise. If you give Master your children to raise, he will raise them to work for his children. Your job is to keep the taxes high, crime high, drug use high and failure high.

"You are just Master's sheepdog riding herd over Master's sheep. You keep hope low, jobs low, education low, and family life low. You have your job to do and you do it well. However, you are not alone; there are many types of sheepdogs. Some, like you, even know you are dogs, you greet each other with 'hey, dog'. Others are the fear mongers that fight anyone that has a plan to leave the plantation. They will not allow any real plan to succeed; Master cannot have a non-performing sheep dog."

"Okay, okay, I get your idea, and for now, I'm listening. Tell me more about this herd of sheep," Jordan replied.

"Well, the sheep is motivated by fear; don't ever forget that. It cannot do anything without the sheepherder or his sheep dog. The main fear of the sheep is this great, unknown thing called 'the wolf'. 'The wolf' will get you if you leave the master's pasture. 'The wolf' will get you if you do not follow the herd, and the wolf will surely get you if you do not respond to the sheep dog."

"Most sheep has never seen a wolf, never smelled him, and do not know anything about this wolf. Most sheep have all of their knowledge about the wolf from the sheepherder and his wolf-like creature the sheep dog."

"While the sheepherder tells the sheep he will take care of them, he is only taking care of himself. While the sheepherder takes the sheep to good pasture and keeps them healthy, he does not do this out of love for the sheep. The sheepherder loves rack of lamb and the soft feel of sheepskin on his chair. Ask yourself this question; who kills more sheep, the wolf or the sheepherder? But we are afraid of the wolf, not the sheepherder. I say, let us take a closer look at the wolf; he may very well be our friend."

Jordan did not understand that then, but he was beginning to. He really did not respect the women hanging out in his gang set. He really did not respect the men he hung around that much. As much as he hated to admit it, he knew any one of them would give him up to get out of real, hard time. If he really respected them, he would respect their mothers, sisters, and girlfriends.

CHAPTER FOUR
LOVE LIFE AND LOVE OF LIFE!

Just as he thought about girlfriends, around the corner came his girlfriend, Iris. He did not have time for Iris; he was on his way to be with the set. They had something to do, and Iris always took a lot of time, especially lately.

Iris was a beautiful teenage girl. She was intelligent and happy. Her only worry was her boyfriend, Jordan. She had known Jordan all of her life; they met in Kindergarten, and he had been her boyfriend ever since. She didn't know why she liked Jordan so much. He was her baby boy in every since of the word, and he needed her and that was attractive to her. She tried to be the type of girl Jordan wanted, the type you see in the rap videos.

She was pretty sure that Jordan liked her as much as she liked him; after all, her protected her and defended her. He liked the way other men wanted what he had, and she thought that was a source of power for her.

Iris wore revealing clothing, not as a reflection of her character, but of Jordan's. She sported long hair and tight jeans so Jordan could show her off to everyone. Iris found it a little annoying and did not like the attention she got from others, but it was a necessary part of her plan. She truly believed that her love and attention would change Jordan. She thought Jordan's behavior was just a matter of maturity, or the lack thereof. If she simply showed him the error of his ways, he would conform to her idea of a great man. Iris was making the same mistake her mother made; the same mistake women have made for thousands of years.

Despite her mistakes, however, Iris was really growing into a beautiful young woman. Not just in her height and figure, but she was developing a beautiful mind. Iris was beginning to notice some things about where she lived. One thing she noticed was that she did not plan to live there long. She would not live in fear; she would not live in a community of fear, and she would not live with a man that she feared.

Iris really liked Jordan, but was not feeling loved or appreciated by him. She had known Jordan all of her fourteen years of life. They started school together, and had been in every class together since. Iris thought she knew Jordan better than any other person. Iris remembered what Jordan was like before he decided to take on the thug life. He was sweet, interesting, and talented. Jordan used to do things in class just to make her laugh. He had even asked her to marry him with a candy ring when they were small. However, many things had changed. He was more distant and cold these days, trying to maintain his street reputation. Every now and then she caught a glimpse of the Jordan she had loved all of her life, but it was rare. He used to be excited about her, but now he took her for granted. As she approached him, she could tell he did not want to be bothered with her. He probably was in a hurry to meet his low life friends and get into trouble.

She knew what being Jordan's girlfriend meant to her and to him. She knew that Jordan wanted a "video girl"; the kind that all of the guys wanted but could not get. She wore sexy clothes that revealed her body. She did it to add to Jordan's reputation. Her skin was light, her dark hair was long down her back, and her midriff was always showing. This was the image Jordan wanted, and she gave it to him.

However, she did not like the sexual attention men gave her. She did not like the looks other women gave her. Iris had not earned the reputation she had in the neighborhood, but she has accepted it. Being Jordan's girlfriend came with a lot of power, and she wanted that. Therefore, if he wanted a "Hoochie Mama," she would be that. That was, until she could get out. Iris was working on getting out. She already had a job working in a library, and looked forward of getting out of the neighborhood as soon as possible.

Jordan was not excited about her job. She only worked on Fridays, and only for a few hours. She refilled the shelves at the library and did some filings. That did not bother Jordan; what bothered him was her supervisor. That young, arrogant, White guy, Gilmore Jr.

"Junior," as everyone called Gilmore Jr., liked Iris and everyone knew it. He did not like Jordan, and everyone knew that, too. While Junior had asked Iris out many times, her refusal did not stop him. He seemed determined and even confident that she would choose him over this gang banging, no-good hoodlum she was seeing. He continued to put pressure on her at work. Not only promising her favors, but also pointing out the differences between him and Jordan.

Just that day, while they were filing alone in the administrative office, Junior mentioned going to a movie. She turned him down as usual, but this time he grabbed her. "Leave me alone, Junior," she demanded, "You'd better leave me alone; I'll tell Jordan." Junior responded with total disrespect of Jordan. "Tell Jordan? That punk, what is he going to do, a drive-by? He does not even have a car. He will be in jail most of the year and then you will want my attention.

"I control Jordan, Jordan does not control me. Why don't you stop playing with that player and hang out with someone that can treat you like a woman? When are you going to date a man that does not have a probation officer?" She looked at him as if he was out of his mind, but he continued. "Listen, in ten years where will we all be? Do you want to be here taking collect calls from the state prison, or hanging with me at my dad's club? Jordan is as mature as Jordan will be. He has achieved all in life he will ever achieve. His future is limited by his past and yours will be, too, if you hook up with him. What are you going to do tonight, get a bottle and go shake your butt somewhere? You think that is what is expected of you, and you cannot pull out of it."

Iris tried to defend her man. "Jordan is twice the man you are. He has respect; no one respects you. People fear Jordan; they only hate you. Jordan doesn't have to make money; he can take it from punks like you. Now since you are my supervisor, I will do you a favor. I will not tell Jordan what you said because if I do, he will rip your lily-white heart out and beat you to death with it. Now, LEAVE ME ALONE!"

That really hit the nerve with Junior and he got angry. "You are nothing but a Chicken Head Ho! I don't call you that; your man calls you that. You are just a wench, today you are Jordan's wench. Next week I may be able to pick your broke butt up on the corner at a discount. I'll just wait until you to need money for your babies' food because your punk boyfriend cannot support you. You are mine if I want you, you just don't know it yet. There will come a time when Jordan himself will gladly give you to me. In the meanwhile, shake your hoochie behind over here and get the filing done."

Her feelings were hurt, but she could not let him know. There were some truths to what he said. She was also afraid that Jordan would end up in jail and she would be alone. The fear was that she could not make a good man out of a bad one. Why did she spend so much time with the bad boys? This idiot was right about some things, but his attitude towards her was horrible. "You're just suffering from Jungle Fever, as all White boys do. What's the matter; can't get enough loving from the skinny behind White girls; need a real woman?"

"No," Junior shouted back. "All you Black girls are to white men is PRACTICE! We use you all up while you are young, and then marry those little thin White girls. You are just community property, wench, and you always will be. This is my world, and you are just a useful tool in it. The bottom line is, I do what I want, and eventually you will do what I want also. Jordan is destined to be in jail, he can't protect you from me. You don't want a man to treat you like a woman? Then I will wait and treat you like a whore. There will come a time when I will be the only person you can turn to. In addition, because of your attitude, the only thing I will require from you is for you to turn a trick. THE TRICK IS ON YOU."

"Well" Iris shouted! "It must be something your mother did not have (as she placed both of her hands on her hips) since you are begging for it over here begging for what you can get free over there, while she was pointing to the receptionist desk. I guess White girls are so bad you do not want it even when you can get it. I know Ann at the reception desk likes you, and you do not even talk to her. Man! It must be pretty bad when an ugly, skinny, pimple faced, White trash boy like you won't even take it from your own when they're throwing it at you. I feel sorry for her and I feel sorry for your sorry butt. You think you got it all White boy; but if you had it all, you would have me."

Ann, watching the bitter exchange, turned red with embarrassment. It was bad enough to see Iris strutting around the library every day like a video girl who's lost her camera crew, but to listen to Iris denigrate her in front of everyone was too much to bear. Ann wasn't confrontational like Iris was; she was passive-aggressive at best, and then only in the company of other Whites.

So, defenseless and speechless, Ann just turned bright red. She really did like Junior, and it really was a pitiful. She had the natural blond hair, the blue eyes, and the slim build; why didn't Junior respond to her? Ann knew she didn't look like a movie star, but she had all the qualities that White men wanted in a wife and mother. With a little makeup and confidence, Ann was actually a nice looking girl. But, because she was quiet and modest, she was often overlooked. Junior wasn't even an attractive White man; however, he was funny, intense, and came from a successful family. That was what made Junior attractive to Ann. But, because Junior was young and Iris was sensual, he was drawn to Iris and was completely oblivious to Ann. He rejected her subtle advances without even realizing she had made them because he was so oblivious to her presence. It all made Ann sick, and Iris' arrogance made her angry.

"That's alright," Ann thought. "Her day is coming and so is mine. When Junior grows up and starts looking for a real woman to be his wife, Iris will be somewhere overweight and dying from diabetes while I'm looking good and climbing the corporate ladder. He may want to take her to lunch, but in a few years he'll want to take me home to meet his mother. I hate that wench. Ugh. Glad Junior finally put her in her place." Ann, bitter and embarrassed, stood up, wanting to finally open her mouth and give Iris a piece of her mind. However, flooded with fear and even some sympathy for another girl who had been rejected by Junior just for being unwilling to change who she is to please him, Ann just deflated and went to the restroom to cry by herself in a lonely stall, nearly bumping into Iris as she rushed out of the room.

Iris left in tears and looked for Jordan. She had her paycheck and needed to cash it at the store, but she had a more pressing issue to speak with him about. When she saw him on his usual corner, she tried to find the right words to say to him. With Jordan, you had about five seconds before he became impatient and lost interest. However, she had a problem. A big problem and she need to talk to her boyfriend. She could tell that he did not want to talk, but he had to. "I got to talk to you, Jordan." She stood there with her hands on her hips and her head cocked to one side. She was not moving and Jordan knew she was serious.

Boy, she has been serious lately, and he could not figure out why. However, he knew he had to listen to her if he wanted to get on to meet the set.

"Yeah, baby, lets talk and walk, I'm in a hurry." He tried to take her arm and lead her across the street but she pulled away. "No Jordan, I need to sit down and talk to you. This won't take long; give me a minute." Iris did not wait for him to answer but took a seat on the bus stop bench.

"Okay..." Jordan relented. He knew it was easier to listen to her and get on down the street than deal with her complaining about him never giving her any time. She just did not understand how hard it was to listen to her while he was sitting at a bus stop. What if one of his enemies drove by he would be a sitting target.

As Jordan took a seat beside Iris, he could not help but noticed how beautiful she was. He really did like this girl. She was nice and smart, and would do anything for him. However, he knew he could not allow her to know how much he liked her because she may stop trying so hard.

However, he really did look forward to spending more time with her; he always thought they would be together forever. She would grow up to be a beautiful woman, and he would keep her around. So what did she want? What was so important that he had to take this important time with her? The set was waiting and they had an important job to do.

"What, girl; I have to get going. Tell me what's on your mind."

"Jordan, I think I'm pregnant!"

"PREGNANT?"

"How could you be pregnant; whose baby is it?" Those words just came out. He knew whose baby it was; but he could not accept that. If she was pregnant, he was going to be a father. If he was going to be a father, he had to take care of her and the baby. If he had to take care of them, his plans of selling dope and pimping women had to change. Jordan did not want to change, so he could not accept being the father of this child.

"Jordan, you need to stop playing; we got to talk about this. I'm pregnant and we have to take care of this. It was an accident, but it happened." Iris said sternly. "ACCIDENT MY BEHIND; YOU HAVE ALWAYS BEEN TRYING TO TRICK ME INTO YOUR LIFE!"

"Yes Jordan, that's it, I have always wanted to trick some fourteen year old, Black, high school drop out, gang banging criminal to be the father of my baby. If anyone was tricked, it was me." Iris started crying and became angry at the same time. She knew that crying always make Jordan angry but she did not care.

"Naw, wench, this is not my baby. It's that White dude's you work with. I know he's been trying to get your attention. You gave it up to the white boy! What did he promise you, a better job?" She looked at him through her tears. This is what she was afraid of; his negative response. Sure, Gilmore at work liked her and has asked her out, but Jordan was the only man she knew. It was Jordan's baby, but he was already trying to deny it.

She looked at him in anger. "Well, at least he has offered me more than heartache. At least he wants to work and has a car. What do you have, a rep and a record? Maybe I should go out with him." She stood up over him and shouted! "At least he makes me feel safe. He can protect me what can you do? You have taken me off all of my dreams and given me your nightmare!"

Jordan stood up and drew his hands back to slap her. How dare this Chicken-head speak to him that way in public! Who did she think she was talking to anyway? As she raised her hand to protect herself, he saw a flash of her belly from the mid-drift blouse. She had a little pouch showing. She really was pregnant.

For a split second, reality hit him square between the eyes. His father had gotten his mother pregnant with him around the same age. He abandoned her, and they have hardly spoken since. He grew up without a father. He remembered the birthdays and Christmas holidays that his father missed, and how he made a promise to himself. He made the same promise over and over again. "I will never abandon my child!"

He stood there frozen in time. He had become his father. Iris stood toe to toe with Jordan, but was not scared. If he was going to hit her then let him; they were going to deal with this today. However, Jordan did not hit her; he lowered his hand and quietly sat down beside her.

"You are really pregnant, that's tough. That is really tough. How long have you known?" He spoke with his voice lowered and his eyes looking down. He was going to be a father. That could not be. Many of the boys he hung out with were fathers, but they did not see their children and acted as if they did not want to. Nevertheless, this was Iris, he still remembered her as a little girl.

"I am eight weeks along and have known for a week. I thought I was, but I wasn't sure. I went to the doctor, and he said I was going to have a baby. I haven't told anyone; I wanted you to know first so we can decide what to do."

Jordan snapped out of it with those words. "Decide what to do?" He was only fourteen years old; what could he do? His mother would take care of the kid; he had things to do. She could give the baby to her own mother or her sister in Atlanta. "You decide, you do what you want, I have nothing to do with that. I'm only fourteen; I can't deal with a child right now." Jordan wondered what his homeboys would say about it. Some would congratulate him on having a baby so early, some would tell him to dump her.

Jordan stood up again; this time not angry, but hurried. "I got to go and I do not care what you do. This baby may be mine, but you are not mine. You just do you want to do, but leave me alone." Jordan walked away from her and did not look back. She called to him but he kept walking. That is just what he needed, a baby. Man! What a break!

After she spoke to Jordan, Iris continued down the street. She had to meet Lynette, cash her check and go shopping. Maybe she would tell Lynette about her condition tonight, after they had a good day shopping. She walked to the bus stop to wait for Lynette's bus to arrive. She watched the people pass by and wondered what she would do.

Lynette was a little late; she had missed her regular bus and was ten minutes late meeting Iris. She was really looking forward to shopping with her. After they cashed their checks, they would have a little girl time to talk, eat, and shop. She was in a hurry and was very happy to see Iris on the bus stop waiting for her when the bus pulled up to the corner.

"Hey girl; how you been?" Iris always called Lynette girl because they were so close in age, but it was out of respect for her. "Sorry I'm late Iris; let's get to the store as fast as possible to cash our checks before it starts to rain. I want to get to Harry's store before 7 pm. The crowds get pretty big this time of night and it looks like rain."

Lynette had her umbrella out just in time for the rain. After a blinding bolt of lightning flashed across the sky, it began to pour down. Iris sheltered herself under Lynette's umbrella as they hurried along the street. "I guess the first thing I will buy is an umbrella." declared Iris as they continued, almost pushed by the thunder.

CHAPTER FIVE
PRISONER OR SLAVE!

As Jordan approached the park where he was to meet his homeboys, he could see they were already waiting. Jay-Low was there still sporting the scar Uncle Thomas had given him. Jordan wondered to himself if Jay-Low would be coming over for Sunday dinner. At nineteen years old, Jay-Low was the eldest, so he came up with the plans for all of their activities. They did not really have a leader, but Jay-Low came close. He had been in jail and had friends that could supply them with the drugs they sold. Without Jay-Low, most of the set would have to pimp or steal from houses to feed themselves.

With Jay-Low was Randy Boy. Randy Boy just wanted to hang around. He was only eleven years old and would do anything they asked just as long as he could stay around them.

"Hey, man; you're late!" Jay-Low always wanted an explanation. "I had to deal with mama before I left. Are we going to do this or not?" Jordan asked. He was nervous and a little frightened, but he was also excited.

They had been selling dope on the corners for some time without really making any money. Well, they made a lot of money, but most of it belonged to the supplier. Everyone thought they had made a ton of cash selling drugs on the corner. If it had really been their money, why would they be living in the Hood and driving these hooptie cars?

When Jordan was arrested, it was on the news. They showed him being handcuffed and the cops pulled hundreds of dollars out of his pockets. He was recorded making eight hundred dollars a day on that corner. Those idiot television announcers made it seem like he kept all of that money himself. He had to give most of it to the guy he bought the dope from. He then had to share the rest with the gang members and try to buy more dope. The gang paid off some people downtown including cops and politicians, and the money flowed back and forth into the community.

Some people were making all the money, but it was not Jordan. It was the big movers, the risk takers, and those offering the protection. He understood business. Nobody makes all the money, if you do not share the cash flow, it will not be flowing. The biggest dope dealers in the city were doctors. Jordan figured that was all they were, legalized dope dealers. They paid the system to go to school, so the system licensed them to distribute drugs to the community through a network of pharmacies and hospitals. The system protected the doctors by running freelance dealers like Jordan out of business because Jordan did not pay into the system with cash flow. Some other street dealers bribed cops, judges, and prosecutors and just to stay on the streets.

Jordan had seen which prostitutes stayed on the streets; the ones that provided the most valuable information to the man. He understood the game and would participate. People pay for one thing; knowledge! Jordan had some, but he needed more. The knowledge Jordan gained after his arrest told him that the days on the corner selling dope was over. Jordan had to find a better way.

After a few months on the corner, every cop knew they were selling and every undercover cop knew when they were selling. Jay-Low knew it was only a matter of time before they were set up and busted. He knew they had to make money without anyone knowing it was them. They had to rob someone. If they could do a good robbery, they could buy enough cocaine to put more members out selling. That would make Jay-Low a distributor, and he could get off the streets.

Jay-Low was turning twenty years old next month, and did not want to go to jail again on a drug charge. If he could get some more money, he could keep Jordan and Randy Boy out selling for him. It was perfect.

"Yeah we're gonna to do it!" Jay-Low said. "You got the piece?" He asked Jordan to produce the gun they had hidden in his house. Since Jordan had the gun and was only fourteen, they decided that he would carry and produce it in the store. They figured, if caught, he would not get as much time as Jay-Low and Randy Boy was too inexperienced to trust with the job.

They had decided to rob the liquor store down the street. They knew the routine; it had been robbed before and they knew when the most money was present. It was the fifteenth of the month, and welfare checks and payroll checks were coming out today. The neighborhood did not have any banks and most people here did not have bank accounts, anyway. The liquor storeowner always tried to carry a lot of money to service his regular customers, like Jordan's mother. They could get their checks cashed even when they got off work late. It was the only place near by with such service.

Just as they reached The Pass, thunder began to roll. Lighting bolts danced across the sky as the group hurried along the path. The slight rustling of the grass and trees almost seemed to call out a warning to them. The creek never ran very high; even with the rain it should have been no problem for them to get across. In fact, the rain could help if dogs chased them, their scent might not be as detectable. Jordan was thinking, "Let it rain; today is freedom day."

As they walked towards the store, Jordan remembered one other thing. This store was also the store Iris used to cash her checks. It was Friday, the fifteenth, and both his mother and his pregnant girlfriend would be in the area when they pulled off the robbery. Boy! What a day this has been; it had to get better.

The three took the long route to avoid being seen by too many people. They crossed the baseball field to the wooded area behind it. A little ways into the woods was a small creek, and after that was the industrial park. On the corner, off the freeway on ramp, was the Liquor store they were going to rob.

As they walked towards the creek, Jordan was trailing the others. He was getting excited about the job and the clout he would have in the community. He would be a leader on this block and have much respect. Even his Uncle would respect such a daring move. As Jordan approached the creek, he looked down to find the stepping-stones leading across. Just as he stepped on the first rock, something caught his eye. It was a small stone, white and rugged, but pretty at the same time. It was not shiny like a diamond, but rough; almost like glass from a bottle that had been worn in the creek. However, it was beautiful; even Jordan could see that. He stopped for a second to pick it up, wiped off the dirt, and examined it.

It was a rough stone that had obviously been in the creek a long time. Jordan wondered if someone had lost this a long time ago. Was it valuable or important? Jordan was not an expert on jewelry, and this did not look like it was worth much, but he decided to keep it anyway. Maybe he could clean it up and give it to Iris as a gift. She would like it although it was not shiny. He stuffed the stone in his pocket and walked across the creek to catch up with the others. As he crossed, a bright explosion of lighting precluded a loud clap of thunder, and a light rain began to fall.

It was 6:30, and the storeowner's wife would be upstairs where they lived. She started to prepare dinner around 6 every evening. The husband held down the fort until the midnight closing and she returned to bring dinner and help around 7:30. If they hit at 6:45, it would be just before the rush home from work.

Most people arrived home around 7pm. On payday, they stopped at the store to cash their checks. At 6:45, the money would be there but the crowed would not. That is why Jordan could not be late. He had the gun, and he would be doing the robbery.

As they approached the store, Jay-Low made one last statement to Jordan. "Just walk in and put the gun in the dude's face. Tell him to keep his hands up and shut up. Give you all the money and you will not kill his dumb behind. He knows the routine and he has insurance. He does not want you to kill him, and he does not want to shoot a fourteen-year-old boy if he does not have to. Got it?"

Jordan looked at him and said, "Let's get this done man!" Jordan walked into the store. Jay-Low stayed near the woods as a look out of course if the police showed up he would have no way of letting Jordan know, but he felt safer staying back. Randy Boy entered the store with Jordan as his decoy, pretending to shop.

Jordan did not hesitate; he walked up to the counter where the owner was standing. Jordan already had the gun in his hand hidden by his long jacket sleeve. As he approached the counter, he lifted the gun towards the owner. "This is a robbery dude! Give me the money and I will give you your life!"

The owner looked at the gun in total silence. He knew words would only make matters worse. He also knew his life was in danger. There was a young gang member holding a gun on him who may very well be willing to take his life from him. His wife was upstairs and his child would be coming into the store; he must get this thug out of his store fast.

The fastest way was to give him the money. He opened the register and dumped the contents into a bag. Jordan motioned to owner to go to the safe. "Hurry, get your punk behind to the safe before I blow it off."

After the owner emptied his safe, he gave the bag to Jordan. Jordan snatched it from him and backed out of the store. Randy Boy was watching from the front of the store and began to signal Jay-Low that they were coming out. As Jordan left the store, he turned around and began running towards the field.

As soon as he turned around to run, he knew he was in trouble. They had not planned the getaway as well as they thought. They should have planned it later in the evening or earlier in the year. The sun had broken though the clouds and was still up, and the field was a long way off. Jordan was horrified at seeing the distance he would have to run before entering the woods. The storeowner would be able to get to the door and see them if they did not hurry. If he got a good look at Jay-Low, they would all be caught.

Jordan and Randy Boy ran as fast as they could. Randy Boy had exited the store before Jordan, so he was ahead of him. Jordan ran as fast as he could, watching Jay-low and Randy Boy leave him behind. What could they do but run? It was all up to him now to reach the edge of the woods before he would be free.

They reached the edge of the field just as the owner appeared in the doorway. He shouted to the three to stop, but they kept running. Jordan almost laughed to himself as he ran. "Stop, man I am almost free now, I not going to stop now for nobody." He continued to run across the field. Because lightning flashed and thunder clapped at the exact moment the gun went off, he never heard the shot...BANG!

Just before the shot rang out, Lynette and Iris were approaching the store to cash their checks. The women hurried along the one block down the street to the liquor store. As they got half a block away Iris looked up and shouted, "Jordan! Is that Jordan leaving the store?" Lynette looked up just in time to see her son running out of the liquor store with Randy Boy leading him around the corner of the store. Lynette did not know why her son was in such a hurry, but before she could call out to him, he disappeared around the corner of the store heading for the open field called 'The Pass.'

"Where is he going?" asked Iris. A few seconds later, the storeowner came out carrying his rifle. "Oh, my God!" Lynette shouted as she began to run. Iris was right behind her as she realized what she was witnessing. Lynette and Iris reached the corner of the building from where Jordan had run just as the shot ranged out. BANG! As the cloud of steel blue smoked cleared away, Lynette and Iris could make out Jordan stumbling, holding his head, and falling to the ground.

It felt like someone had punched him in the back of the head with their fist. The blow was so hard it knocked Jordan to the ground. He was dizzy and his head was ringing. "Who hit me?" He remembered running and thinking, 'How could someone run up on him and hit him in the back of the head?' He turned over to look back and see who could have done this. That was when he saw the storeowner with the rifle in his hands. "I've been shot! Jay-Low, I've been shot!" The warmth running over his body was blood, his own blood. Jay-Low and Randy Boy stopped for a second but as the owner raised the gun again; they took off and left him alone in the field.

"No! They shot my boy! Jordan!" Lynette and Iris rushed passed the storeowner. They saw Jordan's friend Jay-Low and Randy Boy vanish over the creek. They did not even look back. They rushed to Jordan as he lay on the ground. His eyes were dazed and he could not speak. They did not know if he recognized them but they kept calling his name. The women screamed for someone to call an ambulance. They were panicked and lost. What happened? How did this happen to Jordan?

The storeowner stood shaking, still aiming his rifle, unable to move. The old Asian immigrant had hoped he would never have to use the gun, but he knew in his heart that this day was coming. Thugs like Jordan had robbed him before, and his wife and family lived in constant fear. He couldn't continue to be a victim and not fight for his right to run his business in peace. He had come to this country as a young man to find opportunity and build something he could pass down to his children and his grandchildren. He was not about to let no good punks like Jordan take his children's inheritance. That business would fund their futures. Although he was not a violent man, the storeowner knew that freedom was worth fighting for. He just regretted that he had to shoot someone else's child to protect his own.

Jordan laid there in the grass, his body lying in a pool of blood. He heard a loud scream from a woman. "My baby, they shot my baby!" Lynette had arrived to cash her check just as the shot rang out. She saw her boy fall to the ground and ran across the field towards him. Right behind Lynette, also screaming, was Iris.

By the time they reached Jordan, he could barely hear their screams. He could only hear this ringing in his ears. He looked at his mama and saw the tears and horror in her face. Who would protect her? Who would keep her safe? As his eyes grew dim and numbness fell over him, he glanced towards Iris. He reached out, held her hands, and looked up at her. All he could do was squeeze her hands together. The rain began to fall a bit harder, causing some to run for cover, but others onlookers stayed. The crowd gathered over him. Many knew him. Some were angry with the storeowner for shooting this young man that was running away. He was no longer a threat to him and he had his back turned; why did he have to shoot him in the back of the head like that?

Others recognized the terror of the block.

"That is one gang member gone from the hood."

"We won't have to worry about him again."

"He's the one that stole my purse last week!"

"Somebody call an ambulance!"

"Somebody call the coroner…"

Some were calling out to others, and there was general confusion at the scene. Jay-Low had kept running through the woods and over the creek. They only started walking when they heard the sirens of the approaching police.

Iris was standing over him in total shock. There was her man, covered in blood. She stood there looking at him, and he looked up towards her. She knelt down and allowed him to take her hands. She did not know if he knew who she was because he just stared at her. He squeezed her hand and continued to gaze at her. The rain began to pour down and the crowd began to dissipate. Only Lynette and Iris remained. Only those who truly loved him stayed with him. There was Iris, who should have been looking to protect herself, especially after Jordan rejected her; here she was trying to help Jordan hold on as he grew weaker and weaker.

He wanted to say something to her; he opened his mouth to speak, and Iris began to fade away. He wanted to tell her not to worry, that he would be alright. But the words only came together in his head, not in his mouth. He saw her but could not speak; he loved her but could not tell her.

"Don't you do this to me!" Iris screamed at him. "Don't you leave me here alone." Everyone left her; her father, brother, and now Jordan was laying there bleeding to death. Jordan laid there and could only think that he did not want to die in that field.

That field was called "The Pass." No one knew why, but probably because it was "The Pass" to the neighborhood without going around town. The field had never been developed because of the creek behind it and the flooding problem. The children always played there and lovers met there at night. This is where he and Iris use to come after they left his friends' house. It was probably where she got pregnant.

The ringing became dimmer, and there was the slight sound of a police siren. The light faded to dark. Jordan closed his eyes and laid his head on the ground. Jordan was about to come face to face with reality!

CHAPTER SIX
THE PLANTATION MENTALITY!

June 1855

"Get up Jordan! Oh, Lord helps us! Get up, Jordan; they are coming! Please Jordan, get up, please, get up!"

His mother was still calling him. He thought he was dead, but he was not. She was pulling on him to get up on his feet to run. As he struggled up to his feet, he noticed Iris was also there. She was looking back towards the road, looking fearful, yet she kept looking back. Something had changed. His mother was not in her work clothes and Iris was dressed in rags.

"Mama, what's going on? Why are you dressed like that? What's going on?"

"You been shot by the slave hunters, and they comin' after us. We got to get out the field into the woods." Jordan was now on his feet and could see that he also had different clothes on. He was barefoot and had a slight bullet wound to the head. But what was this talk about slave hunters, and why did mama have to escape also? She did not rob anyone; did she?

Jordan heard a sound he had never heard up close before; horses galloping! He was hearing horses coming up the road. The road had changed also. Where was the freeway? What happened to the industrial park and the liqueur store? Jordan was confused and his head was hurting, but that horse noise was getting closer and the women were getting more scared.

"OH LORD, MASSA DONE FOUND US, WE'S CAUGHT; OH LORD, HELP US!" It was Iris crying like some old woman. What was this? Where was this?

Jordan rose slowly to his feet. Maybe he had passed out and was near the city park. Yes, that must have been it; the city park had police on horseback, and they were after him. "Okay, let's get to into the woods" Jordan said to the women. He would have to figure out why they were dressing and speaking this way later; now he had to escape.

As he began to run off, the men on horseback came up on them. "There they go, stop dogs; where are you going, dog?" "Did that cop just call me a dog?" Jordan thought to himself. He turned around and shouted, "Who are you calling a dog?" The horseman rode up to him, slapped him across the face with the butt of his whip, and kicked him to the ground. As Jordan lay on the ground dazed by the fall, other slave hunters jumped on him.

As they were tying him up, he heard his mother and girlfriend being attacked. "Leave them alone, they have done nothing!" Jordan shouted. "Shut up, boy! They have left Master's plantation without papers, and that makes them runaways like you. Shut up; get up and start walking."

Jordan was confused about some things. He was dazed, and in the woods with some crazy cops. He figured he had better play it cool until he got a lawyer.

Jordan and the others were led back to the road and placed in the back of a horse drawn cart. As they got into the back, they began to talk. "Are you guys going to read me my rights?" Jordan asked. "Rights? Boy, you done have no rights that a White man need to bother with. The only right you have is to live or die, and I decide that."

"Where am I, and what happened to my shoes? They were two-hundred dollar gym shoes!" Jordan shouted, still confused and frustrated. The others thought the boy was crazed from the bullet; you could buy a slave for two-hundred dollars, and he was talking about a pair of shoes. As Jordan settled down in the back of the cart, he began to look around. He had on rags for clothing, no shoes, and was bleeding from the head. Why didn't they call the paramedics for him, and where were the uniformed police?

Sitting in the cart with him were his mother and girlfriend. They also were in rags, and had no shoes. Iris reached over to him and wiped the blood from his head with her hand. Jordan turned to look at the two men up front. They did not look any better than the Black folks in the back. They were slightly better dressed and had old shoes on. Their hats were worn, and their clothes were torn. They were poor trash, and Jordan knew it. It was always the poor trash that called you 'dog'; they were living to close to your lifestyle, and it scared them. There is nothing more disgusting than a poor White man in America. Therefore, they must be bounty hunters or just good ole' boys helping out the law.

Jordan figured he would just wait until these rednecks turned them over to the police and then file a complaint. He would get a civil rights lawyer and sue for all the pig sucking money these broke bastards had. He looked back at the three men following them on horseback. They were the same miserable trash as the guys up front. Dirty, poor, and trying to look down on him to feel better about themselves. He probably made more money in a weekend than these idiots did in a teeth-picking month.

One of the horsemen turned around and was staring at Jordan as he looked up, so they locked eyes. A mean looking guy with a bandana tied around his neck. Jordan did not like men to "mean mug him"; that is, to stare at him with an attitude. Jordan stared back at him and mouthed the words, "See you in court." The redneck laughed and said, "Court? The only time we see dogs in court is when they are being sold. I got your court right here, boy." and he held up a long rope.

It was then that Jordan realized that it was no longer 2007, but he was in slavery America. "How did this happen?" Jordan thought. "How did Black people end up here? We are not weak; we are strong!" He turned to his mother and asked, "How did we get here?" She looked at her son and tried to answer him, "Mr. Gilmore bought your granddaddy; we've always lived here."

"I have not always lived here or lived like this; I lived in the city in a house!" Jordan protested.

"Jordan, I live in Master's house, and you live in the slave quarters. I make breakfast and cleans Master's house, and you tend to his fields. Sometimes Master lets you come up for a visit, usually on Sundays, and we have a chance to visit." his mother replied, hoping he would remember.

"What about Iris? Where does she stay?"

"You mean Siri? Siri use to stay in the fields, but this spring she got a job with Junior; that be Master's son. So she stays in the room with me in the Big House."

"So, I got a job. How much do they pay a brother?"

"If you lucky you get paid no attention. It's not a job; Jordan they chores. You get them done because you were told to get them done."

"Mama, what about my brother and sister, are they still around?"

"Yes, I have bred three children for Massa, and he's let me to stay close to all of 'em. Massa has given me your daddy and two other good bucks, so my children are valuable. But I don't want valuable children; I want free children. Massa tells me to take some man to my bed, and I have to. That man don't care; he don't have to take care of the baby, Master do it. He just make the babies, and Master raises them to serve him."

"What kind of Black man would allow himself to breed like a dog? Where are the strong warriors?"

"I ain't never seen no strong warriors, Jordan. The type of men that allows theyselves to be bred is the only types that are making babies. So, I guess we making men with the mind to be weak and just obey Massa. They never let the strong ones breed; they mostly die early, usually fighting each other. The bucks fight each other, too. They take a lot of useless pride in how many babies they done made for Massa. They think it makes them a man to make babies; but nature takes care of that. You just a boy and you can father a child. Some women have husbands that stay with them and help raise them children; now they the real men.

"What the Black man don't understand is that Master knows he has fathered his own replacement. Master knows it saves money to work that man to death and bring his young sons into the fields. The Black man dies early because the White man will not take care of a dog he can't use. That's why you don't see many old Black men, but you do see a whole lot of fatherless babies. That's because old men can't pick cotton.

"So, since the young bucks done lost they reason to be proud of manhood, they call the women wenches; and that means they are dogs. They'll be calling themselves dogs pretty soon. Next thing you know, they'll be calling each other saying, 'Greetings, dog!' What will become of us?"

"Mama, we'll be alright; things will get better! I promise we won't always prey on our own; we will have freedom one day. We will become citizens in this country. We will own our on homes and businesses. It'll be okay, mama."

"Boy, what are you talking about? We may own our own businesses, but Master will own us. We may get our own homes, but they'll still be on Master's property. Unless we get rid of

Master, we won't get nothing. Ford Everything is for Master. He's the problem, and we can't have a solution until we get rid of the problem."

This could not be happening to Jordan. Who were these people, and why were they so negative on things? Why didn't they demonstrate and protest? What they needed was a good old-fashioned race riot. That would put old Master on notice. However, who would send out the National Guard to protect them? Who would help? All of the people that sacrificed doing the 1950s and 60s had to suffer quietly to bring freedoms to all. They were beaten and murdered so he could pimp women and sell dope. They died integrating schools so he could drop out. They fought for dignity so he could debase himself on some corner.

He was afraid to tell them what the future held for them. One hundred years later, they would still be living in the same neighborhoods, doing the same things, but just looking better while doing it. The two-hundred dollar shoes that were on his feet were gone, but the men still wore their hats on crooked and wore their baggy pants. Only this time, the hats were crooked to follow the sun on your face while you worked, and the pants were baggy because they did not fit. How could he tell them that men were calling themselves dogs? They were still breeding babies for Master and allowing Master to raise and educate them for him.

He could only remember Black people entertaining White America. We could sing and dance for them, play ball for them, and make them laugh. However, why didn't we compete against them in ownership and leadership? He had gotten his girlfriend pregnant and abandoned her immediately. She was not his girl; she was Master's girl. He had destroyed their block to make it safe for him to sell dope on the corner. Dope that further depressed his block. Nothing had changed in two-hundred years, and he did not want to tell them about the future.

Somehow, Jordan had been transported two centuries back into time. This was during the slave days. What had happened to him? Who were these guys, and where were they taking him, he wondered. As they travelled in the back of the horse-drawn cart, Jordan was able to whisper to the others traveling with him. His mother told him he was shot and was just struck dumb for a while. He would survive if he could get back to the cabin for treatment.

Siri told him they all lived on Master Gilmore's property and were his slaves. They had tried to escape north to freedom because of the cruelty of Master Gilmore's son, Junior. They would surely be beaten for this escape attempt and maybe even worse.

CHAPTER SEVEN
BROKEN SPIRITS!

Jordan and the women were taken to a large plantation with many other Black folks. As they came up the lane that led from the road through the plantation, Jordan could hardly believe his eyes. The gorgeous, plush landscape, the majestic white house with a porch as long as two or three houses together in his neighborhood; it was all so different. There were trees like in the park, right there in front of this big, beautiful house. But as they continued to ride, he saw vast fields of cotton, full of poor, dirty Black people who were all staring at Jordan in horror as he passed by them. He could even see afar off the slave quarters that occupied the dusty land that was too dry to farm. All of this was new, but Jordan couldn't focus because of the overwhelming fear welling in his chest.

As Jordan's heart raced his eyes began to well with tears. For the first time in his life he was truly afraid; he didn't feel tough here at all. Back in the future, in his old life, Jordan caused others to fear for their lives, and now he feared for his own. The control he seemed to have in the neighborhood was gone, and all that was left in its place was uncertainty and fear of the unknown.

That and sweat.

As the cart pulled into the plantation Jordan was overcome by the smell of sweat. The big house was surrounded by beautiful trees and sweet smelling flowers, dainty and white. However, going further into the plantation revealed the harsh reality of the fields and the despair of the souls who worked them. Their pain, their toil, and their hopelessness – they seemed to be covered in it, each wiping it from his or her brow as they worked. As the cart came to a stop in front of the overseer's quarters, Jordan's nose was filled with the odor of sweat mingled with moonshine. The suffering of the slaves and the cruelty of the overseers. He thought, "How did I get myself into this?" Jordan knew he wasn't dreaming anymore; this was a nightmare.

The slaves all watched in fear as the slave hunters drug them back. "Boy, I guess no one is going to call 911 now" Jordan said murmured to himself. SLAP! Across his back was the whip of one of the slave hunters. "Boy, were you just counting? Did I hear you say nine and eleven? You trying to act smart? Who learned you to count? It is against the law for a buck to be counting. That is probably where you got the idea to run; there is noting worse than a learned dog. I don't like is a smart slave. I expect you to stop acting smart or I will take out your tongue. I like my dogs dumb in more way than one." The other slave hunters laughed at his joke, but Jordan was still feeling the pain and did not understand what he had done.

Lynette went to comfort him and held him in her arms. While she was holding him, she whispered in his ears. "Now Jordan, you listen to me carefully. Old Massa don't like his slaves to be to smart. If you done learned to read and write then keep it to yourself. Master only wants a slave to know how to work on the plantation and get the crop in. Stop talking around White folks; it can only get you and all of us in trouble."

"Stop talking around White folks? What do you mean, I can't talk to them?" Jordan asked defiantly. "No Jordan, you can't talk around them! Don't say anything around White folks 'less you be answering them. They don't need to be bothering about us dogs, and we don't want them to. Let White folks take care of White business; we slaves will take care of White folks, if they ask us too." Jordan could not believe the words coming out of his mother's mouth. Take care of White folks; was she crazy? He was not going to take care of any White people. However, something had happened to him, and his life depended upon him figuring it out fast. He had better play it cool until he woke up. Dream or not, that bullet hurt, the foot to the chest hurt, and that whip hurt. Something was terribly real about this dream.

Siri and his mother were taken off to another place and Jordan was placed in a cell. It was really a small wooden shed with a dirt floor, but the arm and leg shackled fastened to the wall indicated that it was a place where wayward slaves were routinely detained. There were no windows, so light only came in when the barn-like doors were opened or when a lantern or candle was lit inside. Master's son came into the room and Jordan was shocked. It was Gilmore Junior from the library. Only he had a mean look on him and a gun in his holster. When Junior came into the room, Jordan stood up and spoke. "Hey Junior, I think there has been a mistake, I want to see my girlfriend and mother."

"Junior?" he replied with contempt, "Boy, they said you were wounded in the head; I guess you are still a little confused. I have not allowed you to call me Junior since we were little boys playing out in the fields. All my dogs call me Master, and so will you. Don't let that bullet to the head get you a foot to the behind." Jordan began to understand where he was and how he had to react. This was slavery days, he did not know how it happened, but he was on a plantation and this racist cracker was the son of his master. If he was going to survive, he had better play the game. Play the game until he learned enough to escape.

"Yes sir Massa; I's sorry! Do I belong to you?"

"You are just my dog! You do not have any opinions or wants. You are my dog, and your wench is my wench. I will do to her what I please, and you will act like you like it. If you behave, I may let you lay with her sometime. However, understand boy; even the sex you get comes from me; understand? Now go fetch me something to eat."

"Yes sir, Massa. But, Massa Gilmore, there will come a time when you won't be master. There is come a time when I'll take care of my own woman, and you won't have control over her."

Junior laughed. "Boy, let me tell you something. You dogs are so stupid that even if freedom came to you, you would still whore your women and seek to work for me. You don't know anything else. If you get the freedom you're looking for, you will still serve me. If you get the right to vote, you will still vote for me. Your only wish will be to vote for the best master, and your dumb behind would call that freedom."

"No Master, we won't let that chance go by. Freedom is too much a prize to give it back once it's found. If that was true Massa Gilmore, why aren't the slaves that are escaping running back to you? Why do they not only escape, but also come back for others? If we love you so much, why do you lock your doors at night? You seemed to be afraid of something Massa; if it's not me, who is it?"

"Boy, that bullet to the head must have really messed you up. Good thing I know you is just a dumb dog, or I might take offense at the way you are talking to me. Freedom is bad for you, boy; understand that. If you be free, how are you going to take care of that wench you want? Who will hire a free dog? You need White folks to eat and give you a place. If you run off after them damned abolitionists, who will feed you? They do not even want slaves up North with them; that's why y'all keep running back down here. They are sending you South because they want us to shoot you in the back of the head; how's that head doing anyway, boy?"

"My head is getting better everyday, Massa. I feel like I can get back to my job just any day now. Yes sir! I think it's about time to get back to work, sir. You have a nice evening Massa Gilmore, and a good night sleep."

"I sleep well at night, boy! I take good care of my dogs and they love me. My dog managers keep close a look out for troublemakers. I do not fear my dogs because I have them fear each other. You would rather kill your very best dog friend than harm my children or me. Why? Because you are my dog."

"Yes sir, Massa, I may be your dog today. However, you will not always call me dog. Someday, one day, you will not call me dog."

"Yeah, you may be right! The way things are going, I may not always call you dog, but I bet you will always call each other dog. What I call you, you will call yourselves.

"I may change what I call you. It may be 'sir,' even 'boss,' but in my heart you will always be my dog and your girl will always be my dog wench."

Junior Gilmore called for someone to bring Siri into the room. An old slave man led the fourteen-year-old girl into the room. She was tied by the wrists, and she was completely naked. Jordan could not believe what he was seeing. "Man, you got my girlfriend naked in front of this old dude. Put some clothes on her, PLEASE."

"Please my behind," Said Junior Gilmore. "I treated you like my friend because we grew up playing together, I give you a nice job in the house to keep you warm and what do you do? RUN! You run away from me. Do you know how much money you cost me, sending those hunters after you? Well I am going to get paid back."

The older slave took Siri and tied her to a hook on the ceiling. Now she was barely standing with her hands stretched up towards the sky. She was dangling naked, and her eyes were fixed on Jordan.

Junior Gilmore walked over to her and looked her up and down. "Nice looking wench we are growing here. She is going to be a good breeder. You want to be her buck, Jordan?" Junior rubbed her naked back, and Siri hung her head in shame. Junior had a reputation among the slave girls for his late night visits to the slave quarters. She had run away partly because of his attention to her. She knew it would not be long until he forced himself on her as he had most of the young girls.

Jordan stared at Siri she stared at him, but Junior was only looking at Jordan. Jordan had become very strange lately; he was talking back, not working, and stirring up trouble with the other slaves. Now he had run away and was getting completely out of control. Junior had to do something to bring order back to the plantation, and he had to bring Jordan under submission. Maybe he had been too casual with him while they grew up. His father had warned him about getting too friendly with the slaves.

They would think they were your equal if you played with them and ate with them. He would tell Junior to be nice to his slaves but to remember they were only pets; a burden he was responsible for. Junior's father believed the White man had an obligation to take care of his dogs, but in return, they should show gratitude by doing their work. "They don't have to worry about a place to sleep, food or clothing. Every slave on the plantation has a job; hell, White folks are going without work so we can employ these dogs. Another thing son, NEVER call a Black female lady. You only call White females ladies. Black females are called 'woman', 'gal', or 'wench', but never a lady."

Junior was seeing that his father was right. Trying to teach Jordan to read was fun when they were children. To have a reading dog was entertainment for him and his other White friends. However, as Jordan grew up, that reading led to trouble.

Jordan had started reading about freedom, going north, free states, and the writings of those pesky abolitionists and their Underground Railroad. Jordan had stirred up the other slaves on this freedom thing, and showed great disrespect for all the kindness Junior had shown him.

Well that night, it was going to end. Father was right, he was wrong, Jordan was just a slave and he was the master. "Jordan, I am going to show you what happens when dogs like you get out of line. It will not be you that you hurts, but the whole slave community. Since you tried to run away, no one on the plantation will get traveling papers to visit off the plantation. That means they cannot visit husbands and wives on other plantations, and cannot get to the odd jobs they do for extra money. You have hurt everyone, and I am sure they will talk to you about it.

"Meanwhile let's understand this little wench we have here. Everything on the plantation belongs to me, and I control it. This girl is mine; I can do with her as I please. I know you want her, and I could give her to you. However, not only did you want to steal my best young buck from me, but you were stealing my dog wench, too. Now I am going to beat her Black behind to let you know it is my Black behind to beat and to keep."

With that, Junior took the whip and hit Siri across the back. She screamed and so did Jordan. "Stop it, Massa, don't hit her again! I understand and I won't run again." Junior looked at him and said. "I did not ask you to speak. I do not care if you run again or not. I have plenty dogs to replace you. However, if you run, I will beat every slave on this plantation. After I finish beating this dog wench, I am going to beat your mother. Then I am going to sell your mother away from you. Siri, I will keep her until I am done with her, and then I may sell her, too."

He continued to beat Siri mercilessly until he grew tired. She screamed until she could not find the strength to scream anymore. Jordan could only look at her and she stared at him. Finally, Junior left and the older slave cut her down. Jordan and the slave covered Siri and began to take care of her wounds. Jordan looked at her and told her how sorry he was that his actions had gotten her into this. He knew she must have really hated him and the other slaves must have hated him, too.

Siri could not speak, but kept holding his hand and staring at him. Finally, she looked up at him and whispered, "We almost made it, Jordan. Please tell me you will take me away. Take me from this; don't leave me here. I would rather die free in the woods than live here with him." The old slave, who had not spoken while Junior was there, finally addressed Jordan.

"You got to be more careful next time. Travel at night, sleep during the day." Jordan did not understand. Who was this guy, and why was he trying to help? Wasn't he the same guy that had tied Siri up for Junior? What kind of place was this? "What is your name?" Jordan asked. "What's my name? Boy, I'm your uncle; I am your mother's brother, Thomas. Don't you remember?" Jordan did not recognize his Uncle Thomas; he was a broken old man. His back was bent from years of back breaking work, and his heart was broken from years of witnessing what Jordan had just witnessed.

CHAPTER EIGHT
NEW LIFE OLD STRIFE!

"Uncle Thomas, I don't remember anything except being shot. Please tell me what's going on and where I am," Jordan asked.

"Boy, you is in trouble, that's where you is," the old man replied. "First thing you have to do is get over that memory loss and pay attention. You live on a plantation, and talking to White folks the way you talked to Massa Gilmore will get us all kilt."

Jordan felt like he was in the twilight zone. The grassy knoll and the Big House, the white rows of cotton that seemed to go on for miles, the big, red barn where the mules and the supplies were kept; it was all very new and very strange. The slave quarters looked a lot like the projects, except with a couple of small vegetable gardens next to certain cabins where slaves were allowed to grow yams, cabbage, greens, and other special treats that Master didn't particularly care for and therefore didn't care about. The plantation even smelled strange. The country air was fresh, but the fields smelled like sweat. The barn smelled like animals and alcohol, and the slave community reeked of fear and hopelessness. Jordan hoped that he wouldn't be there long enough to get used to it.

"Let me tell you where you are and how we live," his uncle continued. "Slaves depend on each other, never Master. If Master is the problem, he can't be the solution. Look to the future for relief from the wrongs done to us here. Look for the future, not the past. We will be free one day if we look for the future. Meanwhile, we got a good but poor community; low crime, small drug and alcohol problem, crooked slave drivers and community leaders. But we are heading for freedom. You must try again; you may be the one to go tell them." Jordan was confused. "Tell who and tell them what?" he asked. "Boy, we need slaves to get North and tell them northern White folks what's going on down here. They think we like being slaves; Master tells them that we sing and dance all day long, happy to serve him. Someone needs to get up North and tell then about the killings, beatings, and rape. We thought maybe it was you.

Uncle Thomas rubbed his balding head in frustration. He wiped the sweat from his forehead and took a deep breath. Jordan may not have been the one to make it this time, but he could still be the one. The old slave was holding onto hope, despite the insurmountable odds that were stacked against him and all the other slaves who dared to hope for a way to freedom. His once caramel complexion and wavy hair were singed and dry from years of exposure to the unrelenting southern sun. His wide, thin frame was bent from tireless work and malnutrition. Thomas was once a tall, strong, attractive man, and it was a curse to him. The grandson of Master Gilmore's father and a slave woman, Thomas was too fair skinned to be fully accepted by the field slaves and too large and intimidating in stature to be a proper house slave. So, Thomas was forced to work the fields, often in isolation. Over time, as his body became broken and his skin darkened from exposure, he was accepted by his once jealous brothers, but by then Thomas' bitterness and resentment toward them had taken root and defiled his spirit. For years he would undermine the other slaves, refusing to protect, assist, or comfort them when he could for spite and refusing to share any of his meager resources with anyone. Anyone except his sister Lynette.

Lynette and Thomas has the same mother, and in their early years she was the only person on the plantation who was always kind to Thomas and judged him for who he was and not who he looked like. Thomas' father was a mulatto house slave, so he inherited his father's European features; however, his frame was large and muscular, a result of his African genetics. Because of his looks, he was essentially hated by everyone on the plantation except his younger sister. All Thomas wanted from his fellow slaves was to be judged for the kind of person he was, not who his grandfather was, and all he wanted from the Gilmores was his freedom and a chance to be his own man, with honor. These basic respects would elude Thomas, and he learned to look to the future for his hope. By the grace of God he and Lynette remained on the same plantation all their lives, which gave Thomas something and someone to live for. Had she not been there, Thomas may have killed or been killed as a result of his anger and resentment toward both his oppressors and his brethren who rejected him. In time,

Thomas learned to understand the jealousy and fear of the other slaves toward him and the disdain of the Gilmores that he endured. He learned to accept who he was and the realities of the plantation that were imposed both upon him and the other slaves. He learned to think beyond his emotions and see what the problems really were. Thomas learned to love. In so doing, he gained the respect of the older slaves and eventually the entire slave community. He also realized that he had to look after his nephew Jordan with the love of a father. Lynette and Jordan were all he had in the world, and he was determined to help them get to freedom any way he could.

"Master tells them abolitionists that we are happy all day long. He tells them that only a hand full of trouble making slaves are leaving. Rumor says that if enough of us go, the Northerners will come. We want those Northerners to come, when they come, they bring freedom with them."

"How can I be the one; how can I help?" Jordan asked with fear and uncertainty. Uncle Thomas lowered his voice as he spoke, "You see, society has concentrated on getting a new system dedicated to serving Black folks; freedom is coming, and old Master is fixing a new slave system under a different name. No justice, no courts, no police help.

Escaping North was the dream, the only dream. Master will only train you to work for his children. Training is for service. Work is for service. Family don't exist for us and is not encouraged. Happy is taking care of Master so Master will take care of you. If you keep this picture in front of old Master, he will relax and feel secure. We can then work on a better plan of escape."

"I got a better plan! Let's kill that demonic punk. Let's kill him and put him in the woods to rot!" Jordan was angry and scared, He could not fathom someone having this much power over him.

"You will only die that way, son. It is too late for dying; we should have died in Africa on our own land. We should have defended our own land. I don't want to die on the White man's land. I want freedom, not death. So live boy; let him call you dog as you learn to read a map. Let him call you his buck while you plot the stars at night. It does not matter what Master does, it only matters what you do. The only power Master has is your fear of being free. If Master can make you more afraid of freedom than slavery, Master wins! Even if you never get free, make sure you raise your sons and daughters up to seek freedom.

"Master relies on your fear to keep you self-regulating. By suspicion, anger, and guilt, we continue to support Master and push each other away. We are afraid of success; ours and that of those around us. If they make it, they are just showing that I am lazy and incompetent. If you are angry, you are justified in your failures. Each group can systematically grow on its own failures and feed on the recognized success of the 'oppressor group'.

"It takes fear to accept this concept, not strength. You must fear the future and feel inadequate to make personal changes to join this group mindset. Most of us are being told that "they," are different than "we", and that "we" must come together to protect ourselves from "them." "They" will stop "us" from getting "there." We have the field slaves against the house slaves, the small plantations against the large ones. Those with rich Masters are against those of poor masters; all are slaves, and all are looking for a reason to feel better than the other."

Jordan did not know about groups except his set back home. But he thought about them for a second. They were a collection of like-minded people. All agreed on the code, the purpose, and the acceptable behaviors. So the gang was his society; what was wrong with that? The gang provided identity, social interaction, and purpose. What was so wrong with that? The gang gave Jordan his identity and his future. He was a member of the Roberts Street gang; that's who he was.

Uncle Thomas took Jordan to his cabin. It was a musty cabin with a dirt floor and no light. The slave drivers could not afford for the slaves to enjoy too much privacy because they might conspire together and revolt, so there were no locks or securities of any kind on the doors. They offered minimal protection from the elements and easy access for the overseers and Master. There was no furniture except a table and a couple of wooden chairs and no comforts. Jordan couldn't believe that Black people had to live like this.

The Gilmore Plantation reminded Jordan of where he came from. The white folks lived in luxury, or at least respectably. The Gilmores inhabited the big house, lavish and ornate. The grandiose architecture, high ceilings, and polished cherry wood floors were breathtakingly beautiful. Even the overseers lived well in furnished cabins of a reasonable size. They were not elite like the Gilmores, but they lived comfortably; the overseers' quarters were built to be cool in the summer and retain heat in the winter. However, not far from the overseers' quarters were the slave quarters, and the stark difference was mind blowing. The quarters themselves were only cheap shanties built to contain the slaves; nothing of comfort was provided. The way that these people all lived together on the same land but with such different lifestyles and accommodations made Jordan think of the city where he lived. Only a few miles separated the suburbs from the inner city, but the people who lived in these places were worlds apart. The class separation in the future was the same as the slave days! There were significantly more blacks concentrated in distressed areas than in suburban areas in the future that Jordan knew. Just like urban blacks in the future, when slaves did earn money, they had to spend it outside their own community because no one in the community owned anything. They didn't even own the shacks in which they lived. Jordan began to realize that he was sent back to this time to see how things had changed without really changing. There were different clothes and different laws, but the behaviors of the people were generally the same. Slaves would never be respected or free, whether they were in physical bondage or economic bondage; slavery was still slavery.

Other slaves were there in Uncle Thomas' cabin, and they were eager to talk to Jordan. They wanted to know about the escape attempt; how far had he gotten; had he seen freedom? Jordan could not help them because he did not remember the attempt. Jordan sat down to eat, and an old slave came to sit by him. "What is your name, sir?" Jordan asked. It was the first time he ever remembered calling another Black man 'sir'. He would call the police, judge, or probation officer sir, but never another dude in the hood. "Names are not important here, son. I have been called by many names, and they change often. Names are for those folks that has a family, a future, and a past. Massa don't want us slaves to connect to either. That's why they call us different names, so we can't connect to anything. But I am known as The African; I guess you can call me that."

"Can you tell me about Africa, old man?" Jordan wanted to know. "Are you from Africa?" Jordan had never met anyone from Africa before. He was eager to learn as much from this old man as possible. He felt it was important in some way, even connected with getting back home.

The African began to tell him about his father, who was captured from the Motherland. "'In Africa', my father said, 'Boys your age are warriors. You have strength and you are fearless. You are a respected part of the village. We look up to you for protection and for hunting'."

Jordan said, "Boys my age are warriors where I'm from, too. We are feared by all and we protect our territory. We have our colors, flags, and hangouts. You can even say we have uniforms."

"That sounds like a great group of warriors, son. Who is your king? Where is your capitol and what is your source of money?"

Jordan had to admit there was no real king, just a loose association of like minds and smaller groups. The warriors did not have a capitol, not even a city, but they did have some control over small parts of the city, especially at night. The warriors' source of money came from the bounty they took from passers by.

With that information, the Old African looked wearily and said, "Sounds more like a roving band of bandits to me, son. If you give the streets up in the daytime and do not patrol them at night, you do not have any control over your nation, city, or community. Your gang becomes a burden on the community because those with the real power will be attacking you because of the trouble you and your crowd start.

"My father came from Africa, East Coast; they took the fourteen year old male into rituals of manhood, warrior class, built on respect of the woman and the family. The warriors were the protectors, not the predators of the community. Whenever an elderly person came across a warrior on the path, they knew they were safe. There was no fear of our young people. The father passed wisdom and knowledge to his sons and the mothers to their daughters. Language was important. We did not change our names; your name gave your family history. It told the culture and the development of our beliefs. Marriage was vital to the community because it gave direction for the training of children. We passed knowledge from one generation to the next by marriage.

"An African slave system also existed then. It was not the cruel, mean, system that old Master has. The Africans would capture each other in war and serve as slaves in that village. If you were a doctor in your village then you would be a doctor in my village, except you would be my slave. When the White folks came, the African chiefs had no reason to believe their slave system was any different. They traded slaves for supplies that made them stronger against their enemies. They got blankets, better weapons, and better food. It was not the horror we see today. My father said no one knew of the death so many suffered. Now, if you were a doctor in Africa you would still only be a cotton picker here."

"Honor to elders and tradition were normal. We knew our history; therefore, we knew our future. Hope for the future gave patience and courage. Justice was fast, and understood to be fair."

The wise old man told him about Africa and the reasons they were taken into slavery.

"My father was from Africa. He told me a lot about the old country. He was not a king or a nobleman; he was just a hard working African. When I knew him, he was just Master's field slave. However, to hear him talk about Africa, you know he was more than that. He walked slow and talked slow with a bow in his stance.

"He learned how to survive being a slave, and he passed on the survival to me. However, he was not a slave; he was just a prisoner. He always wanted to be free, and never gave up on the idea." Jordan wanted to know more. "Tell me more about the old country; what was it like?" he asked.

"My father was a warrior; most young men his age were. It was not something unusual, just something expected with the coming of manhood. He was a skilled hunter, and had a wife and a nice home to live in. The funny thing about his life in Africa, father said, was that the slave quarters here are better than the mud hut he called home, but he spent many nights longing for that mud hut."

"Why? Why would he rather have the damp mud hut in the jungles of Africa, to the slave quarters made of wood?"

"Because that mud hut was his mud hut, not the master's. He told me that it did not matter how nice Master's possessions are, they are never better than those of a free person."

"So what happened in Africa? How did your father get here?"

"He said he became a slave the day he became selfish."

"Selfish? How did becoming selfish make him a slave?"

"Father said that he had other wives in other villages, and felt that he should protect each one of them. When news came about the White men taking slaves near the village, the warriors had a meeting. It was determined that they could not defeat the White men with the weapons the warriors had. It was determined that they needed to join with other nations so that could resist the invaders. You see, the White man did not have free run of Africa. There were some places he had to avoid going. The warriors decided it was best to go to these places and build a defensible area.

"There were other nations that the White men could not over power. The White men were not an army, although they had better weapons than Africans had. They were just a group of sailors and traders. They could not stand up against an organized African tribe that did not want to become slaves.

"The others wanted to take the village and travel to another country where the warriors were strong enough to keep the slave traders out. My father had other wives in other villages, and did not travel with the warriors.

"He left one wife to go to another wife and was captured by the slave traders. He told me that was the reason; his culture of having more than one wife made the culture weak. The men did not have a reason to stand and die, so the community died. One man, one woman, equals one nation. One man and two women equal slavery."

"Wow! That's deep." Jordan said aloud but almost to himself. He immediately thought of himself with Siri and Jay-Low and his bag of wenches. His outlook on the neighborhood was different from Jay-Low's, maybe because of the difference in how Jordan looked at women. His opinions were still rough and he still had a long way to go before they could be considered respectful, but compared to his friend, he was a saint. This philosophy on community showed Jordan something he had not seen before.

"Father said he was chained to others; men and women and walked for days to the beach. They did not eat the entire trip, and only had water once, in the morning. When they arrived at the beach, my father saw the slave ship for the first time. He and the other slaves spent two days in a fort while White folks bargained over them.

"Finally, he was loaded on the ship in chains. He only had enough room to lie down. There were men, women and children all together at the bottom of the slave ship. There was not enough room to turn over or sit up. It was less room that you would have in a coffin."

Jordan wanted to know how they went to the toilet. The old African told them that they went where they lay. The worst thing was to be placed at the very bottom of the ship. Those poor souls had to endure the suffering of all above them. There were four of five layers of slaves lying down on the slave ship. The human mind cannot imagine lying in body fluids, excrements of all types, and the death of those chained next to you. Some slaves went completely out of their minds.

He told Jordan about the trip up top side to eat. You got a short chance for fresh air, but also new horrors. Captives who refused to be slaves threw themselves over board. Sometimes, if they were blessed, they took some of the others with them. The old ship captain used to torture the slaves for entertainment.

The captain's income came from delivering live cargo, not dead cargo, so he was careful. Some of the slaves tried to die from not eating, and Master would force them to. He would break off their front teeth and tie them backwards over a rum barrel. The captain would then order hot coals placed on their bellies to force open their mouths. Any slave that saw that either began eating or found a better way to die. Some slaves would just die from setting in a corner. They would be out for the feeding and just sit down and die.

His first stop was an Island off the coast of America. It was a place called the Caribbean's, and there were hundreds of Africans there. All it seemed to be was a place for the Africans to get used to beatings. They broke your sprit and taught you enough English to follow instructions in the fields. There was unspeakable brutality, with death everyday and no hope for relief.

The Slaves were taken on board a ship for the final journey to America. His father was placed on the auction block and sold. He spent the rest of his life looking for a way to get free. He died never seeing freedom, but gave the love of freedom to his children. The old African still had the bright hope of freedom in his voice. You could tell he still desired it. Master could not quench it after two generations of trying.

As the old African spoke, many gathered around to hear. They were always interested in what he had to say. His stories of Africa gave them a sense of pride in who they were. Africa had nations the White man could not invade. That was nice to know. But no one asked the question of "What happened?" If we were kings and queens, what happened? How did this terrible thing come to us? Could it all be the result of not having honor for womanhood and childhood? Jordan did not think so; he still had a low opinion of women.

In his mind, all these women wanted were your money and your babies. They just wanted to keep you tied to them and you to pay for their babies. Jordan said, "I have as many women as I want because I am a real man. I'm a player and they take care of me. I won't die for any woman. Forget that mess!"

"I understand young man," the African replied. "Master understands also. He knows that he cannot allow you to fall in love with a woman and her children. If you fall in love, you will give your life for her. Master wants fear; if you have fear, you will give your life for him. You are a warrior and he must give you a war to fight. You must fight each other and not him. You must have no respect for your woman, but have respect for him."

"I do not respect his woman, either." Jordan said, defiantly.

"Yes, you do. You will work all of your life to protect and provide for his woman. You will be in the fields and work in the sun to keep her in the shade. Even if Master dies, we will all be expected to carry on the work of providing for Ms. Ann. The Black man will work himself to death and raise up children for Master's fields but will not work one day for our own women or children."

"Well, tell the Black woman to respect her man and maybe we will respect her. She is always getting the best jobs, thinking she is better than we are, and always demanding more from us."

"She does not have to respect you! You should be the king. If you are the king, she will treat you like the king. In fact, she will probably treat you as the king long before you become the king. Stop worrying about her respect for you. Respect yourself and everyone else will, also.

"Do not make her a victim of your slavery. She knows you are a slave, and she knows you do not have the power you want. She does not blame you, so do not blame yourself. Your freedom comes from her. She will give you the reason to go North. She will give you the reason to get free and stay free!"

"So I need to find a good woman and get busy?" Jordan asked sarcastically. "I need a string of hoes working for me. I all need to do is count my money. Wench better have my money."

"No! You need to find a woman; they are all good. We are the problem, not the woman. We owe women a lifetime of thanks; they have kept the Black man together, waiting for us to get it together. Do not worry about getting a good woman; just choose one and get busy building freedom. If not for you, then pass it down to your children."

Jordan becomes embarrassed at the situation he had helped create. He was really working for Master. He understood why they did not want him to speak the language of success, demand that schools prepare him to compete for jobs or a business, and why there was so much disrespect for women and families. He now understood that he has been tricked; the same old trick.

He was determined to make this work this time. He was determined to escape North and make a new life for himself and his girl. He would spend his time in the 1800s and work for a better future. He must escape this plantation mentality and get free. He now understood that freedom meant responsibility, and responsibility means you must be in charge. So the decision was made to try the escape route again. It was still late Friday night. The other slaves were beginning to return from the fields. Tomorrow was a free day for most of them, and they were preparing to let loose.

Jordan visited his mother in the Big House. He had learned that field slaves were not to come up there without having a good reason. So, any field slave who needed to see a house slave brought milk, water, or firewood as an excuse. His mother was in the kitchen cooking dinner for Master and his family. The other slaves did not like his mother because she worked in Master's home and ate the same food Master and his family ate. But what was she supposed to do? She was just a slave like the rest of them; she ate what Master said she was supposed to eat. Jordan did understand how great the food was up there. MEAT! They had meat up there! Meat was so rare to the slave diet it was a commodity. That was a word Jordan learned from Master Gilmore for cotton; they called it a commodity.

Jordan was awestruck when he approached the kitchen door at the rear of the Big House to visit his mother. Compared to the primitive slave quarters that he was staying in, Master's house looked like something from MTV's "Cribs." The country mansion was like something out of a movie, with perfectly painted white woodwork for less than perfect White residents. The kitchen itself was a sight, with a large island in the middle for food preparation and a range stove and oven that was obviously state of the art for that time. A beautiful eggshell white, the rectangular kitchen had cast iron skillets and copper pots hanging overhead and fine china in the cabinets. Jordan would have given anything just to be able to sleep in a corner where his mother worked. He had been there a few times now, but the Master's kitchen, so unlike his mother's kitchen in his time, still captivated him.

As she cooked, he talked to her, trying to make sense of everything that was going on. "Mama," Jordan said, "Where's my dad?" Lynette hung her head in shame. "Boy, you really done forgot everything, huh? Your daddy's gone," she replied. "I knew it! Some things never change!" he exclaimed. Confused at Jordan's reaction to the news, Lynette began to explain: "Son, your father was a breeder; a stud. His name is Ox, and Massa sure did work him like one, too. Masters only keep breeders for as long as they are obedient and don't cause any trouble. Being tall and strong is a curse for negro men just like being beautiful is a curse to us negro women. Your daddy started drinking too much so he started talking too much. He talked back to Master Gilmore one day, and after he had been beaten within an inch of his life he was sold up the river." Her eyes began to well with tears, and Jordan's heart broke for her. "Did you love him, mama?" he asked. "Yes," she replied, "But I'll never know if he really loved me." It hurt Jordan to see his mother hurt all over again because his father was gone. However, living in slave times and learning how complicated the lives of the slaves really were, he began to realize that black men in the future were often complicated, broken people, too. Right now, as complicated as life was, Jordan was just glad to be able to smell meat cooking. That simple thing reminded him of home and gave him hope that there was something better somewhere, that life might get back to normal.

Jordan's mother was cooking ham, pork chops, and bacon, all from Master's plantation. His mother would slip him a piece from time to time to keep him healthy, but the other slaves in the field had never even seen this type of meat. "Mother, they feed us worse than the cattle. We are lucky to get one bowl of meal for lunch, and we get no meat at all. The only vegetables we get are given to us by the slaves that have the skills to grow their own. We get no sleep and get nothing to eat. How does Master expect us to live?"

"That's just it son; maybe Master don't want you to live. Master is only thinking about his crops and his profit; he isn't thinking about you. You had better be thinking about you."

"I need to get more meat so I can grow stronger, mother. It's my plan to escape this place. I can't live here, so I may as well die somewhere else."

"Son, you tried to escape before; these White folks will not let their profits escape. Even if you get off the plantation, other White folks make their money from this plantation; they will not want you to escape either."

Jordan looked at his mother for a moment; he understood why she was so afraid to leave and why she was afraid of him leaving. She had seen her son beaten down by Master; she had also been beaten down. She was more afraid of the beating than she was of the life long existence on the plantation. "I understand mother, but this time we will make it. Last time I didn't study and I didn't plan. This time I will know the way and I will know who we can trust before we leave. Trust me mother, I will not let you down again. I used to like your cooking and will enjoy it again. You used to prepare pork chops for me and the other children. I remember how much I liked your corn on the cob; now I only see the cob when old man Jenkins lights up his pipe. I miss those days when you would come home and cook for me mother."

His mother looked at him with a tear in her eyes. There was her son, talking out of his head again. Since the bullet hit him, he had been talking like he had been to another place. She knew they had never had such a meal, but she did not want to upset him. Jordan said a lot of strange things about the futures of her and Uncle Thomas, but now he was using this belief to try to escape. Escape back to where he had never been. She was really beginning to worry about her son.

Meanwhile at another part of the Big House, Junior Gilmore had something on his mind and needed to speak with his father. Junior was being prepared to take over the plantation and wanted to make sure he was on top of it. With so many slaves trying to escape maybe he was not qualified to run a plantation. He needed to have the comfort and wisdom of his father.

Gilmore Jr. needed to speak with his father about runaway slaves. He could not understand why Jordan would try to run. Junior saw Master Gilmore relaxing in the study, and thought it would be a good time to go in and speak with him.

"Father, that Jordan really surprised me. I would have never thought he would try to leave us. We have been taking care of him and his mother since I was a boy. We give him food, clothes, and a place to stay. We take care of his health and provide him with a decent job to do. Heck, I was even thinking of giving him that wench for his woman. Why aren't those slaves more appreciative of how much we give them?"

Gilmore Sr. looked at his son and said, "I really don't have an answer for you son. I asked my father the same question. I guess a dog is just a dog, and you cannot expect anything else from them. It's just the White man's burden, Junior. We, the intelligent race, must accept our position as protector and provider of the weaker races. They will never be thankful son; most think they are equal to us. They try to escape because they think they can survive without our help. It is their small brains that make them act that way.

"You and Jordan played as children but he stayed a child. He was a wonderful little playmate for you, but by the time you were five years old he began to fall behind. Now, Junior, you must take your role as master, not as a friend. He will never be a good friend again; he will only be your slave. You must be the master; their only hope is for us to help them. If we did not have this plantation, they would still be in the jungles of Africa hunting each other. Look at that young buck Jordan; strong and powerful but helpless to take care of himself and his girl. Look at her; she is strong and fertile, but would not be able to feed her own children without our help. It is a burden son, but we must maintain control for their own sakes.

"It will be your job to feed and take care of all of your slaves when I am gone. You really must understand a few things before you can become an effective master. I know you like those dogs and think of some of them as your friends. But son, it is just a business. If they do not get the cotton in, you will not eat. If they all escape north, you will not eat. If you let them destroy your crop in the fields, you will not eat. Now they will not eat either, but they do not care because they think you are supposed to take care of them."

Junior understood he had been training for a long time to take over the plantation. But Jordan was his childhood friend. It was going to be hard looking at him as a slave. "I don't understand father, why do we need to take care of them? Why not just let them stay in Africa and take care of their own?"

"Its nature son; the strong always take care of the weak. Remember when you were a child? Everything you needed required me to act. When you were four years old and wanted to eat, go outside, or anything, it required my action because I was the parent and you were the child. As you matured, you were able to do things on your own. Now, if you wanted to go to town, you could saddle up a horse and take off. A few years ago, you needed me because you were still young. Well son, Jordan has never left the four-year-old stage. He cannot read, or even speak in complete sentences; he is still a child and needs you to guide and even chasten him." Gilmore Senior was serious as he spoke the hidden truths to his son.

"Okay, father; I must be the master for Jordan's own good. Otherwise, he will be unable to live in society around other White folks. What else?"

Gilmore Senior continued, "Be careful of the language you use around them. Never call an adult wench a lady. You can call her a woman, but only White women are called ladies. You never want a Black man to think his woman is equal to your lady. Neither you nor the Black man must ever show any respect to the Black woman. She is to be a wench to you and her man. Her duty, Junior, is to breed and take care of your household. Never give her the idea that she is strong, and never give her the idea that her man can protect her. She must look to you for her protection. She must raise her children to look to you for food and clothing, never to the Black man. Be very careful of the language you use around them, they will follow your lead; make sure you are leading them into servitude."

Gilmore Junior understood what his father was trying to say, but did not know how to put it into action. "Tell me father, how do I lead them? What do I say, and in what direction should they go?"

Gilmore Senior understood the question. It was as old as life on the plantation. "Since a slave cannot think rationally, you must teach them some simple clichés to live by. They can remember clichés and that will lead them. Ever hear a slave say, 'Don't forget where you came from?' Junior had heard this before from many slaves talking to their younger ones. "Sure I have father; why?"

"Well son, have you ever heard a White man say that to his son? No, you have not, and here is why: if you keep your mind on where you came from, you will never go to the future. You will celebrate the past, never the future. 'Don't forget where you came from' for a slave is an invitation to go back deeper into slavery. It keeps his mind on slavery, not freedom. 'Don't forget, you are just a slave.' That's the message, and that is why we always encourage that as wisdom in the slave community. Have you ever heard me say that to you?"

Junior thought about it for a moment. "No, father, you never say that, but you do say something close. You say, 'Do not forget where you are going!' Now I get it; that means I keep my eyes on the future not the past. I look for better ways to do things and not worry about the past. I see father, I should keep my mind on the future, not the past."

"Right, son." Gilmore Senior knew his son was getting the idea of how to be master. "One more thing son; you always hear slaves talk about giving something back to the community, yet they don't have a community. A community is a gathering of like-minded people aiming for the same goals. It is a group of planters like us; father, wife, and children all wanting the same things in language, education, and future. We are striving for that as individual families in a location called a neighborhood or town. We have common languages, religion, and standards. But the community is based upon family, not groups. Well, the slave community is definitely not based on family. The last thing you want is a dog looking at his wife and children as part of his community. Do not forget son, your main goal in life is to keep that buck thinking of you as his community.

"If he thought his wife and children were the community, he would want the best for them, and to his small mind the best would be freedom. He would teach his children about freedom, so we must control the education and teach his children about slavery. He would protect his wife, so we must replace him in her eyes.

"'Giving something back to the community' for the slave cannot mean family; it has to mean groups of slaves. Either the house slaves or field slaves, the slaves getting the cotton to the market, or the slaves doing the planting. Their sense of 'community' must always exist within groups that we control, so when the buck talks about giving something back to the community, he will be talking about giving it back to us. We want his labor, honor, and fear; then we want him to die."

"Die? You want them to die? I thought they were too valuable to us. Why would you want them to die? If that's the case, then why are we paying the slave hunters to go after them; it's the same as dying to let them go, right?" Junior could not understand what his father was getting at. They spent a lot of money on keeping the slaves alive and healthy enough to pick cotton. Why would he say he wanted them dead?

"Well, son," he began. Master Gilmore always liked baiting Junior with perplexing statements. "Yes, we do want them healthy and strong, and they are indeed valuable to us. That is, until they get too old to work. When a slave gets too old to work, he is also too old to sell. He will be of no value to you or anybody else. You cannot do anything with him except feed him and take care of him until he dies. A good slave owner would keep the buck healthy until he is around 27 years old, and then let him die. It is better for the buck and better for the profit."

"Hmmm" Junior was thinking. "That's why you seldom see an old Black male? He works hard then dies. How do you get him to die?"

"That's easy." Gilmore Senior laughed. "Just feed them poison over the years, and they will die in time. Ever wonder why we don't feed them very much meat? Why such a low protein diet of grits, vegetables, and meal? Two reasons son; while meat gives you energy, it first takes it away. You would have those dogs trying to sleep until noon if you gave them a full meal. They would be so lazy nothing would get done.

"The second reason we give them that diet is because it includes high salt and other things that wear out the body. Don't you think we know they go after our garbage? I know it is illegal for a slave to have meat unless it is a reward. So why do we throw the slaughtered pig out where they could find it? Because after we take the pork chops, ham, and bacon, those dogs take the guts, clean them out, and make chitterlings, they take the skin and fry it into crackling, and add salt to make it into a snack. Then they use the nose, ears, tongue, toes, tail, and even the brains to make food for their children. Those wenches are teaching their girls to cook like that and the boys are marrying women who cook like their mothers. So, even if slavery ended, the diet would not end. They will continue eating like good slaves and continue to work themselves to death for us. That is why you want your slaves to die; it is good for your business."

"So the diet is to make them strong early and weak later in life? They can work hard and make babies, we take care of the babies and take the profit, and when they are old they lie down and die like good little dogs." While Gilmore Jr. was beginning to understand this philosophy, he also understood why the White people could never think of slaves as humans. You could never treat humans like this. They must be sub-human, because they were treated worse than the cattle and pets. Junior felt that if father says we must then we must, because father was the wisest man he knew. Junior was thinking that he really had to keep that dog Jordan in line. It would be a shame to have to kill him; he had been his dog for years.

CHAPTER NINE
LEARN AND EARN!

"It's party time, the work is done, gonna get shined up and have some fun." This tall lanky slave walked into Jordan and Uncle Thomas' cabin from the fields shortly after the horn blew. Many friendly slaves congregated there after work from time to time, so the tall slave's entrance was not unusual, even though Jordan did not recognize him. He looked a lot like Jay-Low, but he was much skinnier.

"Hey Jordan, sorry to hear about you," he said. "I told you not to take off. Master will get angry at all of us. I hope you don't try that again." Jordan wondered about this guy; who was he? He looked a lot like his old friend Jay-Low. A lot thinner and unclean, but he did resemble Jay-Low.

"I'm sorry, but my head was hurt and I have memory loss; who are you? Do I know you?"

"Sure you know me; I been your friend all of your life. It's me, Too-Hi; we came here together as children. You mean you don't remember your best friend?

"Well, if you were my best friend, why were you not with us when we ran away?" Jordan asked.

Too-Hi looked confused. "Because I didn't think you could make it. But if you did, I would have followed you." Some how Jordan did not trust this guy, even though they were supposed to be best friends. There was something about him that did not fit the rest of the slaves. Then he noticed it.

"Hey Too-Hi, I noticed all of the slaves are bare footed, but you have shoes on. Where did you get the shoes?" Other slaves begin to notice his shoes also. "Yeah," someone asked, "You did not have shoes on this morning Too-Hi; those are not your winter shoes."

Uncle Thomas walked over to Too-Hi, "Boy! What did you have to do for Master to give you shoes in the summer time? Master only gives us shoes in the winter time except we do something special for him."

Uncle Thomas explained to Jordan that he had a problem with the slave hunters finding them so easily. Sometimes the other slaves will tell of the plan of escape. "Why, why would they turn us in?" Jordan asked, completely devastated.

Uncle Thomas looked at Too-hi and said, "For a pair of shoes or a piece of meat from Master's table, right Too-Hi?" Too-Hi denied it and said he found the shoes in the trash. It could have been true, but suspicion among the slaves was high because Master set them against each other. Jordan wanted to know more about the "sellouts", as he called them. "Sellout" was a very negative term for slaves. It was reserved for the slave that would sell out his mother's plan to escape, all for a scrap of meat. Master kept the slaves' diet so lacking of protein that most slaves went most of the year without any meat.

Master would slaughter a pig and throw away the garbage. The slave women would take the pig guts and make chitterlings, and they took the skin and make crackling; they would use whatever they could to keep meat on their tables. So, the slaves developed a way of cooking the toes, feet, neck, tongue, brain, ears, tails and other parts of the slaughtered pig. When a slave girl had a baby for master, he would give her a slice of bacon before she went back into the fields. The meat was so valuable that Master could use it for payment on most anything, thus the term, "sellout."

"Well Jordan, you had better get to bed; we got work to do tomorrow" Uncle Thomas said, already taking off his shirt.

"Work? Tomorrow is Saturday; I thought it was a day off." Uncle Thomas explained to Jordan that normally Saturday was a day off given to most slaves to take care of personal things. Things like, washing, taking care of their gardens, and courting each other were done on Saturday. However, this was late spring, the crop of cotton had to be taken care of, and Master's cotton came first.

"Where do I sleep?' Jordan asked.

"I don't care where you sleep; I am sleeping over here in the corner." Uncle Thomas had spread a blanket over the ground in the cabin and was lying down for the evening. Jordan realized that his bed would be on the floor. The dirt floor! He could use the blanket for covering or for a mattress but not both.

It had been a long day for Jordan. He sat on the floor to think about it. He did not know where he was or how he got there, but he did know it was trouble. He thought about his family, Uncle Thomas, his mother, brother, and sister; how did they get here? He understood that he might need to be punished for something, but why were they in slavery? And poor Iris, or Siri as they call her here. Such a beautiful girl and he could not protect her. He remembers the way she looked at him as Junior was beating her. It was not hatred or fear; it was just a look. She knew he could not help her, but she did not blame him for it.

He had to let her know he still cared for her. She had to know he had not abandoned her. Then he remembered the white stone he had found on the way to rob the store. He could give her that; it was not valuable, but it was all he had. It would mean they would be together forever. Jordan reached into his pocket to get the stone. But it was not there! He must have dropped it when he was shot and fell to the ground. This really hurt Jordan; yet, he did not know why. It was only a worn out white stone, but it was also the last gift he had for his woman. Now it was gone forever; lost, like he was.

He lay down on the floor and tried to sleep; it had been a long day, and even the damp, cool ground could not keep his eyes open. Even the slight feeling of insects crawling up his back was not enough to stop the slumber. After all, maybe he would wake up in his own bed.

BANG! BANG! BANG! BANG! What was that? Who was banging that bell? "Time to get up Jordan. It's already 4:30 am and we got to get ready for the fields." Uncle Thomas as already dressed and his blanket folded up in the corner. "We got to be in them fields when the sun gets up. Don't let Master catch you here when the sun is up. We work from sunup until sundown, except when we have a full moon. Then we just work. I hate the Harvest moon; you get no rest."

"What about breakfast?" Jordan asked, hurrying to fold his blanket. "Yeah, grab an apple on the way to the fields; you get a 20-minute break at high noon. Let's go, Jordan." his Uncle replied.

Jordan came out of the hut and thought how crazy this was. No toothbrush, no deodorant, and no breakfast. In addition, they expected you to work all day long. As Jordan left the cabin, other slaves had already formed a long line heading out to the fields. They carried rakes, bags, and hoes with them. Jordan was following Uncle Thomas because he did not know what was expected of him.

"What do we do all day in the fields Uncle?"

Uncle Thomas looked at Jordan and said, "Cotton son, we do cotton all day in the fields. Sometime we plant it, sometimes we chop it, and sometimes we harvest it. However, what we do is always cotton. Just follow me and remember, do not talk to the White folks."

Jordan already got that. As he approached the fields, he noticed White men on horseback. These were the overseers, whose job it was to make sure you did your job. They were paid based on the volume of cotton produced. The more cotton that reached market, the more pay they got. These were poor crackers that lived just a little better than the slaves. Some resented the slaves because they got all of the jobs.

The overseer did not care about you being tired or sick, only productive. They could not get work anywhere else because of the slaves. Who would hire a White person at White pay when your slave was a more experienced carpenter, blacksmith, bridge builder, planter, or tracker? The slaves were putting poor White folks out of work.

You would think they would support the anti-slave movement. Some did, but most did not. They were stuck by the false pride that slaves needed their care and were to proud to admit they needed the jobs. Therefore, Master had them both on the plantation. Both working for him and both working against each other.

The poor White overseers and the Blacks slaves were both going to die broke and broken. If they could see their plight as Master saw it, they would be in rebellion against Master. Jordan saw this and wondered why the civil rights movement had White folks in it also. They saw that freedom had to mean total freedom. No one is free unless all are free. Where had he heard this before?

Jordan worked in the fields all day. He did not mind the work even though it was the hardest thing he had ever done. However, it gave him time alone with his thoughts. Everyone worked alone and in silence. Except from the occasional order barked by the overseer of the work songs by the slave, Jordan could think and figure out what had happened to him.

"Chopping cotton" was what they called the work the slaves would be doing that day. What they really meant was "pulling weeds." The cotton was planted and the rains had come early. Now there were weeds coming up with the cotton. The slaves had to pull the weeds out before they chocked the cotton. Since Jordan did not bring a hoe or a rake, he had to use his back and hands. All day Jordan bent his back and pulled weeds out of Master's cotton field. He pulled weeds and thought.

'I still can't believe I'm here in this mess,' Jordan thought, 'and I can't believe in two-hundred years we are still in it. My God!' As Jordan learned more about the antebellum south and plantation living, he marveled at the similarities to his future neighborhood. Slaves grew mostly cotton, tobacco, and alcohol-producing grains like corn and barley. In his old neighborhood, the most in-demand products besides illegal drugs were cheap clothes, cigarettes, and alcohol. 'In one era we grow the crops, and in another era they fill our communities with the cheap products,' Jordan thought. 'Since the slavery days, these crops have created industries that rob us of our dignity. Old Massa still has his slaves. Dang.'

He thought about how much easier it would be sitting in school. He thought how much easier it would be cutting his mother's grass. Hanging on the corner with his friends would be a pleasure right now. Even dealing with his probation officer would be a welcome relief from dealing with these overseers. Nevertheless, Jordan also thought about escape. Maybe he was 'the one' or maybe he was not, but he was the one to lead himself to freedom; that was for sure.

He had only seen his mother for a short period. She came down to the fields to tell the overseer something. She was able to tell Jordan that Siri was alright and that she was glad to see him. Then she was gone back to the Big House. When she left, the other slaves began to talk about her.

"What is she doing down here? She only spoke to her son; is she too good to speak to us? All she does is sit in the Big House eating Master's food; she thinks she's better than we are, but she's just a slave like us." Those and other comments reminded Jordan of the division he was warned about. Not only were the White overseers fighting the field slaves, the field slaves were fighting the house slaves. All were fighting each other for a better position on the plantation, but none were fighting to get off of Master's plantation.

It was all a game to Master. Pitting the field slaves against the house slaves. The light complexioned, half-White slaves against the dark skinned, "pure African" slaves. They had the skilled slaves (blacksmiths, carpenters, engineers, and preachers) thinking they were better educated and thus better slaves than the unskilled cooks, gardeners, and horsemen. All just as oppressed and all living on the same slave plantation. Master had them all worried about their position on the plantation instead of how to get off the plantation.

Uncle Thomas was working behind Jordan to keep an eye on him. That bullet just grazed him, but he was acting very strange. They had been in the fields almost half a day by now. The sun was getting high in the sky, and Jordan was picking up his job pretty well. But Uncle Thomas noticed that Jordan still did not know how to keep the sun out of his eyes and off his face. The sun was your enemy in the fields. It would suck all of the energy out of you and drain you of your strength. As the slaves moved down the straight path, they could not keep the sun out of their eyes except by moving the brim of their hats to match the sun's movement. As the sun passed over in the morning, their brims moved over their heads. When lunch break came, they were too tired to move the brims over their foreheads so they just kept them were they were. You would see some slaves with the brims over to the left of their heads; others had them to the right. Some slaves had the brims pulled down the back of their heads to keep the sun off their backs. It was the look of field slaves, who could not even control the sun beating down on them.

Then there was the dust. The dust from the fields and the barns that soaked into your pores. The dust from the animals, cotton, and dirt would cake your body and layer your skin. Most slaves could not wash everyday, so they had to find other ways to keep the dirt off. Most covered their heads with a rag while in the fields or working in the barns. Some would use them to place behind the hats to keep the sun and rain off their backs. Jordan did not have a hat or a scarf and was beginning to suffer. Uncle Thomas touched his shoulder to get his attention.

"Boy, you gonna need to keep out of the sun. Take my hat and scarf until we can get you your own. You must have lost it when you ran. Master don't like his slaves being uncovered. If you're uncovered, you don't look the way a slave supposed to look.

Master may think you are trying to look like a free Black. You always want to look like a slave so Master won't get nervous."

"Look like a slave? How do you look like a slave? I thought all Black people were slaves or at least under the control of White folks." Jordan looked confused.

"No, Jordan; many Blacks are not slaves. Some have bought their freedom, escaped to freedom, or waited for old Master to die, hoping he left them their freedom in his will. Some Blacks own their own cotton fields, and a few even own their own slaves. A free Black would never wear his hat like he had been working in the fields all day, scared of the whip. A free Black would never speak with his head down, looking at his feet. That's why old Master doesn't want you to read or write; that's for free people, not slaves. Here boy, put this scarf over your head, take the hat, and turn it around. We got work to do for Master."

Jordan worked all week like this. He ate lunch with the slaves (only a cup of soup) and slept with the slaves. He did get to see Siri or his mother. He could go up to the Big House if he approached it properly, but he had to carry his hat in his hand and walk humbly. He could never enter from the front, only from the kitchen.

His mother worked in the kitchen most of the time, and they could talk while she worked. He did not understand why everyone in the fields thought her job was easy. At least he was off work when the sun went down. However, that was when Master came home to eat.

She worked all day preparing the meal, and then served it to Master's family in the evening, and she spent most of the night cleaning the home and preparing for breakfast in the morning. Jordan would try to get by the Big House every day to help his mother and the other women in the kitchen. He was tired and had little time, but at least he could do some heavy lifting and carry some water from the well.

However, Jordan was growing weary. He was tired of watching grown men being beaten. He was tired of watching families being separated and he was tired of lying on the floor of the cabin at night. He was especially tired of the sounds. The sounds at night of the women being abused by the overseers and Master. He was tired of the dead slave songs in the fields and he was tired to the grunts of men and women working themselves to death for the profit of Master.

Jordan lay on the dirt floor, trying to find rest. He worked so hard that sleep usually came quickly. Not tonight, however. Tonight he could not sleep; he had to think. Boy he missed being on the set with the other guys. He wished he had it to do all over. His hands and back hurt from all the hard work and back home he would not even cut his mother's grass. He would pick cotton all day from sun up to sun down for this White dude but could not work in a fast food restaurant to buy his own shoes. He had rather take the money from some other hard working person.

He missed the television, cell phones, and his bed, but what Jordan missed most was freedom. This place was worse than juvenile hall. He would rather be there where you had rights and protection. This old White man and his crazy son could kill him and no one would care. Someone had told him that if thought, he could not stay a slave. Thinking was the key to freedom. Jordan had forgotten who said that to him, and at the time, it was said he did not know what it meant anyway. But now that he knew what slavery was, he realized what he had was freedom. He wanted it back, and if thinking was the key, he was going to lie there every night and think his way to freedom.

As they headed back from the field one day, Jordan noticed that Too-Hi was staring at one of the slave girls, smiling. "Is that your girl, Too-Hi?" Jordan asked. "My girl?" he replied, almost indignant. "You mean that wench? Man, when will your head get right? That's just one of my wenches that Master Gilmore gave me to breed. She ain't my girl; I don't have a girl - I have all the girls. I'm one of Master's best breeders, and I make lots of babies for him." Too-Hi was very proud of the children he had produced on the plantation.

"But Too-Hi, man, look around you. You see more children than old people. The only slaves you see are working slaves or children. Maybe Master wants you to make babies so he can let you die off when you can't pick his cotton anymore. Maybe you are breeding yourself out of your own life," Jordan suggested. Jordan was right, but Too-Hi could not hear him. He was very proud that he could please Master. All he had to do was have fun with the slave girls and Master would reward him for each child born. He did not have to take care of them, protect them, and did not have to worry about the girls. This girl was a breeder too. Most of them liked the little benefits they received for giving Master a baby; they would get a little more food and a lot more attention. Too-Hi figured that Jordan was just jealous and probably worried about that fine little wench he had his own eye on. "Boy! Now that is a cutie," Too-Hi thought to himself, hoping Master Gilmore would choose him to breed with Iris.

"Hey Jordan," Too-Hi began, "Man, let me ask you a question: why is it so important for you to run away? Why do you hate us slaves so much? Do you think you are better than us?" Too-Hi considered himself a part of the plantation. So, any attempt to change it or escape from it was also an attack on him and his lifestyle. Any slave who did not maintain the slave culture was against the slaves. Too-Hi was worried his friend Jordan was trying to act like he was better than the slaves on the plantation.

"Too-Hi, what does my attempt to leave here have to do with you?" Jordan answered. "Whether I stay or go, you will still be in those fields tomorrow morning. If I make Master happy or sad, you will still be his slave. What I do has nothing to do with your relationship with Master or this plantation. It is not your plantation Too-Hi; it is your prison. What kind of world do you live in, Too-Hi? If all the slaves sang Master's songs all day, picked cotton with smiles on their faces, made more and more money for Master, and then died when they could not work anymore, what would that do for you?"

"Jordan!" he snapped. Too-Hi was getting frustrated. He could not seem to get his friend to understand that there was no life for him except a slave life. "Who will give you a job? Who will feed you? Jordan, no one will deal with slaves except his master. What's so bad with this life, anyway? We pick a little cotton, make some babies, and keep Master's family; so, what? We get free food, shelter, and no responsibility except to be obedient. Then some smart behind slave like you come along and try to tell us we should be free. That would upset Master and that would change my life. What if Master decides not to give us shoes for the winter? What if Master gives us a higher goal for picking cotton? What if Master gets so tired of your foolishness that he stops caring for us? Your beliefs are against the safety of the slaves; that is why someone told Master you were running, and that is how you got shot!"

Jordan looked intensely at Too-Hi as he listened to his words. "What do you mean, Too-Hi; who turned me in?"

Too-Hi glanced down to the ground almost as if he was ashamed; but his apparent remorse lasted only for a moment. "Man, you cannot threaten the lives of people and not expect them to protect themselves. Do you know how angry Master gets when slaves escape? Think of what a slap in the face it is to him. Usually, it's the slaves who Master has given the best jobs to that escapes. The drivers who gets to go to town, house slaves that can take money, or his best field slaves who he has taught to ride and go on errands for him. Any one of these slaves would not want to make Master angry and could surely make Master happy if they told him about your plans of escape. You see, Jordan, there is another way of getting along in life. You think freedom is escaping the plantation and living on your own. I think getting along is showing Master I will look out for him and take care of his family for him.

"Master gives me the best jobs, and I live better and better. You are very smart Jordan; why don't you try to give Master the proper thanks for all he has done for you? After taking care of your mother and her children, giving her the job of feeding his family, allowing you to go up to the Big House, and playing with his son, how do you thank him? Escaping from Master is like saying you do not want to be taken care of! That's foolish; a slave cannot take care of himself - you need Master and Master needs you. He knows he and his drunkard son cannot get this cotton to market. We are doing good here, Jordan, and you are giving us grief."

Jordan could only stare at his friend. Was he saying that it was him who turned in the plans of escape? It couldn't be; but he probably knew who did. "So, if I get free you will become more of a slave?" Jordan replied to his now suspicious friend. "That makes no sense. My freedom has nothing to do with you. I am not your father or your keeper. You take care of Too-Hi and I will take care of Jordan. You can remain a slave; but I have never been a slave. You see Too-Hi, you are a slave; I am only a prisoner. As a slave, you think getting the best job on the plantation brings you freedom. As a prisoner, I will only be free when I get out of here."

How could Jordan say that he had never been a slave? What did he know about freedom? "Then that will be when you go to your grave Jordan," Too-Hi replied indignantly, "and it will probably be an unmarked grave out in the woods somewhere." Too-Hi was a little worried about his friend; but only a little. He was on his career path to becoming the head slave. One day he would have the best choices of slave girls, the respect of the slaves, and special access to Master and his sons. Soon he would be one of only a few slaves who could even approach Master. He had an important position on the plantation and he had Master's trust. But Master also knew that he and Jordan were old childhood friends. Jordan's attitude could make Master doubt Too-Hi's loyalties. Too-Hi was determined that no one would get in the way of his lifestyle plans. "That is why I am your only friend, Jordan. People think you are crazy. They don't understand why you are trying to start trouble. All the slaves say you are a danger to us and cannot be trusted. You make Master angry and that makes everyone angry at you. You think you are leading people to freedom! Jordan, we do not want freedom; we want you to know your place and stop acting uppity. You are just a slave, Jordan; your father was a slave and your son will be a slave. The other slaves think you are a fool, Jordan!"

Jordan just looked at Too-Hi; that's all he could do. He held his gaze for a long time. Jordan knew that would be the last time they would talk about anything. He wished his old friend would see the light. Either you are a predator or a protector; but the two cannot communicate with each other. They were on two different roads going in two different directions. Jordan knew he and Too-Hi had reached such a point in life where they were growing into manhood with two different views of the world. This was goodbye for his friends. "Too-Hi, why should someone else's opinion of me mean more to me than my opinion of me?" Jordan asked. Too-Hi had no idea of what Jordan was saying.

Jordan remembered a conversation he had just had with Uncle Thomas. It was about Too-Hi, Uncle Thomas thought he was one of the 'Sell-Outs' and Jordan did not know what it was or how to recognize them. "They call them 'Sell-Outs' Jordan, Uncle Thomas had said. Be careful of those slaves who will sell out your plan to leave the plantation. They will get paid just a block of bacon or winter shoes for giving Master information on your plans. They will try to become your friend because those are the ones you trust with information. But they do not want you to be free because it would make them look bad. They wish to serve Master, so you cannot let them in on your plans. You cannot trust anyone except those you are escaping with, and then only trust them with the information they must have to leave."

"How can I tell a Sell-Out before he sells me out?" Jordan needed this information more than he needed to learn which way was North. Without knowing who to trust, he could only make the trip alone and that would be very difficult.

"The Sell-Out usually starts off trying to discourage your plans. They say it will not work, Master is too strong, or the time is not right. When that does not work, they stay around and listen. They listen for information and try to discourage others around you. Then, after all of this fails, they start asking questions and looking for information. They have already decided to tell Master, but they wait for more information on your plans and those going with you."

Jordan could not believe what he was hearing. Back home, in 2007, the Sell-Outs were the people trying to leave the neighborhood. Those people living in the Suburbs, sending their kids to "white" schools. The Sell-Outs were the ones not down with getting more benefits from the White people. Now it seems the real Sell-Outs were the ones trying to keep you on the plantation, not free you from the plantation.

There was one man on the plantation that seemed to have the respect of both the slaves and of Master. He was a slave that could approach master directly and ask for special things for the slaves. It was the preacher. The Master allowed the slaves to have church service on Sunday morning. In the barn, they would gather and sing hymns and have a service. The preacher was the only slave allowed to get close to learning to read. As long as it was the King James Version of the Bible he read from, Master did not mind.

The preacher did not have a name; everyone called him "The Preacher", and everyone respected him. Master would not have respected him if he knew what Jordan knew. The preacher was the focal point for the Underground Railroad.

Since Saturday night partying and Sunday morning service were the only time the slaves were allowed to meet without a white person present, they used the Sunday meetings to organize and plan. The Saturday evening partying was just that, partying. It was used as an escape from the daily toil on the plantation. However, church and the preacher were the tools used to plan the escape from the plantation.

Saturday morning, Jordan went down to the stables to visit some of the other young slave boys. Boys about his age hung out at the stables to get away from the adults who always had something for them to do. It was a great place to discuss things among themselves.

It was also a good time to hang around older men, pick up ideas, and listen to the stories. The older men gathered to fix tools and cut each other's hair. Saturday afternoon was preparation for Saturday night. Gambling, women, and drinking homemade liquor were part of the fun. But it was also a chance to socialize.

One old slave that hung out at the barn did not like Jordan very much. His name was Tim. Tim was the wise slave that everyone listened to. His last Master traveled a lot and took Tim with him. He was his personal servant, and spent most of the day with his master as they visited some of the largest cities in the South. Tim had even visited the North.

Being a well-traveled slave made his knowledge something others wanted to talk about. Tim could read a little and was always giving his take on the world. But this young buck Jordan who had been shot trying to escape and now could read and write and speak about the North as if he had been there was a threat. The slaves were beginning to talk with Jordan more than they did Tim, and that bothered him.

"So, here comes the seer," Tim announced as Jordan stepped into the barn. "What do you see for today, Jordan? Is it going to rain?" Jordan looked at Tim with a little respect because he did know a lot about this life, and he had to get as much knowledge as possible if he planned to escape. "I don't know about the weather Tim, just about my future."

Tim said, "Yeah, but your future still has us as slaves; your future still have us living where Master wants us to and still has us working for him. You really don't know the future Jordan; you just know slavery."

CHAPTER TEN
EDUCATION OR INDOCTRINATION!

"The bigger the fool, the better the dog!" Master can only stay master if the slave stays a slave. Not only should the slave not learn, he should not want to learn. One day Jordan visited his mother Lynette in the Big House. It was Sunday, and all the White folks were at church. With no one home, Jordan decided to look around the house. He soon found the library and started picking out books and newspapers.

Lynette came in and warned him about looking at books because Master did not like reading slaves. Jordan understood, but continued to read the books and newspapers. He picked up a flyer advertising a slave auction a few days from then. It read, "Hard working kitchen wench. Good for breeding. Trained to serve the household. About 30 years of age, good teeth. No visible scars. Good cook, seamstress, and obedient, goes by the name Lynette. $500 offered by Mr. Gilmore of the Gilmore plantation. Auction house, County Fairgrounds, Sunday the 15th!"

Lynette was going to be sold! Master Gilmore was going to sell Jordan's mother in a few weeks. "Mama, you are going to be sold! Master Gilmore has announced your sale date; we gotta get out of here." Lynette looked in horror at the paper. "Are you sure boy? That paper says that?"

"Yes, it says they want five hundred dollars for you at the auction house on the fifteenth." Lynette still did not understand how Jordan learned to read and write. The slaves thought it was a gift from God because it happened after the shooting. However, was this true? Was he able to read Master's pamphlets?

"Oh, baby, Master will not sell me. I have been his kitchen wench for years now. I have served this family all their lives." Jordan new his mother was not going to believe him. Master had promised her a lifetime on the plantation for a lifetime of service. It would not matter what he said; she would believe Master.

Jordan had to get to the auction and see the sale of slaves. He had to know what was going on and see for himself. The only way he could get to this week's auction was to convince Junior or Master to take him. Master Gilmore attends the auction most Sundays after church. It gives him and the other plantation owners a chance to get together and socialize. If Jordan could convince Master that there was a benefit to taking him, he could see the auction for himself.

Later, when the White folks arrived back home, Jordan was in the kitchen with Lynette. Junior walked in with Master Gilmore and saw Jordan. "What are you doing up to the Big House, boy?"

"I was just helping Lynette carry in water for the night, Master. I figured you all would need to wash up before dinner, and I wanted to make sure there was enough water."

"Good Jordan; that is using your head." said Master Gilmore. That was all the opening Jordan needed.

"Master Gilmore, sir," Jordan started, "I been learning to drive the buckboard back with the cotton. I'm also leaning how to control the horses, so I was wondering, could I be your driver when you go off the plantation? That would give me more of a lesson than just taking the mules from the fields to the barn."

"Sure Jordan, if you can make time after your chores, maybe you can take me and family to town. But only after you finish your work. I have my dog driver and do not need another. However, it is good to have another trained dog in case I need one."

"Thanks Master Gilmore, I just want to learn to get the best job on the plantation. Since I'm off on Sundays and come up here to help Lynette, why don't I drive you to church next Sunday? That way, I can start learning on my off days."

"Sure, sure, see Jasper in the stables and tell him you will be driving the carriage next Sunday. Now get back to the quarters; it's almost night time, and you got to be in the fields early, boy."

"Yes sir, Master Gilmore, I will be right on my way." Lynette glanced at Jordan as he left, thinking, 'That boy is really learning fast. Maybe he is the one to lead us all free.'

The next Sunday, Jordan was waiting outside Master's house, dressed in the best clothes he could borrow. He had the carriage clean and the horses washed. He did not want anything to get in his way. He had to get to that auction. Lynette was due to be auctioned the next Sunday.

Master and his family came out and got into the carriage. He did not speak nor look at Jordan. Sitting with Jordan was another slave. His job was to help the ladies in and out and assist the driver. His real job to Jordan was directions since Jordan did not know where he was going.

The first stop was church. The master's family attended church every Sunday out of duty, not conviction. The slaves stayed out back in the barns until their masters were ready to leave.

Jordan met many other slaves and had hours to talk and learn from them. They all had the same stories. Rape, beatings, and being sold. There was one old man named Jake that was very wise. Jordan sat down in the shade of a tree to talk to him. Jake had heard about Jordan, the young buck that tried to escape and had been shot. Rumor had it that he could read now and was a prophet.

Jake had the letters "RS" branded on his face for "Running Slave." His master had placed it there to remind him of his failed escape attempt and his slave status. He also carried a deep cut on his right angle that master gave him to keep him from running away. It cut his ligament, and old Jake walked with such a limp that the only job he could do now was drive White folks around town.

Jordan noticed that most of the slaves had scars of letters burned into them. They looked like branding iron marks. Some reminded him of the tattoos so many of his friends were being placed on their bodies. Master branded his slaves and we were branding ourselves. Jordan thought that was amazing. He wanted to get a tattoo with his gang name on it. It would have looked just like the markings master was putting on his slaves. Jordan wondered why he never saw White boys with their arms branded with signs. Even here, Master's sons were not expected to have brands unless they were prisoners.

Jordan had learned to deny any ability to read, but did confess of having some memory loss. He asked the old slave to tell him about slave life. What could Jordan expect with life on the plantation?

"Well son, let me tell you." Old Jake sat back and pulled on his old corncob pipe. "Master is cruel, very cruel. So all you can expect is cruelty. Some will burn you for the fun of it. They will work you to death just for the money. I understand from some that you can see the future. What does the future say about old Master?"

Jordan did not know about old Master in the future. He only knew about him. His future was going to include freedom the enjoyment of freedom. As they waited for the Sunday service to end, Jordan wanted to know about the auction.

Old Jake told him about the time he was auctioned to his current Master. "Capt'n Green had grown tired of my running and my rebellion, so he placed me up for auction. You could only beat a dog so much before he begins to lose value. When you see a slave with a badly whipped back, it shows the buyer that he's trouble, so no one will pay top dollar for him. Branding was okay, but whip marks on the back took the value away, so Master sold me before he was stuck wit me.

"I stood there on the block with women and children. I remember White men coming and placing their hands in my mouth to look at my teeth. These were the same White men I saw examining certain parts of the cows and horses that was up for auction. I also noticed they did not wash their hands. With the same dirty hands, they would fondle me and the men and women on stage.

"Women were stripped down to show if they had scars on them. Good breeder women were still valuable even if they had scars. However, if your woman had been burned or crippled on purpose, that was a bad sign.

"Some slaves were sold because the Master had died. They went first because they usually already had buyers for them. Other local owners knew the slaves or the dead owners. The other slaves were runaways and they were saved until the last. Some still bleeding from the whippings and some half dead from the torture.

"I remember Aunt Burk from the Wilson plantation. She had run away once, and Master beat her badly. Then she and her husband ran off, so Master killed him and scalded her with hot water all over her chest. He strung Aunt Burk up naked on the old oak tree. He kept her up there for two days so everybody could see what happens when you run away.

"When Aunt Burk grew too weak to scream, Master would rub brim and salt over her body, which would give her more strength to holler. Master wanted to teach the slaves what happen when they run away. All it did was showed us what happen when you were caught.

"If you run Jordan, and I know you will, do not get caught. Go the path of success. There is a way to freedom and there is a way to slavery; make sure you are on the path to freedom."

Jordan asked the slaves if they thought Master could change. Uncle Rumpus said he thought Master would never change. "Don't forget Jordan, Master is breeding the Black man to be a slave, but he is also breeding himself to be Master. He cannot breed cruelty into us without breeding it into himself. He will become what he places into us. If Master is cruel today, he'll be cruel in the future. That's why you can't talk about the future; Master is just as mean there as he is here."

"Yes sir, you may be right, I've never thought of that. However, Black men are stronger. If we recognize Master, we can defeat him. We do have power in the future, but Master is good at hiding. He does not look the same as he does here.

"Here you got White folks that will help you get free and in the future, you will too. However, you can tell the Master from the freedom fighters here. That is a little harder in the future."

One of the slaves spoke up, "You can tell a slave from a free Black here. Those free Blacks will speak to White folks straight in the face. You will get a beaten if you speak to Master without bending your back and speaking broken English. Free Blacks, especially those that own property, speak proper English and look White folks in the eye. Boy, I can't imagine a time when I can look old Master straight in the eye and tell him what's on my mind."

Jordan wanted to know how a slave stood and spoke; he wanted to learn so he could survive until they escaped.

"Just remember, speak to your feet, not to White folks. Don't say anything to them unless you are answering them. I remember an old buck name Jessie. Jessie was always giving Master his mind until one night he caught Master drunk and in a bad mood.

Master made Jessie take hold of a hot pot full of boiling water with his bare hands. He told old Jessie that if he did not hold that pot in his hands, he would pour that boiling water over his head. Well old Jessie had no choice, he grab hold of that hot pot and it burned him very bad. Of course, Jessie was not an ignorant slave. He dropped that pot on the floor and old Master was too drunk to wait for another one to boil again."

Jordan asked why free Blacks could speak to White folks and slaves had to look down to their feet. If it was Black folks the master wanted to control, why did the free Blacks get away with it? The other slaves explained to Jordan that White people were not the real problem; it was slavery. Master did not want to control Black people, Master wanted to control slaves. Slavery had to be cruel to work; nobody would take it any other way. Master did not hate Black people; he loved the power and control of the slave system. If you were a slave, the Southern culture kept you in your place and kept you down. If you were a free Black, you did not fit into the system. A free Black person had restrictions, but did not have to act like a slave to survive.

Jordan continued to sit and listen to the slaves talk and teach. He realized how much wisdom there was in old people. He learned the history and lessons on survival. If he did not get these lessons from them, he would learn them the same way they had; by the whip.

Church was over and Master and his family came out. The wife and children would be going off to shop and socialize, but Master and the other men would be going down to the auction. The auction was more than just an auction. It was a social gathering for the planters, traders, dealers, and merchants. There was a bar where patrons could drink, meeting space for important community members, and opportunities where one could even find a job.

They drove up to the auction house and Master got out. Jordan followed him into the office carrying his grip. The company that ran the auction had an office for patrons to register. They were given a sheet of paper that described the slaves being offered. If you were bringing in slaves to be sold, they were taken from you at the office or bought from your plantation by the company.

The owner and one or two helpers ran the slave auction. The business also included a slave whipping service. This is where masters from all over the county sent their slaves to be flogged for various reasons. There was a charge for each lash ordered. Masters like this system because the professionals did their job with minimum damage to the property, and it freed master from any guilt or responses to begging.

When the slaves arrived, the manager would examine them and ask questions that would be used in the auction, questions about skills, duties, medical history, age, and others. The teeth were examined to try to judge the age, and the muscle and bone structure were observed to reveal any arthritis or weakness. The slaves were placed in groups determined by their jobs. Field slaves, house slaves, market slaves, and children. Some slaves were sold as families, but most were sold as Master wanted to bid.

Well trained house females would sell for around five hundred dollars if they were grown. They sold for up to nine hundred dollars if they came from a good family or had special training. The other house slaves that were well bred and trained would go for anywhere between one thousand to twelve hundred dollars if they could be used as formal servants for dinner parties and special entertainment by Master. Skilled slaves brought in the most. In demand were engineers that built the roads and laid the foundation for buildings, carpenters that kept the house in order, and the blacksmiths that made the tools and repaired the wagons. They sold for up to eighteen hundred or two thousand dollars. The least valuable slaves were the unattended children and adult males that were badly scarred by beatings. No one wanted an undisciplined slave.

A chronic runaway always caused trouble with the other slaves. Now his mother and girlfriend were going to be sold, all because of Master's contempt for him. Jordan figured his mother would be worth eight hundred dollars to Master and Siri even more. Master could buy two field slaves for the price of his mother. That means Jordan had less value and was more of a threat to Master. Jordan knew Master would kill him if he tried to escape again, especially if he took his valuable slaves with him.

The atmosphere was like a carnival. People ran around playing and shouting. Other folks sold food, drinks, and merchandise like whips, chains, branding tools, and such. Some vendors even sold clothing, tools, and equipment. All were directly associated with and dependent upon the slave trade.

People up North could not understand how poor White folks put up with slavery. It took jobs away from them, which kept many of them from taking care of their own families. But looking at all of the businesses that thrived because of the slave auctions, one could see the direct benefit for poor Whites. There was a lot of money in the selling and movement of merchandise directly associated with slavery.

These auctions would offer up to a thousand slaves for sale. The slave traders and handlers were paid for moving as many slaves as they could as quickly as possible. They would separate slaves by male and female and then the children without mothers. The auction offered slaves that were skilled and unskilled. Blacksmiths, engineers, carpenters and house managers were the most valuable male slaves. Women got high prices if they could cook for prominent parties or were exceptional seamstresses or breeders.

A buyer would walk up and down the rows of slaves to examine them. It was no different that going to a horse or bull auction. The merchandise was presented and examined, and the offer was made. Slaves were stripped naked, thrown down, and pushed around in an attempt to test their strength. Husbands and wives, if you could call them that, were often sold to different masters. Even the married slaves were often paired up with other slaves to force breeding of more slaves.

Jordan knew he would escape and he knew he could not be caught. He had to find the organization that helped slaves get away. He had to get help for his mother and his girlfriend.

Master Gilmore was not there to buy or sell this week. He was there to socialize with his friends. Jordan had to watch, learn, and listen. He had made up his mind; Master was not going to sell his mother at this auction. Master was not going to beat his girlfriend anymore, and Master would not reap the benefits of his labor again.

CHAPTER ELEVEN
Stay right or be left!

Jordan only wanted to get to know the slaves with "RS" branded on their foreheads or their arms. "RS" stood for "Running Slave", and was placed on them by Master to keep them from running again. Since the brand caused White slave hunters and other owners to stop and question those baring the mark, RS slaves were not sent off the plantation for errands. They were restricted and less valuable to Master. Master did not like to have to brand them because it indicated to any potential new owners that the slave would be a problem.

But Jordan sought out RS Slaves to talk to. He wanted to know as much about escaping as possible, and knew only those slaves who had tried would be able to let him know what was down the road. The first thing Jordan learned was which way north really was.

Master had tried to get the slaves to think north was in the southern direction. A slave who believed Master would be heading deeper into slavery while thinking he was getting closer to freedom. The first thing Jordan learned was how to tell if he was on the right path. No more listening to those slaves who were afraid of change. No more listening to the beaten down slaves. No more! He understood those who were too tired to go. He understood those who had seen so much. But he could not let their fear stop his motivation. He would be free one day.

Jordan also asked the older freedmen about freedom and what they had experienced. Jordan had learned the importance of getting information from those who had been around longer. Experience was valuable. The slaves told their stories, and now it was time for the freedmen to tell theirs.

He used to want nothing to do with these types of men. Men who had gotten enough of poverty and misery. He would never learn from these men. That was, until he met the old slave named Bones. Bones could not stand long and had lost most of his sight. But he stood for freedom and never lost sight of it.

Bones was eager to tell Jordan about the eight times he had run away. Bones would have tried again, but Master blinded him in a rage after his last attempt. Bones used to be a tall, strong slave but had grown old fast. He had taught himself to read a little and could navigate the stars. He had been North once before being caught and returned. All of the slaves prodded him for information. "What did freedom look like?" "Was it like heaven?" "Do Black folks be free and have jobs?" They asked him questions all the time, and he never got tired of telling what he knew.

As Jordan walked into the barn to visit Bones, the old man looked up sleepily. "Hey Jordan, I expected you would be coming around. They told me you see visions of the future now that your head has been healed. I hear you talk about things gonna get different in the future. You say we gonna be free one day. They even say you can read and write a little. Set down son and tell me about the future."

Jordan pulled up a stool and sat down with Bones. Bones could not work any longer, so Master allowed him to stay in the barn and clean up while the other slaves were in the fields. He was sitting on a stool repairing the horse bridles, so Jordan grabbed one to help while he talked with him.

"I just want to know all you know about escaping Bones. Teach me all you know about getting out of this place. I want to leave and I will never stop until I am free. They tell me you are the best person to talk to about freedom Bones; can you help me?"

Bones lifted his shirt, stood up, and showed his chest to Jordan. "This is all I can teach you Jordan." On Bones' chest were the branded letters, "RS."

"They burned you?" Jordan asked. He could not believe it. He had a brand on his chest that matched the gang tattoos he use to have. "What does it stand for, is it the mark of one of your old Masters?"

"No, Jordan" he replied. Bones let his shirt down and sat back on the stool. It means "Running Slave", and Master Gilmore gave it to me when I ran the third time. After that, I should have remained on the plantation. I could not get thirty miles with that brand on me. Even if Master was to free me, men would still capture me and bring me back to the South. I can't go anywhere or visit anyone. This brand allows the slave hunters to keep tabs on me and to know if I am out of my place. It has been my mark ever since; branded like a bull. I will tell you all I know about running, but you got to learn more than I know. After all is said and done, all I know about running is how to get caught. Learn how to reach your goals, boy. Take my knowledge, but add to it or all you can be is what I am...a slave. I will meet you everyday, we can do our work together and I will answer your questions. One thing Jordan, when you get free...tell them about us. The Master is telling White folks up north that we like being here; you go son and you tell them the truth."

Some slaves cautioned Jordan about running away. One in particular interrupted Jordan's conversation with Bones to offer some slave wisdom. "Who's gonna give you work? Do you think dem White folks gonna give a slave a job up North? Them abolitionists really hates you Jordan; they want you to leave the plantation were Master feeds you so you can starve in the woods. Master is only trying to protect you from harm. Freedom is bad.

"Maybe ole Master is cruel at times, but he takes care of us. We get food twice a day, a hut to stay in, and even a little garden to plant our vegetables. Master provides us with a pair of shoes a year and a few pair of pants. All you got to do Jordan is pick his cotton for him. Is that so bad? Slaves don't even get whipped unless they really insist on it.

"I hear tell, up North a slave has to get his own clothes, feed his own children and buy his land to work on. How can a slave do that? No, Jordan, those folks coming down here talking about freedom really hates us Jordan. Stay here with Master, Jordan."

Jordan looked at the slave hard. He seemed like some of the guys hanging out at the barbershop back home. Tired, beaten, and giving up on themselves. Because they had not made it off the plantation, they did not want anyone else to. If Jordan succeeded, his success would also prove they were failures. Jordan's success would prove these others were just lazy or did not want freedom enough.

Jordan asked, "Sir, you are a grown man, don't you think you could buy your own clothes, land, and seeds? Why would you expect another grown man to take care or your everyday needs? When I was a small boy, every problem I faced required my mother to do something. When I was hungry mother had to act, when it was time to go to bed, get dressed, or work, mother had to act. That was because I was a boy. I am now a man and do not need to be taken care of. Every problem you have requires Master to do something, because he treats you like a small boy. And you accept that view of yourself." Jordan did not accept the fear perpetuated by those scared slaves. But could he be sure Bones had not yet weariness turn him into one of them?

The other slave's name was Rusty, and he had been on the plantation a long time. Jordan wanted to hear more from him because he wanted to get to know how someone who had seen so much still wanted so little from life. "Tell me Rusty, why do you really think serving Master will get you more?" Jordan was using an old trick from the streets; let them tell you all about themselves.

"Well, look Jordan," Rusty continued, "We cleared this land, we plowed it, and we planted it. We take care of the crop from sun up to sun down. We work these fields until the harvest is in, then we work them some more. Why shouldn't we get some of the benefits of Master's harvest? We get the hut, he gives us food, and he takes care of our babies. Now we can all see that the Black man is kind of fragile and don't live as long, but even that does not stop old Master from showing how much he cares. Even when an old slave can't work any more, Master still takes care of him and gives him what he needs until he dies.

"This has always been our home, Jordan, and some of us are proud of how good it looks and how well it functions. I'm proud when this plantation grows more cotton than that Mr. Lewis' plantation down the road. We the best slaves in this county, and I'm proud of that. Now I hear talk among the White folks of those Northern Yankees coming down here to spoil it for us. Well, I tell you, Jordan, they can come if they wants to, but we gonna whoop them dang Yankees when they get here."

Jordan knew what he was dealing with; a lost soul. He preferred serving Master over freedom because he had served him so much. He thought he was part of the plantation and could not be free from it. Success to Rusty was getting the best job or the most respect on the plantation. Jordan knew there was nothing he could say to Rusty; he just had to keep Rusty where he could see him. Rusty was never to be trusted with any plans or information about escape. Rusty would be left behind to build Master's fire for him at night.

Jordan sat on the stool by the old man and continued to talk to Rusty, who was discouraging him. "Look, I know you have been through a lot and suffered a lot. I understand in your youth you wanted to be free of it. Now you may have to accept you condition. Maybe freedom is too heavy a burden for you. But do not discourage me. Let me gain the freedom you once desired. I still have the desire; help me, teach me, and my victory will be yours too."

Just as he finished speaking, the Preacher came to Jordan in the barn; he had been watching Jordan and was curious.

"Jordan, can we go for a walk?" The Preacher had come to Jordan after the work was done and everyone was visiting. It was not strange to see him walking and talking to slaves all day. Even the White people recognized that there were some things you only wanted to discuss with your pastor. It would not raise anyone's suspicion to see Jordan and the Preacher walking down by the creek.

They could have been going fishing, looking for bait, or just talking. As they walked, the Preacher began questioning Jordan on his head wound and how he felt. Jordan had been around long enough to see there was another reason for the visit. Jordan could not figure it out, but he felt he was being sized up for something.

They walked along the creek for a while and entered a large clearing around the bend. It was still on Master Gilmore's property, so it was okay to be there. It was known to be a place where some of the younger and romantic slaves met by moonlight. It was a field called "The Pass."

The field was beautiful; the green grass and the sapling trees scattered about almost formed a path, inviting you to stroll throughout and just enjoy the glory of God, or get lost on a blissful lane, leading to an unknown place. The creek ran along the outermost part of the field, separating it from the woods beyond and defining its border. In the center of the field, however, was a mighty oak tree with branches that seemed to touch the sky. As they walked, a gentle breeze blew and rustled the leaves of the oak so that they sounded like resounding applause. Jordan instantly knew that this was a very special place, and he wanted to know why.

"Why do they call this field 'The Pass'?" Jordan asked.

"Interesting question, Jordan. They call it 'The Pass' because many slaves had walked down this field and never came back.

Some slaves think it is a doorway to the North. Some think it will lead you to the future, Jordan."

"What do you think, Preacher; will this field lead one to freedom?"

"That depends Jordan."

"Depends on what?"

"It depends on who you meet in the field, and where they are going, and if you choose to follow. Jordan, I hear you been telling people about the future. You been saying things about were we are going. Jordan, are you a prophet?"

Jordan thought that was funny.

"No, sir; I'm only caught up on this plantation like you. I'm not a prophet; I am only a prisoner."

"Has God shown you the future of his people, son? Do you see visions?"

"I don't see visions Preacher, but I have seen the future. It's hard to explain what I mean, so I've stopped trying to explain it. However, I feel like I am not from this time but from another time and place. I see things differently, and I don't seem to fit in."

"Sounds like God is working with you for some reason, son. I know that many slaves are looking for that visionary to lead them to freedom, and many are always claiming to be that person. But you have not claimed that; you have only proclaimed what you see in the future."

"It's not the future to me, Preacher; its home. I want to go back home. How do I get to that future?"

"Well, I only know you can't go to the future by waiting on it to come to you. If you want to go to the future, you need to be moving. Are you moving, Jordan?"

"What do you mean, Preacher?"

"If your future is not on this plantation and you are not making plans to leave, you will never get to your future. Your future will not come to you; you must go to it. Where are you going, Jordan?"

Jordan had heard about the secret Underground Railroad all week. He knew there were secret songs in the field and hand signals. He even suspected that there was a major plan of escape going on. Someone had to be leading it; could it have been the Preacher? Was the Preacher trying to test him to see if he was willing to go?

"Yes, sir, I am ready to go to my future, but do not know the way. Do you know the way, Preacher?"

"No, Jordan, I do not know the way for you to get to your own future. However, I do know that if you seek, you will find. If you are looking for the way, you will see it when it reveals itself. Keep your eyes open and always focus on your future; you will then have a clear heart, mind, and eyes. The truth will be revealed to those seeking truth."

Jordan understood, shut up, and paid attention. He had found a conductor on the Underground Railroad. All he needed was a ticket.

"One more thing, Jordan; I believe you are a visionary and a prophet. If I am right, may I ask you a favor?"

"Sure, Preacher. What is it?"

"When you find this future, will you come back and get me?"

"Why would you be willing to follow me? I am only a slave on this plantation. You are the most respected slave here. Why would you look to me for a way out?"

"You are right, Jordan, I am very well respected by slaves and Master on this plantation, but I would rather be unknown and unnoticed and be free."

"Why haven't you left before, Preacher? Rumor has it that no one leaves without you making the way. Why haven't you made a way for yourself?"

"God calls us for what he wants us for. God does not explain the reason. I have been called to be the deliverer, not the delivered. However, I think it is time to retire. I believe God will let me see freedom here before I see freedom in heaven."

"If I find the future, Preacher, I will take you."

They left "The Pass" and made their way back to the slave quarters.

Jordan noticed how some of the slaves kept to themselves and did not talk or visit with the other slaves very often. They were liked and respected, but he knew they had a special role to play on the plantation. These slaves had a way of communicating that the other slaves did not. They spoke with their hands and used the same words as the other slaves, but with different meaning. The words were designed to educate the slaves without warning Master. It was important to develop a different way of communicating with each other. They used hand gestures and double meaning words. Like the word 'good' meant 'bad', and 'cool' really meant 'hot'.

Jordan remembered being back on the block and speaking to his friends. They tried to have special languages to speak only around themselves. Words like 'peeps' for people and 'rents' for parents could be spoken right in front of these people without them knowing it. Jordan and his friends could pass on information to each other whether they were on the computer, texting, or standing in front of their parents. But here on the plantation it was not just for recreation, it was for survival. The information delivered by these special slaves could cause you to lose your life it you were not careful.

One of these slaves was named Buckeye, and he became interested in Jordan because he thought Jordan was a prophet of things to come. Buckeye came to visit Jordan one Saturday to ask about the future. He wanted to know when the slaves could use proper English instead of trying to hide their meanings with secret words.

"Jordan tell me, in the future, will it not be against the law to speak English to White people"? Jordan did not know what he meant. It was always legal to speak English. But he and his friends would not start speaking "White" because that would have made him a sellout.

"No, it won't be illegal. A time is coming when Master's children and your children will go to school together and learn together. There will be no laws telling us how to speak. What kind of laws would those be?" Jordan looked confused at Buckeye's question, so Buckeye tried to explain. All the slaves had noticed Jordan had changed since he tried to escape; they knew he had difficulties remembering, so Buckeye needed to explain something Jordan should have known.

"You see son, it be a law that a slave could be struck forty-nine times with a whip for learning how to read and write. Teaching a slave to read or write is one of the few crimes a White person could be whipped for. The crime of educating a slave is so harsh that even White children are punished for doing it. So we have to find new ways to learn and share information. We must never act smart in front of White people because showing how smart you are will cause White folks to punish all of us. That be why you find a slave acting smart and the other slaves will warn him to 'stop acting smart in front of White people'." Jordan could not believe himself.

He told them how he remembered going to the shopping centers in 2007 and hearing the mothers calling out to their children to 'stop acting smart'. Buckeye asked, "I bet you never heard a White mother call her children that way. You would never hear a White woman telling her children not to act smart. Sounds like in the future we still have some of the fears from the plantation."

"Yes!" Jordan said, "But I think they are just used to saying it. It is just an expression we used in the future. It will not mean the same thing; it is just slang we use." Buckeye had more questions for him because he was confused.

"Maybe I am hearing you in double talk Jordan. Sometimes we say things with double meaning to confuse others. Let me get this right. In the future, we continue to call ourselves by the demeaning names Master calls us just because we are used to it? We still call ourselves dogs and wenches? Do we still look at ourselves as slaves and free Blacks, or are all of us free?"

Jordan was getting a little tired of this game. Why didn't this old man get it? Did he think Black people of the future were so stupid and dumb to think of themselves as slaves even when slavery was over? They knew they were free, but still had doubts about the White man's willingness to look at them as free. "No, old man, you do not understand, we are free in the future but we still use the old names because that is what we remembered. We hold on to the past. You do not want us to forget where we came from, do you?"

"What? You mean you do not even want to forget where you came from? You really want to remember this? The beating, long hours of work, walking in the winter without shoes, having no freedom? Jordan, son, please tell me we do eventually forget about this place. When freedom comes, I will walk away from this old plantation, never look back, and never think about it. I do not care if Master never gets his cotton planted and never feeds me again. If I am going to starve, I will gladly starve as a free man. Let me ask you Jordan, why do you call this field 'The Pass?'"

Jordan looked at the slave, searching his face for the mood. Was he tricking him; everyone knew the name of this field is called 'The Pass', it always had been. "I have always called it 'The Pass'; that has always been its name."

"No, Jordan, it was not always called 'The Pass'; today we call it 'The Passage'. That has always been its name here. Something happened between your future and slavery. Somehow, the name was shortened to 'The Pass'. Maybe when freedom came, the freed Blacks forgot where they came from and did not need a Passage any longer. Maybe they just wanted to shorten the name. But it has always been called The Passage son, even today."

"What? The Passage? I hear the slaves always calling it 'The Pass' field even today. I just heard that name this morning. 'The Pass' is the name of this field we are standing in." Jordan knew there was a double meaning in what the old slave was trying to say; he knew he was being tested and did not like tests. "What is it you are trying to say old man? Just tell me what it is; I want to know."

"Well, son, think about it. When have you heard the slaves calling this place 'The Pass'?" Jordan thought about it and answered, "I heard it this morning in the barn, I heard it last night when I was helping my mother in the Big House, and I have heard it as long as I can remember."

"Jordan, let me ask you something. Every time you heard slaves call this field 'The Pass', were there White people around, or those slaves who work really close to White people?" Before Jordan could answer, the old slave continued. "We all call this field 'The Pass' when we are being heard by others, but among ourselves we use the real name. The real name, Jordan, is 'The Passage!'"

"'The Passage?' Why do they call it 'The Passage', and why only around certain people?" Jordan knew the answer to his question. His heart began to race; he was finally learning who the freedom minded slaves were and where he could find about where freedom was located. "Why do they call it 'The Passage'; were does this old field lead?"

The old man just smiled. "You have a lot of questions for someone who has no vision. I know you have tried to run before Jordan, and you failed. I don't know if you will try again, but it seems important to me that you gather more information than you had before. Learning where The Passage leads may be important to you or it may not. But if it is important you, need to find out on your own. The answers to all of your questions are there if you ask the right questions. People are watching you son; they think you may be the one to lead them to freedom. Whether it's true or not, it will not stop people from following you. If you have folks following you, make sure you are going in the right direction. Every name is important son; the name you call each thing has a meaning. If you call your woman a wench long enough, she will try to be the best wench on the plantation. If you call a Black man a dog long enough, he will try to be the best dog out there. Just pay attention; some people have called this field 'The Pass' for a long time and they have their reasons. But other people have always called it 'The Passage'. Look at those people and decide whom you will follow. If you follow the ones who call this field 'The Passage', you will know why they call it that and will need no more information. You have the answers to your questions son; that means your future is in your hands."

Double talk! That is what Jordan had just experienced. The old slave was trying to tell him something, but if Jordan told Master, the old slave could defend himself. No real information was exchanged, but vital information was learned. Jordan knew that field lead to freedom. He would keep his mind on that old field as well as this old slave.

The next day Jordan and some of the guys went down to "The Pass" to fish in the creek. Jordan felt really comforted in this field. It was a place for peace and thought. There was already someone there. A White teenager named George. George knew all of the other guys except Jordan. George was from one of the many poor White families in the county. George's father did not have work and only serviced on his own land. George, his father, and his older brother could not afford slaves and could not afford professional repairs to their tools and barns. So, their farm had been run down over the years.

Even though George was poor, he went to school. The slave children knew he was learning to read and write, and felt he could teach them. However, it was illegal for a slave to learn to read and write. It was also illegal for a White person to teach a slave to read or write.

So, ever since they were all young, the slave children would try to trick George and his other White friends to teach them their letters and writing. They would tease them into showing off the alphabet in order for the slaves to learn. Whenever one slave learned a letter, they would teach it to the others. Buy the time the children were ten or so years old, everyone knew about the game. Even the White children knew they were teaching slaves to read and write, but it became part of the normal teenage rebellion against authority.

They would play in the dirt with sticks and write their letters. They would read the headlines on the papers to understand dates and calendars. But most of all, they would read the Bible.

The Bible was important for a number of reasons. Master did not mind the slaves talking and studying about God. Master thought he believed in God too, so it was important for his slaves to understand "Servants, be obedient to thy masters."

Also, the slaves could quote scripture from the White preacher, find the verse with the help of White children who could read, and then study the spelling of the words to learn reading.

"Hey master George! Good morning to you!" It was very easy for Jordan to be polite when he wanted something "How's the fishing?"

"Not too bad." George replied. He did not really trust the slave. He had tried to escape and was shot, and may have been trouble for him. "What are you doing down here anyway? George wanted to make sure he was not trying to run away again.

"Just trying to catch some fish for my mother. The creek is low today, huh? George just nodded and continued baiting his hook. Jordan knew the creek flowed northeast until it ran into the Big River. The Big River was supposed to run straight north, but Jordan did not know for sure. It would be very nice to find out from this White boy, which way the Big River flowed. Jordan could tell by the sun if he was leaving in the daytime. But all the slaves knew that would be dangerous. They would all leave at night under the cover of darkness to escape the eye of the slave hunters. So Jordan needed to know which way the Big River flowed before they reached it. If it flowed south they would walk upstream, if it flowed north they would follow it.

George stared at Jordan for a while. He knew that his own father did not like slavery. His own father found it hard to work and wanted slavery ended so he could provide for his family. George walked over to Jordan, placed his fishing rod on the ground, and sat down. Jordan sat down beside him and they both stared out over the creek.

"You know, Jordan," George was speaking almost to himself. "Folks don't like slaves to have too much information; they tell me it is dangerous." Jordan was quiet; he had learned that you get more from White folks by being quiet.

"See Jordan, if you were educated and had knowledge, you would know that this little creek flows to the northeast until it reaches the Big River. You would also know that the Big River flows north a bit. But what you would not know is that you have to cross the Bid River and walk up the other bank to get to where you wanted to go.

"You see Jordan, the Big River flows through a few towns on the other bank and you have to know who feed and hide folks going North. If you do not know which house to go to, you'll never make it. That is why Master does not want slaves to be able to read or write; it will lead to freedom."

Jordan looked at George and smiled. "Thanks!" He said. "Thanks?" George stood up. "Thanks for what? I am just sitting here with a slave talking to myself. If you heard something, it was because I was talking out loud. Lord knows I would never teach a slave how to escape. That's not what I do." George got his fishing pole and walked away. Jordan looked back at the creek and then looked north. Freedom was waiting for him.

"Redneck…" Jordan thought, "Poor Whites who have to pick their own cotton. They should support ending slavery…"

George was a very strange white boy. Jordan would have never spoken to him in 2007; he was county, poor, and rough around the edges. Even George called himself a Redneck, and he seemed proud of the title. Redneck? That's what they called the racist white boys back in 2007, but this Redneck was a little different. He was still a crazy White boy, but the name had a different meaning here on the plantation.

"Redneck" on the plantation meant a poor White man who could not afford his own slave. So, he had to pick his own cotton and tend to his own work without the help of hired hands or servants. His neck got red from working in the fields all day and when he went into town you could tell he was a poor White man from the redness of his neck.

But unlike the Redneck in 2007, whom Jordan thought was racist and against Black people, George and his father seemed to be against slavery. Maybe it was because of the lack of jobs and prosperity for him and his family. George worked hard with his father, but could not compete with the almost free labor slaves gave their masters. Sure, George could get educated and move about freely, but his stance in life was just above slavery and not as good as many free blacks Jordan knew. Redneck - that would have a different meaning to him from that point on.

It was Friday night, and the slaves were planning to party. The musicians were getting their instruments ready. The folks were getting into their party clothes and there was almost a festive atmosphere on the plantation. Jordan just shook his head. In the same building where they would have church service in the morning they would have a party tonight. The same slaves who drank and danced Friday and Saturday night would attend church bright and early on Sunday morning in the same building! In both instances, the barn was an escape. They tried to dance and party their cares away on the first two nights, and then pray and sing them away the third morning. Church services were often a cover for meetings of slaves who wanted to plan their escape. Rarely was the slave church service truly and solely about God. They did not realize that this practice would come back to haunt them in the future. Many Black Americans in Jordan's time had the same perspective on their spirituality; they partied on Saturday and praised on Sunday, simply looking for an escape from their real lives in both instances. It wasn't about God; it was about using God in some way or another to escape the poverty and misery they were in. Since a loving God would not want them t be enslaved, they used his name to plot their escape without ever really getting to know Him. But, the idea of escape itself, whether physical or mental, excited them enough to keep using what opportunity they had to leave it all, even if only for a few hours. The slaves seemed to have more life in them that evening except for a few of them; they seemed more docile. Jordan noticed them, standing by themselves, stealing looks at each other across the room. He had learned to know when something was about to go down. He did not know what it was, but he kept his eyes peeled.

Finally, one of the women started to sing, to herself. "Swing low, sweet chariot, coming for to carry me home. Swing low, sweet chariot, coming for to carry me home."

Another slave chimed in, "I look over Jordan and what did I see, (coming for to carry me home) a band of angles coming after me, (coming for to carry me home.) They repeated the song among themselves and no one seemed to notice. Jordan remembered the songs from when mama made him go to church.

Old Master Gilmore was walking through the plantation with his wife and even he was enjoying the song. "Listen to them dogs sing. They just love us; we take a walk and they entertain us with song. I keep telling you Carol, them slaves love us." Mrs. Gilmore just smiled and walked along with Master Gilmore, but inside she was filled with rage. She saw how he took pause to look at the slave women as they walked; she could see the lust in his eyes when he looked at certain slaves. Lynette was one of his favorites; whenever Master Gilmore hung around the kitchen, it wasn't because he was hungry for food. "Ah, the slaves really do love us," Master Gilmore sighed, pleased with himself and all he had accomplished. His cruel leadership had been profitable to the family business, and the plantation was bigger that what his father had ever dreamed as a result. He also had a disproportionate number of female slaves; they served double duty as workers and personal rewards to Gilmore for all of their hard work.

'Oh, they love you indeed," thought Mrs. Gilmore. 'They hate you just as much as I do, especially the women.' When Master Gilmore was a young man, wanting a family and full of dreams for his future, he adored Carol. He shared his hopes and aspirations with her, he gave her lavish gifts, he doted over her like she was the most beautiful woman in the world. She even kept herself pure for him to ensure he would love and appreciate her forever. However, as soon as she got pregnant with Junior, things changed. He lost interest in her; she had fulfilled her purpose and was no longer exciting. She was now just a working cog in his machine, doing what she had been recruited to do. She knew how the slave women that he bred felt; she was a breeder, too. She was just desirable for the breeding of future masters, whereas the slave women bred future slaves. Carol's pain was heightened by her lack of understanding of what he saw in the slave women in the first place. 'They are black and ugly,' she thought. 'What beauty could he see in these fields? What is desirable about a house wench who only exists to cook my food? What can she give him that is better than what I give him?' As her thoughts began to betray her, Master Gilmore asked, "What is wrong, my petunia? Why the long face? Do you not like the slave songs? I will order them to stop singing if you wish." Mrs. Gilmore took a deep breath and lied, "No, nothing is wrong. Let them sing. That is all these pitiful dogs have is their music. I am a good woman; I will not take from them that simple thing." Master Gilmore looked at his wife and smiled, "You have always been such a good woman. That is why I don't mind being good to you." As Carol lowered her eyes, Master Gilmore believed it was in humility, and he put his arm around his beautiful wife. He could not see the shame and regret that was all over her face. "Carry on, slaves, carry on," Master Gilmore shouted as they began to make their way back to the Big House.

At that point Uncle Thomas walked up to Jordan and whispered in his ear. "Do you know the signal?" Jordan indicated that he did not, but he knew something was going down.

Uncle Thomas replied that slaves often communicated by codes. They talked with their hands, spoke double meaning words, and encoded Master's favorite songs. So, while they were singing for Master, they were really communicating with each other. "That song just sung was to tell us there will be an Underground Railroad train leaving tonight down by the river." Jordan got it. The chariot was the Underground Railroad coming to take them to heaven, which was freedom. The angels coming after them were the safe house conductors and escaped slaves returning to get them.

Once Jordan understood, even he started humming and then singing the song..."Swing low, sweet chariot, coming for to carry me home..." Tonight he was leaving; he would not stay another day in this place, and he did not even want to see the cotton fields in the morning. He would leave with or without anyone else.

After they left the fields, Jordan went straight to the Big House. He had to take mama and Siri with him. When he walked into the kitchen, both mama and Siri were alone.

"Mama, Siri; we're going to our future. We're going tonight!"

Lynette looked at him with her eyes wide open. "What do you mean Jordan? We are going where?"

"Mama, Siri, we don't have a lot of time, and I'm not going to explain how, when, or where. I'm leaving and want you to come with me. If you are tired of being beaten, if you are tired of being used, if you are just plain tired, then come with me tonight."

Lynette was ready; she had been ready for years. The last escape ended in a serious beating, but that did not damper the feelings of freedom she had those few hours in the woods. Now her boy, the boy Master sent by a breeder, was leading her to freedom. This was wonderful; her boy was the one, and she was leaving Master. However, Siri was hesitant. That last beating had a different effect on her. She was scared and did not know what she wanted. She told Jordan she could not go with him.

She was hurt and in a lot of pain. "Siri, baby I'm so sorry. I let you down and did not protect you. But we have to get out of here. We are going North." Jordan tried to comfort her and reassure her that all would be well, but Siri was afraid; the next time Master would kill them for escaping, and they were caught before. "No, Jordan, I am not going to leave, I will stay here where it is safe. Old Master is not that bad and we need to be safe. I just don't want to be beaten down anymore." Jordan could tell she was fearful of freedom. Just what Master wanted. "Baby, if we all just come together we can make it. We are going north to freedom; we are going on the Underground Railroad to freedom."

At that point, the old African walked into the kitchen, he had been listening. The old African spoke up. Jordan had noticed how much he looked like his probation officer, but he was much older and much more humble. The African said, "In order to 'come together', you must first give up some of that individuality you cherish so much. If not, it becomes the good of the group over the individual and your freedom becomes the first thing sacrificed. However, if you look across the horizon at most of these groups, the 'group philosophy' is usually that of one individual. He has become the social, economical, or political influence on history and society. People gather around him because of the power he has to make them comfortable.

"His philosophy becomes the philosophy of the group. His values become the values of the group, and his standards become the standards of the group. They are strictly followed by all in the group. The dedication is self-perpetuating by succeeding members of the group. Master's morality becomes the morality of the plantation. Leaders that are constantly protesting, angry, whining, and demanding tend to have followers that are protesting about everything, angry at everyone, whining about something, and demanding you do something about it.

"On the other hand, positive leadership brings together positive people. Being around people that are positive about life and opportunity will attract others around them. That is why we are told to leave our friends behind when change is necessary. If you believe, you can no matter what...you will no matter what. If you are around people who believe, nothing can stop you ...nothing will stop you. Even if Siri does not want to go, you MUST go."

Siri looked at Jordan and knew he was leaving. "Come back to get me, Jordan. I cannot go with you now."

"Why not?" Jordan stood there looking at her for a moment.

"Because I am going to have a baby! A baby; I cannot travel now."

Jordan looked at her with tears in his eyes. Now he was torn between leaving her when she needed him the most and going to prepare a place for her and their child. It never crossed his mind to ask or think who the father of the baby was. Her circumstances were not of her doing. If the old African was correct, it was the male's problem to protect her. He had failed her once before, he would not fail her again. He would return for her.

That very night came the signal that the Underground Railroad was leaving the plantation for freedom. The Underground Railroad was a secret network of slaves, runaways, and White folks that lead escaped slaves to freedom. This train was lead by this Black woman named Harriett Tubman, and she was coming to the plantation that night to take folks north. She was risking her very life to save others. Master had a bounty on her head that was big enough to free most slaves. All they had to do was turn her in, and Master would free them. However, no one ever turned her in because that was not real freedom. Real freedom you earn and fight for; that is why Jordan decided to travel on the Underground Railroad to freedom.

CHAPTER TWELVE
NO ONE IS FREE UNTIL ALL ARE FREE!

Jordan wanted to take his mother and Siri with him. However, Siri was scared, so he would have to leave her. Maybe he could come back for her later. Mama, Uncle Thomas, and the old African were leaving with this old lady, Tubman. Jordan could not believe he was placing his life in the hands of a woman, especially a strange woman. They would all meet down by the creek at midnight. It would be a short walk across "The Pass" and on to the first safe house.

Jordan looked at his friend Too-Hi. He did not know why they were friends; everyone said they were, but he could not figure out how he could be a friend with such a low life. Even at home, Jay-Low was a little bit of a bother but at least he was cool. This character was transparent, and Jordan could not see being his friend. But if he was his friend like everyone said then he should give his friend one last chance to go to freedom. He started to speak with him about his plans but the warning of his uncle and others came into his mind. It did not matter if you were speaking to your brother, mother or best friend, some people will not share your desire to be free. You can only talk about freedom to freedom loving people. Too-Hi did not love freedom, he love power and that was too dangerous to let in on the plans. Jordan just left it alone.

As he left the Big House, Gilmore Junior confronted him on the back porch. Junior had been drinking and could barely stand up. "What are you doing up here, dog?" Junior was mean when sober, and much meaner when drunk. He had two of his White friends with him, and that made it more dangerous for Jordan. "I was just helping Lynette with the water, sir; I will be going to the slave quarters now." Jordan tried to get out of a long conversation with Junior and move on down the road.

"Wait, boy! I didn't tell you that you could leave. Lynette has plenty of help in the kitchen, and I am tired of your Black behind being up here. I think you are sniffing around that wench Siri. Is that what you're after, that fine little slave girl?" The other White men with Junior laughed at some inside joke and stared Jordan down.

"No, sir; I was just visiting my mother and trying to help out." Jordan was trying not to upset Junior, who was already drunk and angry. He needed someone to abuse to feel better about himself. His father for had dominated him so long that he had developed low self-esteem. Junior only hung around poor White trash like the guys with him because they looked up to him; they hung out with Junior because he provided the cheap whiskey.

"What do you think fellas?" Junior was trying to get confirmation from his friends to play around with Jordan. "What should we do with this uppity dog trying to get at one of my wenches, right here in my house? How do we handle dogs like that?"

"Let's string him up and whop his Black hide off," one of the drunks called out.

"No, lets see how much pain he can take before he passes out; I got twenty dollars that says he can't last one hour standing on broken glass."

Jordan just stood there staring at the men. He was not going to take any more of Junior's insane and sadistic cruelty. He was going to freedom, probably tonight, and he just was not going to take it anymore. He knew if they got it in their minds to harm him he would have to defend himself. He stood there looking and trying to figure out which one of the three drunken men he should hit first. He realized that once he struck any of them, all bets were off. He would then be fighting for his life and would not be able to stop until all three were finished. If they gave him no choice, he would take no choice.

Jordan was still carrying the water pail he used as an excuse to visit the Big House. He could use it for a weapon against these three drunken White boys. He had already decided to strike Junior first. He would not be expecting it, and it would be the strongest blow. After all, if he were going to die he would still get one good hit in on Junior then take on the other two. If they did not have pistols on them, he had a good chance with the surprise attack and their state of drunkenness. If he could get out of this, he would try to, but they would have to decide how this went down.

He tried to stand relaxed as Junior stood to his left and one of the two guys stood in front of him. The third drunk stood far to his right and would have to be the last one attacked. But this punk Junior, he was ripe for a right hook shot with the bucket in his hand. He would go down like the drunk he was. Jordan planned to quickly strike the second man with the follow through left, and then turn to face the last man. He figured that by that time, he would be shocked at seeing a slave act like a man and hesitate just a second. If he did, Jordan had a good chance to continue to use the weapon he had.

That was his plan, but before he was forced to see it work, Master Gilmore spoke from the back door. "What you boys up to?" Junior was surprised to see his father standing in the doorway.

"Nothing, Pop! Just teaching this old dog a lesson; you surprised us, how long you been there?" Master Gilmore was looking at Jordan as he answered. "Long enough. I have been standing here long enough, but I think you may have been the one surprised by old Jordan, here."

"What do you mean, Pop?" Junior looked at his father, confused. Master Gilmore never took his eyes off Jordan. "Son, it does not matter what we think of these dogs; it is what they think of themselves. If your dog thinks he is a man, he will act like one when he is cornered. You three drunken characters think old Jordan here is afraid of you? Well he isn't. That makes him a danger to you. You are too drunk to see this slave does not think like a slave, so he will not act like one. Hey, Jordan, why don't you put down the bucket?"

The game was over, Master Gilmore made four White men, and he was not drunk. Jordan had to go to his second plan. "Yes, sir, Master Gilmore, I was just trying to get back to the slave quarters when Master Junior here stopped me. Can I leave sir?"

"No, Jordan; we got to fix a problem here. Junior, if you can handle it, place old Jordan in the solitary cell with chains on, and tomorrow we can decide what we will do with him. Maybe a night chained up like a dog will make him realize he is a dog. Now take him away before I place your behind in there with him." "Now that I've saved your hide once again, Junior, I'm going for a walk," Master Gilmore snapped.

The three men led Jordan away, placed chains around his wrists and waist, and forced him into the hot house used to punish slaves.

Master Gilmore had chosen that night to punish Jordan for not showing respect to Junior. Jordan was placed in irons around his wrists and waist for the weekend. It was a typical punishment on the plantation; it was meant to cause discomfort and embarrassment.

Nevertheless, Jordan knew he could get out of them especially the chains around his waist. However, he would need help with the chains around his wrists. Once he got to the other side of the creek, there would be others that could help him get them off. He was going with or without the chains.

He was confined in a cell-like building for added punishment. Master Gilmore would let him out tomorrow, but he intended to have a surprise for old Master in the morning. Like all of the slave shelters, this one had a dirt floor. Jordan would have no problem digging his way out once it was time to go.

It was the night of his escape! Finally! No more slavery; it would be freedom or death. He only hoped he got the codes right. Would the freedom fighters be in The Passage field? Could it be a trap? He had heard the slave songs; he had listened to the elders that had gone this way. He had thought about freedom enough to see it. Everything was in place. Jordan knew this was the best time; this was his time.

He had to get into The Passage field and across the creek. But how could he with the chains Gilmore Jr. had placed on him? He was not sure if he could make it across and he was not sure if he would meet the abolitionists on the other side.

He laid there on the floor in pitch-black darkness, thinking of reasons why he should not try to escape. What if Master Gilmore was right? What if those abolitionists hated slaves and wanted them to die in the woods? He had never seen White folks caring about Black people; why would they do it? Then it occurred to Jordan, Master certainly did not care about the slaves. If Master did not want him to do something then it must be for him to do. What did the old preacher say? "If Master is the problem, he cannot be the solution." Yes, he must remember everything Master told him so he could do the opposite.

Master's warnings would lead him to freedom. If Master did not want him to read, he would learn so he could read the signs on maps to find the way north. If Master called his mother a wench, he would call her a lady to show respect for his future. And if Master said not to go because there is death along the way, then Jordan knew he must go because it must be Freedom's Way.

As he lay there, he could hear the slight sound of thunder rolling in the background. If it rained, it might keep the dogs from picking up his trail. But the creek could rise and force him to stay on this side. He would surely be caught if he did not cross the creek. The thunder got louder and the lightning began to show the outline of the yard. Was this a warning from God, or was it a trick of the devil to keep him on the plantation? It seemed to be warning him to stay where he was, but God would not want him to stay on the plantation, would He?

At that moment, it began to pour down rain! Jordan leaped up to look out of a crack in the walls. It was raining so hard he could barely see the line of trees at the edge of The Pass. But a lighting bolt showed him the path. Master wanted him to stay, but he could leave. The devil wanted him to be frightened, but he could still leave. It was up to him to want freedom or to want safety. It was up to him to leave or stay. Jordan decided it was okay to leave the plantation.

Chains or no chains, swimming or drowning, freedom or death, he was going tonight. Amazing! Once the decision was made, he felt comforted and relaxed. Once he stopped questioning himself and started believing in himself, he felt capable of achieving for himself. Instead of being frightened at the thought of having to dig all the way under the cell wall and out to the surface, Jordan began thinking of the best strategy for the dig. Jordan began digging furiously, but soon grew tired. 'I have to make it,' he thought. 'I can't get tired, I can't give up. I have to be free tonight. If I don't do it now, I'll never do it.' After he caught his breath and calmed down, Jordan began digging again, but this time at a comfortable but steady pace. He realized that he would make more progress more quickly if he worked at a pace that would allow him to keep moving. Short spurts would rob him of his energy and momentum. That would lead to discouragement. If he could just keep things moving, even if they seemed to be moving slowly, the consistency in progress would strengthen his will and his morale. He had to keep moving forward.

As Jordan pressed forward, nature assisted him. The rain water made the soil softer and easier to dig through, but only if Jordan moved quickly; otherwise, the heavy rains would have pooled on the ground and hindered Jordan from digging upward to the surface. He moved with confidence, caution, and speed – and soon Jordan had dug a short tunnel from within the cell to the outside!

Jordan got up and wrapped his chains in the cloth bandana Uncle Thomas had given him. This would keep them quiet while he snuck out into the fields. Once he got away, he would use rocks to break the chains. 'Old Master Gilmore is so cheap' Jordan thought to himself, 'he never uses strong irons to keep us down. He only uses our strong superstitions, jealousy, and fears to keep us down.'

"Swing low, sweet chariot, coming for to carry me home." Jordan was going home with a band of angels. Funny thing, his name was Jordan and he was going to look over the Jordan River to freedom. Jordan made it out to The Passage field and up to the edge of the creek. It was the first test of Master's fear tactics! Master said he would drown crossing over to meet the abolitionists…or would he?

Jordan sat down with his back on a tree, trying to catch his breath before the crossing. He would need to relax and have as much energy as possible to cross over. As he sat there resting, lighting occasionally brightened the night sky. On one such strike, Jordan caught a glimpse of something near the edge of the creek. "What was that? Jordan thought to himself. "It couldn't be, not after all this time." He put forth his hand and pulled a white stone out of the mud. "My God!" Jordan exclaimed to himself. He could not believe it. It was the stone he had found going to rob the store. It was the stone he wanted to present to his girlfriend. He could not believe his fortune in finding it again.

Jordan was sure he would see Siri again; he must give her this gift. The little stone of no real value had become the most precious possession Jordan had. It was his only connection to the future, and he would keep it as a reminder of his promise to Siri. Jordan slipped the stone deep into his pocket, and even pushed a few wet leaves in behind it to make sure he did not lose it again. Now he was ready for anything. He was going to freedom.

What did that old song say he should do at the water? Should he splash into it, hoping to get across before the depth and chains around his wrists took him under? No, that was not what the song said. "Wade in the water, wade in the water children…God's gonna trouble the water…" Jordan was supposed to wade quietly into the water. Less noise for the slave hunters, he supposed. Once his feet touched the water he discovered something.

The creek was not that deep. It had rocks on the bottom! Rocks that would keep his head above water while he walked across. The creek was only up to Jordan's neck in most cases. Master said it was deep, but Jordan could walk across it if he had just tried. Jordan struggled from rock to rock, standing on them to breathe, and then lowering his head and struggling forward in the darkness until he found another rock to stand on.

Gasping for air, he struggled on. Remembering the secret message of the old preacher, 'Jesus would be his rock to stand on.' Was this what he meant? Were these rocks part of the secret code of escaped slaves? Those who know about the rocks must have known that if he rushed into the water, the rocks would become stumbling blocks, not salvation.

Just as he was feeling really good about his chances to make it across, he slipped off a rock and lost his balance. Jordan fell underwater and struggled to get up. He began to panic as he tried to get his head above water for one more breath. As he struggled underwater, he raised his hands up above the surface trying to grab a tree branch or something in pure desperation. He did not want to die like this. What would his mother do? What would happen to Iris? Master would surly use his death to point out to slaves the impossibility of escape. The more he struggled the harder it was to hold his breath; he was going to drown in this field called The Passage.

Jordan remembered one more thing that old preacher said; 'Call on the name of the Lord…' Jordan did not know why; his lungs were bursting for air, he was going to die in this creek, but his dying words, even underwater, were going to be calling on the name of the Lord. He wasn't much of a believer, but those beliefs had gotten him free for a moment. He opened his mouth and gurgled underwater, "Jesus!"

A hand reached out from the dark and grabbed his chains protruding out of the water. A pair of men dragged Jordan out of the creek. He panicked; who were they, slave hunters, Master Gilmore? He struggled with them as they forced him onto his back; there were more men trying to cover his mouth with their hands. "Be quiet son, we got you. Stop making noise; you want to get us all caught?" It was the abolitionists! He made it to the other side, to the first stop on the Underground Railroad.

As Jordan laid on the banks gasping for air, he made out the figures of his rescuers. Some he knew Uncle Thomas, had pulled him out, also he saw his mother and the old African. Some he did not recognize. There was this old woman bending over him. She had a hard face but a gentle presence. "Just breathe son, just breathe. You are going to be alright now. We are not going to leave until you have caught your breath. You are among free Black folks now, son."

Jordan was coughing and struggling to breathe, but he was not going to stay down on that ground one more minute. He wanted to get to freedom. He sat up as the old lady gently patted him on his back. "Who are you?" Jordan asked, gazing into her eyes. "My name is Harriett Tubman, son; I am here to show you The Passage."

Jordan finally knew what the name meant. "This is the Passage?" As he gathered himself up, Harriet Tubman explained what 'the Passage' was. "The Pass Age...Pass the age of slavery, misery and death. Pass the age of men not being able to die for their families, pass the age of women not depending upon their men, pass the age of dependency - it was the Passage! It had to a personal journey, not a group journey. The Passage had to be your own personal experience. When you get tired enough, you will enter your Passage; your own journey. It will be Jordan's Passage, and no one else's.

"But I thought it was just the "pass" to the creek for fishing and swimming," Jordan replied, confused. "It is Jordan, if that is as far as you see. If you are only looking for food or cleanliness, your passage will end at the creek. What are your dreams Jordan? Where is your spirit leading you son?" Only you can see your Passage, only you can complete the journey. While others must help you, you must travel alone.

THE GREAT ESCAPE!

As Jordan and the others walked through the along the creek towards the river every sound was amplified. His heart was racing with excitement and fear. He could hear the sounds of dogs in the far distance; some slave was being hunted down. He strained his ears to pick up any sound of horses or men. No one on horseback this time of night was a friend. There were slave hunters who got a bounty for every running slave returned. More money for a live return, but even a dead slave brought a profit. Every slave traveling with them knew dead or alive, Master still had a value on them.

The slave hunters were just poor White boys trying to make a living. There were not very many jobs for White men who did not own a plantation or a business. Slavery was the only employment in the south. You either worked slaves, hunted slaves, traded slaves or serviced the slave business. Every White person he met either worked in the cotton business, slave auction, sold equipment, or transported cotton. Everyone was making money off the slave trade and nobody wanted him to escape. Everyone he would come across would be a potential slave hunter or Master's sympathizer. He had to be very careful and pay close attention to this woman leading him.

They stopped in a clearing to gather their thoughts. It was then the leader spoke. When they met earlier, she did not say very much. Rumors had it that she suffered from blackouts from a beating her master gave her. She only wanted to know a few things from us.

"Who wants freedom bad enough to die for it?" she asked. If you did not want freedom enough to die, she did not want you on this trip. She was risking her life for your freedom, so it should have been important enough for you to die for your own freedom. Tubman carried a pistol on her hip; they never knew if it was for them or for the slave hunters. She did not say and they did not ask. She had never lost a slave that left with her, and they were confident in her leadership.

Harriett Tubman said, "None are free until all are free; if you want freedom more than you want your life, let's go. If you want freedom more that you want breath, let's go. However, if you're afraid of Master, stay. If you are worried about the overseer or whether or not Master's wife will eat well tomorrow, stay. But, if you are worried that your children will grow up to hate you and love Master, then let's go.

"No questions, just action. I can tell your answer by your actions. Slaves are standing still, free people are walking." She then turned around and walked into the woods. Jordan almost ran after her; he wanted to make sure he did not lose sight of her. When he caught up, he began to walk right behind her. He had plenty of questions, but he knew she did not like questions, so he decided to ask only one and took a chance. However, the questions kept coming.

"Ms. Tubman, how do you know which way to go at night? How do you know when you are free?" Jordan asked.

"Smell that air son. Take a deep breath all the way down into your body. Smell the fragrance that is freedom."

"Ms. Tubman, that is cotton I smell; I have always smelled the cotton fields. There may be a little fragrance of daffodils mixed in, but the smell is no different than it was when we were back on the plantation. I don't smell anything different."

"I know you smell the same things son, but now you smell them as a free person. You are in charge of where you go from here. You smell the world as a free man. It smells the same, but much better at the same time. Now that you are free and have left the plantation, you are now responsible for your freedom and your life. Freedom is never given; it is always taken. It does not matter if you know the way north; it only matters that you want to go north. If your soul wants it strong enough, you body will find north."

They stopped to rest at the safe house. The small wooden house was quaint and cozy, with a flower garden out front and a rocking chair on the porch. The pale yellow paint was peeling a bit, but it was a handsome little home nonetheless. You would have never thought that this little country house was full of runaway slaves in a secret underground cellar. The simple but elegant furnishings inside would never be used to entertain Black dogs and wenches; or so the owners wanted people to think. It was a perfect safehouse along the Underground Railroad.

Safe for the moment, Jordan had a moment to speak with her again. "Tell me the way to freedom, Ms. Tubman." Harriett Tubman was sitting by the fire and she was tired and sleepy. These young slaves always had the same question. She was not going to tell them the directions to freedom. If they were captured, they would be forced to tell about the safe house locations. The conductors on the Underground Railroad lived under a code system. A free Black person was called a Diamond. A Diamond had suffered through the pressures to become free. She would answer his questions in code. That way, he would get the answers he needed and not gain information that could hurt others. "Young man, let me tell you the ten things you must learn to become a diamond:

1. A diamond has become a diamond because it has gone through the pressures. No one can tell a diamond in the rough, from a lump of coal.

2. You cannot win if you do not begin.

3. If you are not willing to sacrifice, you are not willing to succeed.

4. Diamonds are willing to sacrifice what they have to obtain what they need.

5. People like success and successful people like to be around other successful people.

6. You can only have "pride" in your deeds, not the deeds of others.

7. Do not make a presentation to someone without a clear benefit to them.

8. No success without developing the heart of a servant.

9. Success comes from people doing certain things a certain way for a certain period of time. So does failure!

10 Failure is not the enemy, procrastination is."

He understood, but did not understand. Diamonds were those willing to go through what ever it takes to make it to freedom. Others were willing to accept the pressures, but not go through them. They end up as a pile of coal dust on the floor; all used up and discarded. Jordan knew he was willing to die in these woods before he lived another day as a slave. He knew he was willing to listen to leadership and accept the wisdom of those ahead of him. Jordan knew nothing would be acceptable except freedom. Jordan knew he was a Diamond!

Mrs. Tubman was a strange woman. She sat quietly by the fire to warm herself. How could this fragile old woman make such a difference? She was only a woman, and an old woman at that. Every slave on the plantation knew her name and honored her, yet she was so humble and so quiet. What could it have been that drove her so much? The lady of the safe house offered her a cup of soup. Mrs. Tubman thanked her and took it. She sat there with the cup in her hands, looking deep into the fire.

The windows of the safe house had sheets pulled over them. The slave hunters were out all night looking for them. Mrs. Tubman did not sleep; she responded to every noise from the woods. The owner of the safe house was a White man name Mr. Joel Goldman. Joel Goldman was a tall, slender man with graying black hair and the kindest, most compassionate eyes Jordan had ever seen in a White person. When they first arrived at the safe house Jordan had taken notice of his large brown eyes. They were not looking at him with hatred or fear; that was the first time Jordan could recall seeing anything humane in the eyes of any White person since he woke up in the slave days.

Goldman had made a name for himself in the printing business in New York. As more and more organizations and individuals produced printed documents, brochures, and books, he found himself positioned to make a lot of money fairly quickly. He was wise enough to streamline the printing process and expanded his business to serve more communities. He and his wife came from New York years ago because the city was getting too crowded. He was able to leave the business to his eldest son and move to the South where he and his wife could retire to the carefree country life they always wanted. However, when they arrived and began to see what life in the antebellum South was really like, it was anything but carefree. They were appalled at the treatment of slaves in the South and wanted to do something about it. Here were two White people, already rich and free, risking their lives and fortune to help strangers they would never see again. Jordan was amazed.

This was a strange place. Back home, the only White person he knew was that racist Junior Gilmore. Here, evil came in different colors. White folks were trying to help you and Black folks were trying to keep you down on the plantation. Jordan realized that it was the same way back home. In reality, evil always came in different colors. The other gang members were Black, and they did the shooting. The cops had Black and White officers, and they did both good and bad.

His perception of the world did not fit the realities of the truth. If it was not based upon color, then what? So we think we are brave but we really are afraid? We think we are tough but we are really weak?" Jordan began to think, "I understand, is that why we change the meaning of our words? When we call "good" "bad", we are just trying to change our view of our world. Just trying to change the ideal of the plantation we live on. How do we stop the guilt and the fear?

The group kept a steady pace north. They slept in barns, even bails of hay during the day. They had to bugs and dig for roots, but they kept moving north. Mrs. Harriett Tubman really knew her way. The group never got lost, and when she appeared at the safe house, they seemed to have expected her.

They traveled only at night and slept all day. Jordan was surprised to see free Black folks living in the South right next to plantations full of slaves. Some of these Blacks would host safe houses and others you would not want to meet. The number of White folks helping them move north also surprised him. He understood the Northern Whites; they did not earn a lot of money on the slave trade, but Jordan saw many Southern White families giving them the only bread they had, and also and shoes and rest.

It became clear to Jordan that the divide between slaves and free people was not based on color, but on character. It took them weeks of danger and hunger to reach their goal. It took fear and despair to arrive. Some wanted to return; others just wanted it to stop. Mrs. Harriett Tubman only wanted one more mile out of you. She would not let you give up on yourself or on freedom. Although his life was constantly in danger, Jordan began to appreciate the journey. Like any other person, he would have enjoyed being born free and not having to escape the clutches of slavery, but since he had no control over where he started, the only thing he could control was he would finish. However, that was no easy thing. Jordan and other slaves had to overcome seemingly insurmountable odds just for the chance to be free. They had to risk their lives and even the lives of those who depended on them to lay hold to freedom, but what was worth the risk if not freedom? Why waste your life enslaved, and not risk it to be free? A life in slavery was no life at all, and Jordan had learned that. He endured real hardship for the first time in his life, suffering so that he and his family could be free. He both hated and loved every grueling minute of the escape. The road was long and the journey hard, but Jordan understood that it would all prepare him to handle the rights and responsibilities of freedom.

On the final night on their journey, the escaped slaves neared the border of the free state of Pennsylvania and safety. It was a clear, moonless night as they approached the bend of the river. Jordan was walking as close to Harriett Tubman as possible; he did not want to lose her or miss any of the wisdom she often spouted without a moment's warning. Miss Tubman would use any situation or circumstance to educate and motivate the slaves. As Jordan walked alongside her, she suddenly stopped. Their leader stood frozen on the path with her right hand held up in the air, signaling the others to stand still.

Jordan had learned that this was a time to pay close attention to his surroundings. Something was happening; she either knew this was the rendezvous point or she sensed slave hunters. Jordan found himself sniffing the air, peering through the darkness, and inclining his ear to hear. That's when he caught a sound that made the hair on the back of his neck stand up. It was undeniable and frightening. "Dog!" He whispered. "Dogs are coming!" Jordan could hear the faint sound of the hounds on their trail. They would certainly over take the slaves. They were going to be caught or worse.

Mrs. Tubman ordered everyone into an easy trot. She did not want them to panic or run as fast as they could. She ordered them to keep a steady pace, continuing north. The dogs were getting closer and closer, but the group kept the same steady pace. Jordan could hear the sounds of men running towards them as they made their way deeper into the woods along the river.

"Why aren't we running faster?" one of the slaves cried. "They are going to catch us; we should be running as fast as we can." Harriet Tubman looked over her shoulder, but did not lose a step. "Stop worrying, son, and stop talking. Master wants you to hurry so you can get tired out. Those dogs are running faster than the slave hunters are and we are leaving them behind. They will catch us before the hunters, and we can deal with the dogs." The other slaves began to panic just a little. With the thought of the dogs catching them before the slave hunters, their minds were full of the awful possible results.

"Slow down everyone," she cautioned. "We are going to make it. Let the dogs and us get as far away from the slave hunters as possible. Them dogs are trained to hunt, not to kill. Master wants us back alive if possible, and he wants them slave hunters to decide, not them dogs. They will chase us and try to tree us, but they will not bite us. But those slave hunters, they will kill you, so keep moving. I have a plan!"

Jordan's heart was pounding out of his chest as he slowed down to a steady pace. He had learned to listen to the calm voice of this leader. She said she had a plan and he believed her. They must get as far from the slave hunters as possible before they confronted the dogs. He had to keep his breath to help in whatever plan she had. He must protect her as well as fight those dogs. Jordan did not know what plans she had, but he was going to follow them.

Uncle Thomas had Jordan's mother by the hand and was hurrying along the riverbed. The other slaves were quiet and scared as they made their way long the edge of the river. The banks were slick with the recent rain and they had to run high on the banks to keep their footprints down to a minimum. It was hard running on the slippery slopes of the riverbank, but they pushed on.

As Harriett Tubman followed the river, her head kept moving from side to side while she ran. The sounds of the dogs were getting very close, and her head moved faster and faster, looking for something on the banks of the river. Then she found it - a large fallen log from an old tree. "Here, you men, pull this old log into the river. Hurry!" She ordered those following to grab the old tree log and drag it off the banks. Jordan and the other men immediately did as they were told. "All who cannot swim just climb onto the log; we are floating downstream. As the band of slaves entered the water, the dogs came around the bend and were on them.

Harriet Tubman and Jordan were the last on the bank; the others were already taking the log out into the current. Jordan grabbed a branch to go after the dogs but Harriet Tubman stopped him. "If you attack the dogs they will attack you. We got to scare them into leaving us alone. Get into the river son; I will handle this. Jordan did not want to go; he wanted to stay and defend this woman, but he had learned to trust her.

As he turned to enter the river, he saw Harriett Tubman reach into her belt and pull out her .45 caliber pistol. She fired off two shots towards the dogs and took aim for the next shot. The lead dog stopped and ran off into the woods, and the others followed. Then she quickly turned and followed Jordan into the river. As they waded out to the others, she motioned them to remain quiet.

The log had stopped drifting because the water was very low, and it could not go any further. The slaves hid behind the log and waited for the slave hunters to appear. They had heard the shots and would be coming with their pistols drawn, ready to shoot any slave they saw.

The group waited quietly, listening to the sounds of the dogs running further and further away through the woods and the sounds of the slave hunters coming closer. "Foolish dogs," Harriett said under her breath. "A hunting dog will not run from a gunshot, but a chasing dog will. If they had been Master's hunting dogs, we would have been dead. But Master doesn't want us dead unless we are free or too old."

Just then, the slave hunters came into view. They had lanterns to illuminate the river but could not make out the slaves behind the log. They could not find their dogs and thought they still may be on their trail. The slave hunters paused for a moment and held their lanterns up high to look over the water, but seeing nothing, they ran off after the dogs.

Harriet Tubman and the others waited there in that river for more than an hour. They kept quiet, listening to the sounds of the woods for any sign of the return of the slave hunters or the dogs. Finally, Miss Tubman motioned for the others to follow her. "We cannot wait any longer. If we don't make it to the safe house, we will have to spend the day here in the woods and it is too dangerous. We have to make it to the safe house tonight. I know you are all tired, scared, and wet, but that cannot stop you. We only have a little ways to go, but we must keep moving." She turned around and continued to walk away. The others, including Jordan, did not say a word, but kept following her.

The time lost hiding from the slave hunters cost the group dearly. They did not make it to the last safe house until the sun was coming up. This was a very dangerous part of the day. Not only were slave hunters coming back out of the woods, other White folks were waking up and going about their business. Anyone could have discovered the group and turned them in.

They spent that day in the barn of an abolitionist. They were fed and given newer clothes, more like those of free Blacks. This was their final safe house, and tomorrow they would pass over the border into the free state of Pennsylvania. Although they had to remain extremely quiet as they hid in the barn, everyone was excited to be almost there. Those who were hiding close together held hands and cried silently, thanking God for bringing them such a long way. They had overcome so many obstacles and held on for so long. Each day and night seemed like an eternity, and forever was finally here. Even in their silence, the group shared in a secret joy that gave them all strength. Many in the group would continue on to the country of Canada, but Jordan wanted to stay close to the Gilmore plantation. He still had a cost to extract from Master Gilmore; Siri and her baby.

But that was for later; tonight they had to make sure plans for the last few miles of their journey. It had been nearly three months of hiding, running, and trusting strangers for food and shelter. This was the final night of escape; tomorrow they will be free. That was, if they could get past the concentrated group of slave hunters and pro-slavery advocates patrolling the boundary.

The safe house was owned by a Black man named Mr. Wright. He had been born a slave, but was freed when his master died. Mr. Wright had been working as a conductor on the Underground Railroad for ten years, and was an expert at getting slaves past these final few miles. Mr. Wright owned a business across the state line; he was a carpenter and made coffins for the local undertaker in the city of Delta, Pennsylvania. Mr. Wright's shop was in the neighboring town of Whiteford, Maryland, only about five miles away. Every weekend he loaded his coffins onto his wagon and brought his helpers to deliver them into Pennsylvania.

During every such weekend trip, he would pass the patrols along the way. They would look at the load of Black men on the wagon and the professional driver. They would notice the names of legitimate undertakers as customers, and knew Mr. Wright was a free man. It never dawned on them how seldom they saw the same Black men helping Mr. Wright. They should have been suspicious of Mr. Wright, always changing his highly skilled workers. But maybe all Black men looked alike to slave hunters. Mr. Wright never questioned their intelligence or attention to details. He just kept delivering his cargo to the first undertaker; another free Black man named Mr. Anderson. He would pull up in the back of his shop and unload his usual eight coffins with two men helping carry each one into the building. Each coffin was extra large, and could carry up to two adults or three children. In one trip, Mr. Wright could deliver over twenty former slaves to their freedom.

There were many back roads and a few main roads leading to the free state of Pennsylvania, but they were all guarded pretty well. There was even a large river to the east of town that ran right into the Free State, but it was heavily patrolled by the hunters. It was going to take planning and good fortune to slip through on these last few miles of their journey.

The group kept quiet up in the loft of the barn all that day. Keeping out of sight protected themselves as well as Mr. Wright. Even his hired hands could not be trusted with the secret of their location. There were always some slave hunters willing to pay for information of the locations of safe houses. On "special delivery" Saturdays, Mr. Wright would allow his crew to have the day off, and he would take the load in himself or get some of the "local workers" to help out. With the nosey work crew gone, Mr. Wright sent word ahead to Mr. Anderson's business to prepare for the final delivery.

Jordan and his mother crawled into the coffin together, and Lynette almost chuckled at the sight. She knew Jordan was prepared to die for his freedom, but she never thought he would arrive in a coffin. The journey to Delta was almost boring. The horse drawn wagon went undisturbed and no one stopped them. They arrived at the undertaker's office and pulled around back. Those escaped slaves riding as helpers quickly jumped off the wagon to begin unloading their precious cargo. Once the group had all of the coffins in the back office, they began to open them.

When Jordan's coffin was opened, he saw an old, gray haired White man standing next to a very important looking Black man. The White man was the local Quaker preacher, and the Black man was the owner and undertaker. The Black man, Mr. Anderson, extended his hand to Jordan and welcomed him. "Greetings brother; welcome to freedom." Before Jordan could respond, the White preacher touched his head and declared, "Behold, a new man! Whom the Father has set free is free indeed." All Jordan could say was "Amen Preacher, amen," as he fell to his knees in exhaustion. They had made it! Free at last, free at last.

When they made it to the final safe house in Delta, Pennsylvania, everyone was happy. They praised God and thanked Mrs. Tubman, but she told them that thanks were not enough. "Freedom is no good until all of us are free," she said. She wanted them to meet up with others and work for the freedom of those still down in slavery.

They were finally 'Up North'. Jordan had made it to freedom! He rejoiced with the prospect of finally living his life as a free man. The abolitionists took Jordan to a home to rest, eat, and clean up. It was the home of a merchant in town. The home had a place to sleep and a place to wash. Jordan was there with other escaped slaves. All were looking for jobs with the help of the abolitionists. Jobs! They actually paid a Black man to work. They didn't just take his labor and use him, but paid him a fair wage for his labor. For the first time in his life, Jordan was eager for such an arrangement.

The other slaves on the plantation often warned him about "Up North." The slaves said they would never give a Black man a job. Freedom meant going hungry because you would never have Master to feed you. Freedom meant going without clothes because you would never have Master to clothe you. But this was real freedom. Even back in 2007, Jordan knew about welfare, low-income housing, and minimum wage increases. But they kept control over where you lived and how much money you could earn. Today, Jordan was going out to look for work with no limitations of earning. He was already meeting other freed men and was looking for someone to share a boarding house rental.

Jordan had to admit, some White folks were alright. As a matter of fact, most White folks did not care about Black people one way or another. They did not hate, love, or tolerate Black people; they just did not care. Those were the type of White people Jordan preferred. He was tired of those White people with "The White Man's Burden" attitude, always trying to "take care of" and "keep track of" Black people. Jordan now understood to care for someone you had to control them. To take care of someone's home, job, and health required that you control them so you would be better able to provide for them. His whole life, Jordan watched people in his community give up their freedom so the government could take care of them. With a lack of men to take care of their families, many women chose to make the state their children's father, and in doing so sold themselves and their children into slavery to the system. Even more shameful were the men who could work but pretended to be unable so that they could live on government resources. Although some individuals in dire straits did use social services purely for temporary assistance as they got back on their feet, they were few and far between. Jordan knew third and fourth generation welfare mothers – something was seriously wrong. In accepting a lifestyle that dictated someone else take care of them, these people had unknowingly stunted their own growth, taught their children that their welfare was someone else's responsibility, and aborted their work ethic through an entitlement mentality. Once hooked on the system like the drug it is, these dependent families were willing to do whatever the powers-that-be told them they had to do to maintain their 'benefits.' It did not matter how degrading or demeaning the treatment was; if the government said it was a requirement for benefits, those who have accepted the enslavement would comply. Jordan remembered this as he reflected on all that had happened and what he was embarking upon. Jordan was tired of being looked after; he wanted freedom, and he had achieved freedom. He did not need anything or anyone taking care of him; he just did not want you to lynch or beat him when he showed up to compete. But now he had to learn about his new freedom. What could he expect from this new world?

At one meeting, Jordan met a man named Fredrick Douglass, a great speaker and respected member of the Underground Railroad. Jordan asked Mr. Douglass how he developed the courage to lead others to freedom. After all that Master did to place fear in us, how could we succeed? Mr. Douglass suggested that slavery was a self-inflicted wound. Change the people around you to change what's around you. "Master thinks that once you are a slave you will stay a slave and raise your children to be slaves. Master thinks that it will become your culture to please and entertain him. What do you see in your visions, son?"

Jordan had to be honest with this great man. It was clear that many Blacks were moving off the plantation, but his crowd was not. He explained to Douglass that things got better for some and stayed the same for others. Master was forced to stop beating us, so we started beating ourselves. Master no longer called us dogs, but we still called ourselves dogs. Our women were given more respect by Master than by Black men. Master was forced to allow us into schools, but many of us dropped out. In the future, Master had to pay Black women to have his breeder babies and the Black man still did not have to take care of them, so Master was glad to do that for them. Master would spend decades passing down the blood of the Black buck breeder. The results would be a community of male breeders instead of male feeders. Jordan realized that we must first admit our legacy in order to change it. He decided that he would no longer associate sexual prowess with manhood. Manhood would now be associated with sexual protection.

But there were major improvements in the future. Not only would Black people live under the protection of the courts, they would have Black judges, police officers, lawyers, elected officials, and Black men and women serving in the greatest army the world had ever seen.

However, while the future had Black judges, there were still more Black men in prison than any other race. There were Black doctors, yet Black people died sooner than anyone else. There were Black schools, colleges, and Black professors, but still Black children were not going to college. The problem was not with the leaders, however; it was with the followers.

A person leading the Underground Railroad to the future did not spend a lot of time talking about the food or housing on the plantation. He was not interested in any of Master's programs. A freedom fighter was only interested in leaving the plantation life, not improving life on the plantation. So, if you were looking for a better program on the plantation, you would not be led by such a person. Jordan explained that the future had too many Black people spending too much time trying to get comfortable on the plantation and never looking to get off the plantation.

In the future, Black people still fought back and incited riots, but they burned down their own businesses and their own homes. Slaves of the future thought such destruction was getting back at Master because he had to repair and rebuilt. However, Blacks were still dependent upon Master for solutions to every problem they had. If there were not enough income, the slaves would call for a wage increase from Master on the cotton they picked. If they needed better slave quarters they demanded "low-income housing" from Master. If their babies got sick, they needed Master's health plan. If Blacks could not stretch the minimum wages enough to by food all month, Master had to give them a 'government cheese program'. They slaves of the future called it a victory when they got more benefits from Master instead of calling it a victory when the got away from Master.

Jordan told Fredrick Douglass that the future needed more men like him to lead freedom-seeking Blacks. Frederick Douglass said the future needed everyone to be a leader instead of looking for just one. He explained that Master would gladly give you a leader if you were looking for one, but if you were all leaders, what power would Master have? The future did not need better leaders; it needed better followers, followers who would choose good leadership, not just popular leadership. If you knew where you wanted to go you could find those who were capable of leading you to the goal. Following someone just because he or she was leading could lead to failure.

Jordan asked Douglass how he overcame the obstacles he faced before he found the courage to leave the plantation.

"I needed friends and associates that supported my belief in self-determination," he said. "It was necessary to have a support system in place to keep me motivated and give me knowledge. How can you work on your own business if all of your friends and associates believe owning a business is impossible? They would take every opportunity to discourage you, never encourage you. They would only participate in your business occasionally borrowing money from you. These old friends would not even buy from you. They would not mean you any harm, it is just that success is not of their culture; managing failure is. People outside the culture of success cannot understand your willingness to sacrifice your "spare time" to pursue your own business. They cannot understand why you are no longer hanging out and waiting for Monday morning to pick more cotton. They may never understand, and it is not personal."

"But what if your friends really do not understand and everyone thinks you are going in the wrong direction? Don't you give some thought to the possibility that maybe you are wrong and everyone else is right?" Jordan asked, thinking about his own life.

"There are times when we must leave old friends behind. I will see them at funerals and weddings. However, my time is spent with those of the same dream. If I changed political parties or religious faith, it would result in a change of association. It does not mean you treat your old friends much different. It simply means you do not have the same beliefs or standards as they do anymore. If you joined anti-gamblers or anti-alcoholics groups, you probably would not still hang out with your friends at the casino boats or the bar. You would meet new friends that support your new beliefs. It is the same with economics. If you want to change where you are going, change what you are doing and whom you are doing it with; that will change your directions. It will not matter who agrees with you."

"Mr. Douglass, you are saying to turn my back on everyone and everything I believe in? If I accept that, I am saying that I have been played all of my life. I will be saying that everyone I look up to has misled me. How can we accept that about ourselves? They will not allow a Black man to look at himself with that much confidence, will they?"

"You must change your actions from defensive to offensive. If you think 'they' are out to get you and 'they' will keep you down, then 'they' will have more power over your life than you do. If you perceive others as having more influence over your life than you do, you will develop a defensive life style. Your main source of power is your ability to protest and demand from the stronger for benefits for the weaker group. Your life will be full of self-doubt and inaction. You will always be concerned about who has done you wrong.

"Others will look at you the same way you look at yourself. If you think you are inferior, you will be treated that way. When I walk into an establishment, I do not think about whether they like Black people or respect me as a person. I act like I own the place, and in most places, they treat me that way."

Fredrick Douglass continued, "Once I became the reason for all things concerning me, my condition stopped being the fault of others and it became my responsibility. My actions became more positive in response to my self-perceptions. If I needed something, I had to act, no one else. This concept changed my language. I began to speak in certain positive terms. I did not call them positive terms then, however; looking back now I simply recognize that is what they were. I stopped describing my life in negative terms. 'If they would leave me alone, I could make it' became 'I will make it'; no excuses, no blame. 'Why can't I' became 'when will I'. 'They' (the enemy, the man or they system) became secondary to things I had control over. Reading good books and being around good people were within my control. With self-confidence, it no longer mattered whether or not someone liked me or wanted me to succeed. It only mattered that I intended to succeed.

Fredrick Douglass was beginning to believe Jordan was listening. He thought his words were making the young man think, so he continued. "A baby will walk: it is natural to do so. When a woman is pregnant, she does everything for the safety and love of that child. Everything the child needs; warmth, food, comfort, is provided by the mother while the child is in the womb. The child does not know anything but the womb. The child does not know the outside world and has everything provided for it in the womb. However, no matter how comforting and loving the mother is, the child will still struggle to be free of her, because freedom is natural. The baby does not know what is on the other side of the womb. The child does not know if there is another side of the womb. The child only knows that it must be free. It does not hate the mother; it loves freedom."

"I know I am ready to change my life, make no doubt about it. But how do I know which direction to go in? It seems like there is a natural trail to follow. It is like growing from a child to a teenager. No one told me to start liking girls or to grow a mustache; it came when I was ready for it. I think I am ready for the next stage of my life, sir."

"You are right, Jordan; nature will not let you move from one stage of development until you master the stage you are in. But remember, whatever stage you are in, freedom is natural to you. When the child is brought home, the mother keeps the baby warm, clean, and fed. Everything the child whimpers for, the mother will provide. However, eventually the child will still struggle out of its mother's arms down to the ground to crawl, because freedom is natural. The baby will try to walk; why? It has never walked before. The child will fail every time it tries to walk. However, no amount of frustration will keep the child from pulling itself up to try again. You cannot keep the child from walking because walking is natural. The child begins to attempt to run, fall, and even gets hurt, but it does not matter. The child has never run before and will continue to fail at running. Mother warns the child of the dangers of running in the house, but the child will run because running is natural."

"I understand Mr. Douglass; freedom is natural. It takes an unnatural occurrence to make someone accept himself or herself as a slave for another. That is unnatural." Jordan had a revelation, and could see into his condition clearly. "It never changes with the human nature; freedom is natural. The only way you can make a person accept slavery is by having them change their nature. Freedom is natural, and I am a natural person."

"Hmmm, I never thought of it like that, but you are right Jordan, it takes an outside force to convince you to accept slavery or failure." Fredrick Douglass was beginning to learn from Jordan now; this was a big surprise. He did really seem to have a grasp on his life. "The plantation mentality did not matter once I changed my way of thinking. Master believes that serving him is serving your family. Prisoners believe in serving Master until they can serve their families. Master says you should give something back to the community. Never give to your family, give to your community; he owns the community."

Well Jordan certainly understood master. Douglass continued, "Master says, 'don't forget where you came from'! What he means is do not forget, you are just my slave. You never hear Master tell his own children that. They never worry about where they come from; they talk about where they are going. They understand their heritage and their pedigree. Master has his family crest on the wall, but you will find most of Master's time, money and efforts are on gaining the future, not regaining something from the past."

Now it was Jordan's turn to place his philosophy at the feet of this great leader. "What happened in Africa to our ancestors happened, and they had to deal with it. What happens to our children here will depend upon how much we sacrifice for their future. The warriors of our ancestors did not defend the nation against Master. I do not know if Master's culture was stronger than ours was, or if ours just fell apart. All I know is that it could not defend us from this misery. Know who you are by planning where you are going. I noticed a large oak tree in Master's front yard. It must be forty feet tall. However, it only has five feet of roots. It does not need a deep root system to keep it going. It spends most of its energy developing branches and growing towards the future.

"We cannot allow Master to raise our children. He does not love our children; he loves his children. We cannot allow Master to determine what the slave culture is going to be; we must determine that ourselves."

Jordan had so many questions for this great man. His head was spinning with thoughts. He wanted to know if there was a plan to go back and fight Master. Where was the army gathering? He was ready to go back and fight. He thought that the North would go and fight to save the slaves. He wished American History had been a more interesting class. If he only remembered what happened in this county.

Fredrick Douglass told Jordan that the war was coming, but not now. He could join the raiding parties that some were organizing. Slaves found many ways to resist and to fight Master.

There had been too many uprisings to count. Slaves were burning the crops in the fields or destroying them on the way to market. Some slaves fought back by surviving. Raising the next generation was surviving. Master wanted to destroy the identity of the Black man. By raising their sons and daughters, Black men and women were fighting back. Slaves fought back by educating themselves. Learning as much about this culture as possible, mastering every part of it.

Jordan was amazed at Douglass' usage of the English language, considering his background as an illiterate slave. Douglass went on to explain why his language skills were so impeccable compared to other freedmen Jordan had met. "I have mastered the English language because it gives me an edge in this country. If we lived in France, I would master the French language. Get the edge on life; master the culture you live in. It does not really profit you to master the slave culture in its current state. The slave culture does not benefit the slave; you will only become a better slave. However, if you master Master's culture, you will be better than Master in his own country. Master knows that Jordan. Master's greatest fear is a Black man who masters this system. Real freedom is being your own master."

It was not until after Jordan was free that he really began to understand the harshness of slavery. For days, he still walked like a slave and spoke like a slave; he still had trouble looking White men in the eyes, and occasionally he found himself stooping over to walk. It would take Jordan a little time to adjust to being free. It was not that way for his uncle. Uncle Thomas stood up straight his first day of freedom. He turned his hat around straight and tucked his shirttail in. He spoke differently and stood straight, looking anyone dead in the eyes while he spoke to them.

Jordan wanted to have the confidence of Uncle Thomas and asked him to teach him how to act like a free man. "Act like a free man?" Thomas looked at Jordan like he was lost. "You had to act like a slave on Mister Gilmore's property; now Jordan, you do not have to act like anything to be a real man. Respect yourself in everything you do. You are strong, but only act strong when you need to. You are aggressive, but only when you must be. That is what a man is; strong when needed, and aggressive when required. I stand up straight because I am a grown man. I am learning to speak the proper language so I can be more valuable when I start my own business. I intend to build a home for myself and your mother and operate my own business so I can help others escape." Uncle Thomas had a look in his eyes Jordan had only seen in the future. This was the Uncle Thomas he knew back home on the block. He was determined and focused.

"I guess that is giving something back to the community?" Jordan wanted to know. "Not necessarily Jordan. What is the community? Where is it? Is our community part of the Quaker Church doing so much for our freedom? Or would we include sellouts like Too-Hi as part of this community? I am only counting members of my community who look at life as I do. No one is free unless all of us are free. If they agree with me that slavery is an evil existence that must be destroyed, then they are part of my community and I will support them. But we have people even here up North who work to keep the Black man enslaved. Some are White and some are Black; it has always been that way. Our job Jordan, you and I, is to see who they are and place them in the right category. Who is with you, who will stand beside you, who is against you; they all will show it. Don't forget Jordan, give something back to your family, and that will take care of the community."

Uncle Thomas was right about that; Jordan had learned that the hard way. Giving something back to your family, right; but did he miss something? Why was he not feeling complete with his mother and Uncle? Why didn't he feel free like them? He knew the answer, and he knew what he must do. "Uncle Thomas?" Jordan sat down on the chair next to the table. "I still have something to do before I can settle into freedom. I need to go back for my family." Iris was having his baby, and she was part of his family. He knew Uncle Thomas and his mother would not approve of him returning to the Gilmore plantation, but he knew in his heart that it was the only way to complete his journey. He had to bring her out of that misery.

Uncle Thomas looked at Jordan with his deeply piercing eyes. They were both sad and understanding. "Be careful son!" That was all Uncle Thomas could say. He knew Jordan would return for Iris one day, and he knew that he must make that journey alone. Uncle Thomas had to take care of his sister and prepare a place for Jordan to return to. "Let's make sure you are as ready for the return as you were for escape. We have to prepare signals to and from the safe houses along the way. You have to have help all along the escape route, and you must know whom to trust. This is going to be dangerous, Jordan, and your mother is not going to like it. But you are a man now, though a young one, you need to decide what freedom is for you and go for it."

Jordan had found an entirely new society of free Blacks and concerned White people, all seeking a common goal, to free the slaves. He did not know there were so many White people working so hard to free the slaves. People risking their lives and property for the sake of strangers was amazing to him. Once free, Uncle Thomas began to work with these organizations by giving speeches, testifying to the horrors of slavery. He raised money to fund safe houses, and even traveled to Washington D.C. to talk about the need to end the slave system.

Jordan had to reflect on the lessons he had learned. Most compelling were the people who helped him along the way. For the most part, they were business people; successful people with good income and respect in the community. He knew that in order to help others, he had to have the income to protect them. He needed to have a safe house himself to help slaves moving north; that would require learning to run a business. He remembered how he used to rob business owners because they had the money. He thought they were weak, but maybe he was the weak one. Robbing them raised the cost of doing business in the neighborhood. If those businesspersons took their businesses out to the suburbs, he would have called them sellouts for leaving where they had come from. Now, Jordan was looking to them for help and leadership. Having your own business was the key to success; what a thought!

The first thing Jordan had to do was study. He had to remember his history and study the time he was in. He had to learn more about reading, navigating, survival, and hiding. He also had to pick up a trade in order to earn money to fund his reentry into slave country. He studied maps to learn about the terrain and where the obstacles were. He remembered Harriett Tubman's trick with the dogs. That would work with a steep cliff or thick patch of overgrowth. Anything that would slow up horses and men would have the same results, buying enough time to distract the dogs before the men showed up. But he had to learn where these obstacles were and how to find them in the dark. Jordan began to read about the stars and the tides; he knew when harvest season and planting season were. They would come in handy if he wanted to hide in the barns or haystacks. He studied and learned whenever he could; he was determined to make it back to Siri and free her.

One day he was speaking to Uncle Thomas about his plans of escape. Uncle Thomas had become something of a leader in the Abolitionist movement. He had traveled, speaking about the slave system, and had learned a lot about what was going on to end it. Uncle Thomas asked Jordan if he still planned to go south. "Yes, as soon as possible Uncle; I have to rescue Siri from Junior." Uncle Thomas asked Jordan to join him at the table for a little discussion. He wanted to make sure Jordan had all of the information he needed about slavery and the direction in which the nation was going.

"You know Jordan, things are moving pretty fast toward a solution to the slave problem. There are a lot of people in the North and the South that are tired of the whole thing. There is talk, Jordan, about a war coming to completely end slavery." Jordan was not sure if he believed that. "How many Black men could there be to form an army to end slavery, Uncle?"

"No, Jordan, not a Black army, although I suppose many of us would join it, but White men up in Washington D.C. are talking about sending an army of White men to fight Master Gilmore and others like him to end this once and for all."

Jordan was still skeptical. "Now Uncle, for White men to help organize the safe houses and raise money for the Underground Railroad is one thing, but do you expect White men to go down South and fight their own brothers and cousins to free Black men? I have learned to respect certain White men since I have been free, but I have not met that one yet." Jordan was a little worried that Uncle Thomas was getting too caught up in politics to understand what was really going on.

"Listen, Jordan, things are really changing, and changing fast. This is already the end of 1857, and in the last seven years, a tremendous amount of national support for ending slavery has come about. Some good things and some bad things have happened, but all of it is pushing us closer to the war which must come."

"What things, Uncle? What has happened in the past few years to make you so confident this war is coming?"

"Well, Jordan, back about seven years ago in 1850, the state of California had already come into the United States as a free state. That means it would be like Pennsylvania and not allow slavery. Well, to get the state of California, the people in Congress compromised with the Southerners to allow a stiffer Fugitive Slave law. Now that was bad for slaves, because it allowed White men to follow us up North and recapture us. It even allowed for free Blacks like Mr. Wright to be captured and brought South as slaves. Now I know that does not sound like good news, Jordan, but in a way it was. It angered the abolitionists so much that they began to cause all kinds of trouble for old Master. There were more slave revolts, runaways to Canada, and a great deal of debate among White people.

"Two years later in 1852, Mrs. Harriet Beecher Stowe wrote a book called 'Uncle Tom's Cabin' about slavery, and gave White northerners their first real, hard look at what was going on. Boy, Jordan, that book really got things stirred up, and the debate has only gotten more intense.

"Then Jordan, just two years later in 1854, this nation almost broke out into civil war when something called the Kansas-Nebraska Act was passed. It allowed these new states to decide if they were going to be free or slave states. There was a very violent reaction in this country.

"Just this year, 1857, a Black man named Dred Scott declared he was free, but the court said he and no other Black person was free in America. Furthermore, that decision said the US Congress did not have the authority to outlaw slavery in any state. These decisions have the population against the courts and Congress. The people want slavery ended, Jordan, but the Congress only wants to compromise. Now there is talk about a new political party forming from the abolitionists and freethinking people. It will bring the question of slavery or freedom to the boiling point. Talk is that the South will leave the Union if this party takes control. If they do leave, we will go after them and get our people."

Jordan was listening because he knew Uncle Thomas had seen and learned a lot, but he still could not see the nation going into a civil war to free Black folks. "So, Uncle Thomas, if the South leaves the United States, then they would be free to keep the slaves and not worry about the North. How is this good for us?"

"Well, Jordan, if they leave the Union, the United States is saying it will be illegal, and they will force the South back into the United States. That is the civil war we are talking about. It may be ignited by slavery, but the real purpose is keeping the South from leaving. We cannot have states leaving the Union every time a vote does not go their way. Now if they stay in the Union, Congress will have enough free thinkers to end slavery, and the South knows that, so the South will leave, Jordan, mark my word. So you may want to stay here for a while, and if the South secedes from the Union, you and I will march onto Master Gilmore's plantation in the uniform of the United States army. Boy, won't that be a great day?"

Jordan caught himself daydreaming about riding into the gate of Master Gilmore's plantation, right up to the front door of the Big House. He would walk up to those double doors, kick them in with his feet, and personally grab Junior by the collar and demand to know where Siri was. Boy, that would be a great day; but is it only a dream? "Civil War? There may be something coming like that Uncle; I have heard the same rumors. If it was to come, you can count on me to join the fight for sure, but meanwhile, Siri is still sleeping under Master Gilmore's control. I will not wait for some pending civil war; I will not wait for another night longer than I have to. She will be free as soon as I can get down there. Then I will join you in preparing for the great day of this Civil War. Will you help me with the plans?" Uncle Thomas knew Jordan was going back; he knew nothing he could say would stop him. Of course, he had to give him as much help as possible, to make Jordan as safe as possible. "Of course, Jordan; let's make some plans."

Jordan was free, but unemployed. There were societies and organizations that helped the escaped men and women to adjust. Jordan found work in a blacksmith's shop. He kept close ties with the Underground Railroad and the Abolitionist movement. He helped in any way he could. He always sought out information from anyone arriving from or near the Gilmore plantation.

Soon, just getting information was no longer enough. His uncle and mother had found jobs and were helping, but that was not enough for Jordan. What about his woman back on the plantation, Siri? He had to go back for her. He could not leave her wondering what happened to him, and he could not live there without his woman. He had begun to hang around other young men who were seeking to remain free. They talked about the split in the nation over slavery. Free States and Slave States and what to do about the division had become a huge issue. Jordan began to speak to crowds about the future of slavery. Many people still thought of him as a prophet, but others just thought he had wisdom beyond his years.

Every once in a while, in the middle of the night, Jordan would pull out an old tin can. It was where he kept his stone. He called it the 'Iris Stone' because it was promised to her in the future. He would look at it and feel closer to her. He would talk to the stone and wonder what she was doing at that time. He could not be this close to her and not go to get her. This was driving him crazy. Soon it was clear; Jordan had one more journey to complete. Jordan volunteered to return to Master Gilmore's plantation. It had been almost a year since he left. He made his way back South through a series of safe houses, but not the ones from his initial trip up North. They always changed, and would not be the same on the way back. He was led by coded messages left in certain places. He traveled at night and slept during the day. He had to sleep in haystacks, barns, and creek beds. He traveled in the back of cotton wagons and riverboats. Anything to get back and keep his promise.

The first part of the journey was pretty easy. The abolitionists gave him fake papers saying he worked for "Mr. Wright" the undertaker, and was on a mission to purchase supplies. That got him over fifty miles south before the story ran cold. Then he would pick up objects and stories at the safe houses to help him get to the next location. Once, he carried a horse bridle in his hands and when the hunters or White folks questioned him, he would announce he was looking for his Master's horse that had run away. With the fake stories and information, Jordan could travel during the day and much faster than the trip up North. He made it to the county of Master Gilmore's plantation within a few weeks of leaving Pennsylvania.

Finally, Jordan reached "The Pass", that old field on the outskirts of Master Gilmore's plantation. The coded signals and songs had already gotten out to those who wanted to leave. Meeting him at the river were both strangers and a few that he knew. Some did not want to be led by such a young man. Jordan understood and did not argue. It was their decision on who would lead them to freedom.

In the crowd was also the Preacher; it was finally time for him to leave. Master was getting a little suspicious of his church services, so he was heading north. Then Jordan saw the face he longed to see. Siri stepped forward to greet him.

She carried with her a small bundle and presented the package to Jordan. "This is your son, Jordan; his name is James. Now, because of his father, he will never know slavery or ever see the plantation. Thank you for coming back for us."

"Baby I have missed you so much. I tried to get back sooner, but I couldn't. I wanted to see you and my son so much. I have something for you, too. It isn't much, but it has kept me going for all of these months. It's a stone I found and carried with me, thinking of you. I found it here in The Pass a long time ago, and it always makes me think of you. This is for you, baby!"

Jordan took James in his arms and smiled at Siri. With his son in his arms, Jordan reached out to Siri to hold her hand and give her his gift. However, there was not enough time for a conversation. Jordan had noticed many extra patrols out that night; Master was on to something, and they had to hurry. He glanced around to see if anyone else wanted to go. As he looked around, Siri placed her arm on his. "Too-Hi is not coming, Jordan. Master made him one of the slave drivers and he thinks that is his ticket to freedom. His job is to keep us on the plantation and report to Master anything that we do. He is not going to freedom Jordan. He does not want freedom, for you or himself."

As they stood there talking about Too-Hi, a shot rang out in the dark. Jordan fell to the ground. His son fell with him and landed on his chest. Jordan had been shot!

As Jordan lay dying in that old field, the Preacher cradled him in his arms. "God bless you, son, for what you tried to do. To give your life for a friend is the greatest of gifts." Jordan looked up at the Preacher as his face faded away into nothing. He felt the warmth of his own blood again, and it was comforting. Jordan was tired, although he was not ready to die. He had so much to live for, so much to learn. He was leaving his woman and his child again, and that pained him. However, this time, he was dying to make them free; he died giving his son a better life. For the first time he truly understood, in his own way and by his own actions, what a man really is. A real man does not seek to impede the freedom of others or rob them of their freedom; a real man is one who works to be free and then leads the way so that others might be free. This is what his uncle, his probation officer, the preachers and the abolitionists were trying to tell him. This was what he was brought to the slave South to learn. Jordan just wished he would have been around to teach these lessons to his son.

As a deep sleep seemed to come over Jordan and the blood pooled around his body, he, with his last thought, prayed for God to have mercy and somehow allow him and his family to live so that he could point the way to freedom for his son and as many others as he could.

CHAPTER THIRTEEN
FREE AT LAST, FREE AT LAST!

Post trauma: 2007

"Jordan, are you awake? Jordan, wake up son." It was the voice of an old friend. He could hear Reverend Obedi, but was still dizzy from the wound. He opened his eyes to see Reverend Obedi from his mother's church. He was sitting in the hospital room over his bed. HE WAS BACK! It was 2007, and he was back.

"Yes, Pastor I am here." It was the first time he had addressed the Reverend as Pastor. It was a sign of respect and he knew it. He had avoided it for that very reason. It was also the very reason he was using it now. "Have I been gone long, Pastor?"

"No, Jordan; you had surgery for the wound, but it has only been one day. How do you feel?"

"One day? It's only been one day? It seems like it has been a lifetime!" Jordan could not believe his fortune; he had made it back home. He looked around the room to make sure. This was a hospital room in 2007. He saw the tubes running into his arm, heard the traffic outside the window, and there on the wall…a television set! Jordan had found freedom; he was back.

"I feel like a free man, sir!" Jordan exclaimed. "I have so much to tell so many people, Pastor. I want to warn them about slavery and tell them about freedom. I need to find a way to live up to the sacrifices of others before me. I want to prepare for the future, Pastor. I want to serve. Tell me sir, how do I serve?"

"Slow down young man; you have been through a lot, and the first thing you need to do is rest."

"No sir, I do not need rest, I need to free people seeking to escape. Where is my mother sir?"

"She and Iris were here all night. Once they said you would recover, I encouraged them to go home and get some rest. They should be back any minute now. Now I will encourage you to get some rest son."

"I do not mean to be insistent Preacher, but I do not need rest as much as I need to see my mother and my girlfriend. But please, answer me sir, how do I serve my people?"

"I do not know what you are asking me son. You have been through a lot and still have a lot to attend to before you are finished. However, if you want to know about service, let me tell you.

"You cannot serve anyone without serving your self first. You cannot serve yourself without serving your family first. Too many serve just for the purpose of serving. They only serve their own egos; they like to say that they have helped the poor and underprivileged. They feel that they are superior, but they feel justified because they are nice. On the other hand, some serve because they employ the psychology of keeping a potential competitor undereducated, unmotivated, poor, and angry. If they accept this 'help' being offered, for generations they will judge their success on how many failed programs others are given to them in service.

"Both have their reasoning and are a great study in human development. However, you do not have to give in to the history, reasoning, or personal experiences that come your way. Serving the true need is the mindset of true service. Getting to the need!"

Jordan interrupted, "That is why you did not mind serving a poor community that could never reward you financially?"

"Exactly, Jordan. What poor people need is money with little or no debt! What people stricken by famine need is food! They have a crisis and they need immediate relief. They need food, water, medical attention, police and fire services, or other comforts. They need true service. Not committees, not budgets, but SERVICE! Sometimes our politics and our greed get in the way of serving the actual need. But furthermore, after the famine, what are you doing? Why have they been hungry for generations? What can be done about that? That is real service."

Jordan wanted to understand, but his head was still ringing a little. He knew he had to spend to more time with the pastor when his head cleared. It was the first time he was happy at the attention Reverend Obedi was giving his mother. He knew Pastor would be around the house a lot more, and they would be able to talk.

The pastor was on a roll now. He had been waiting a long time to direct this young man's life. He only prayed that this was not a momentary interest out of fear of going to jail. He would continue the conversation and hope Jordan absorbed most of it. "If you serve the need, you will spend far more time increasing your personal success using the lessons you have learned in life. Just because you did not see me working, that did not mean I was just serving. I have a family of sisters, brothers and cousins to take care of, and I intend to do just that. So, I went into a business that allowed me to spend time serving and let the business serve my family. This way, I have built a very successful career and at the same time served this community.

"Pastor, how can I take care of my family and serve the community? Will those goals be in conflict with each other?"

"You need to address the charity needs of your community with a balanced commitment to your family and yourself. As your personal success increases, the more capable you become to serve the true needs of the community. However, your driving force should be to take care of your family and yourself. If you get more satisfaction from giving your direct time in hands on service to the poor than to the success of your family, your family will be poor.

"If you spend more time serving the community instead of serving your family, you will not have the time to put into your personal success. Your family suffers, and your ability to truly help the community suffers. However, your self-esteem is still intact because you are now "serving the community" by volunteering at the "Community Hope Chest for the Hopeless." However, you could have been the donor that built the library and research center to get to the real root of the problem. GET TO THE ROOT!

"What is the real need, Pastor?

"On the immediate measure, they need food in their mouths, but on the cultural, community level they need to change some things."

"Preacher," Jordan interrupted, "I am a third generation poor person. It is all I know; how can you help someone like me?"

"If you are in the third generation living in or near poverty, YOU ARE DOING SOMETHING WRONG! Pay attention; it is not "the system" that is the problem; it is the decisions. Decisions your mother made, your grandfather made, and even your great-grandfather. Those decisions resulted in habits, behaviors, and decision-making skills, which became your 'culture'. If this is true, you must to face "the truth, right between their lies!" You have to admit to having a "poverty based culture." While you are not responsible for the truth, you are responsible for what you do with the truth. Truth is your friend; a harsh friend at times, but a friend indeed. If 'the truth will make you free," then freedom fighters must always seek the truth.

"You are lying in this hospital bed solely because of a decision you made; no one else. Your decisions will always get you where you need to be. Just make the right decisions. The truth is just a useless old wives' tale if it does not make you free.

"Change your behavior and you will change your culture. Change can be positive or negative, but the truth remains, change your behavior and you will change your culture. Does your honest analysis of your family culture show a culture based upon poverty or near poverty? Then change your behavior and your learned responses to life. Since all of us are affected in various ways by our history and the history of the community around us, if we change, it will change."

"But Pastor, really! How can I change others around me if they are affected so much by their history, culture, and traditions? Even if I do not want their values, I am still living among them."

"If you live in a region that serves an industry of low wages, it does not automatically mean that you are destined to work in that industry for those wages. If you stay there and hang out with the sons and daughters of the community, getting a job in that industry will become one of your goals in life. You have just made a series of decisions that will lead to living in the area you dislike. It will lead to doing the things you least like to do with people whom you share few values. The truth, however, will allow choices. Good or bad, negative or positive. If you live on a farm and stay in the area, you will be more likely to become a farmer or work in that industry. If you do not want to live in that culture, you must leave the farm; it will not leave you."

"How can I find the pathway to success? How do I know which way is north?" Jordan asked the reverend. Reverend Obedi thought that it was a strange set of questions, but he was beginning to understand. Jordan felt trapped in a circle of decisions outside of his control. Jordan was looking for someone or a philosophy to follow to find freedom. At the same time Jordan wanted to be sure, he was not leading others astray.

"If you want success and freedom, look at the habits and traditions you keep. If you want a change in your lifestyle, you must change your life. It does not matter what kind of change you want. Whether you "turn it over to Jesus" or "become one with nature," you will have to make some changes in your life before you get a change of lifestyles."

Jordan was still a little confused, but recognized that the pastor would answer all of his questions honestly. He felt like it was time to get some things off his chest and clear up some real serious questions about life. The one thing Jordan did not want to do was fall into the trap of following failed lifestyles. "I wanted to be a businessman, but the only businessmen I saw were pimps, drug dealers and gangs. So I tried them all." All the men getting respect were those destroying the neighborhood. I became what I saw and it became me. How can I change?

Reverend Obedi looked at Jordan and said, "Think it, or believe it? If one day you suddenly 'think you can' and you do nothing else, it was only a thought. If you believe you can and need to do a particular thing, you will make plans today that will bring your belief to fruition. No belief, no action; no action no success. If you need to enough, you will. If the 'why' is big enough, the 'how' will not matter. Jordan, you just did not really believe you had any other possibilities so you never tried anything else."

"Many people go through life making decisions, or in most cases, non-decisions, based upon the possibilities available. Think about it: almost everything is possible, but you will only follow the positive possibilities. It is possible to win the lottery, so you play every weekend because, 'you never know'. Well, it is also possible to lose every weekend, yet it never seems to stop you from playing. Why is that? Because the probability of winning the lottery is very low, therefore, most of us will not spend every paycheck on tickets. It is the probabilities in life that keep us in check."

"But" Jordan spoke up, still faint but anxious to learn more. "We have people in the hood making money off basketball, gambling and many schemes they can come up with. They make it on luck. Will that work?"

"We would rather rely upon 'luck' than thinking it out, as if something about our strong personalities or the relationship we have with our inner consciousness will have some profound effect on matter? However, a reality check will demonstrate that most success around us was made by people that did certain things a certain way for a certain period of time. The possibility of us achieving similar success is increased by following the same patterns of these leaders. However, our human egos get in the way and many of us would rather spend years trying it 'our way' instead of building your business with people whom have shown their probabilities. We hang on to every dedicated, incompetent associate because of the possibility that they may change. If you have to wait until someone grows in to his or her position, you will have to wait before you can make a decision. What do you want in your business; employees that are learning the business or those actually doing business? Make decisions and get busy.

"'Haste makes waste' does not mean stop moving. It means slow down and make rational decisions based upon probabilities, not just possibilities. It's about taking a good analysis from past evidence, and then aggressively going ahead to success.

"Pastor, I have seen slavery and I have seen freedom. I just want freedom for myself and for everyone around me. I understand that not everyone will want freedom, but I will only be around those who do want it. I know you have tried to help me and guide me, and I did not want any of it. I still may not take all of your advice, but I know you are trying to guide me over things you have experienced. I appreciate your wisdom. But I still do not know how to think like a free person; how do I do that?"

"Stop thinking about it and start doing it. Fear of failure brings about fear of starting, and that is failure. Failure is not your enemy, procrastination is. We spend a great deal of time getting ready to get ready, and we never get started."

Jordan knew that Reverend Obedi was a pastor and wanted to talk about God, and he did have some questions about what he had just experienced. "I want to learn a lot about God, but do not know where to start. Can you help me understand why God gives some people second chances and others he does not? Why am I still here and my friend died last weekend on the corner doing the same things I was doing? What is it about manhood that you can teach a fourteen year old boy?"

Reverend Obedi had seen this before. Something happens near death that creates a hunger for life. A life changing experience breeds more vigor for like experiences. He was witnessing it here. He would take the opportunity to share with this young man about manhood.

"Manhood should be celebrated! It was created and ordained by God! The office of manhood was established and sanctioned by God. Men of God should show honor and pride in their manhood.

"I know that male honor and pride are not popular traits in today's world. I hear women criticizing and some men apologizing for 'male pride' or 'male egos', etc. Well, I am male, so if I have an ego, it will be a male ego and if I am to have any pride at all, it will surely be male pride. I make no apologies! I do not have to become less of a man so my wife can become more of a woman.

"How often do we stop ourselves from beginning? We talk ourselves out of it because of predetermined ideas and magical thinking. Some people think their skin color is a barrier to success in America, and they will give you a number of valid reasons for believing it. They will cite past discrimination, legal barriers, and social struggles to validate that the pigmentation of their skin is a strong barrier to overcome. This fear could keep them from the competitive structure, which prepares them to succeed. One may not go to school because of the fear of skin color barriers. 'Why try to get a job, the skin color barrier will stop me.' However, skin color, like all other external and internal obstacles, has only a limited effect on you."

"But Pastor, there are people who will hate you based upon your skin color and they will try to keep you down. I know not all White people are bad, but some are very bad. How do we manage to get around them?"

"Let us examine that person who is convinced that the color of his skin has become an overwhelming barrier to his success. Let us pretend that his skin color disappeared tomorrow. He now has the same pigmentation of the majority of Americans. Are we saying that all other Americans would now support him in his efforts to compete in America? In other words, when he goes for that job interview, competing against people with the same skin pigmentation, will he find them supportive? Will the other job seekers encourage him in their application? Will they give him a chance for the same job? Of course not!

"If you entered a business looking for a sales position and see only women working there, and you are a man, will you give up? Would you say, "They would never give a sales position to a man; they only want women here?" If you were crippled, do you think those walking would not buy a car from you? There will always be differences among us. Every job sought, every sales presentation is a competition against someone else. There will always be someone wanting that job or that sale. They would rather you talk yourself out of it so they can win. It does not matter if you use your skin color, gender, age, or accent as an excuse; if you can talk yourself out of the sale, they win.

"So he suffered without because he doubted himself? The suffering was self inflicted?" Jordan asked, amazed at the revelation. He knew that this reference to self-inflicted suffering went much deeper than the current example Reverend Obedi was using, so he wanted to learn more.

"Yeah, but people are telling you to save for a rainy day and not to place all of your eggs in one basket, so how do you know when to spend?

"Every plan must include a list of sacrifices. If you do not know what you will sacrifice, you do not know what you want. When you were an infant, you could play with all of the other boys and girls in the sand lot. Your only problems were who would share their toys with you. However, every child had most things in common and sand in their diapers.

"A few years later, you get a bike and your best friend from the sand lot gets skates. You and your best friend can still play together with the bike and skates, but there are some differences. You may find more friends with bikes and play with them, but you still keep your friend with the skates. As you get a little older, you get a car and your best friend from the sand lot gets a motorcycle. You can still meet your friend at dances and ball games, but your friendship starts to pull apart because he has more motorcycle friends and you have car friends.

"Now towards the end of high school, you decide you want to go to medical school, and your best friend from the sand lot wants to be a rock star. While you need to go to the library at night, he wants to go to the clubs to meet band managers and agents. You seldom see each other and eventually lose contact.

"What happened? Why did you and your friend grow apart? It happened because as your interests changed you had to change your friends and associates. You had to surround yourself with people of similar goals. You had to acquaint yourself with those that would encourage you and work with you.

"Your rock star friend would not understand why you could not come with him to auditions when you needed to study and keep your grades up. However, your other premedical students would. Therefore, you change your friends and sacrifice your social life for your goals and plans.

"So if I stop gang banging, I probably won't still hang out with my boys? That makes sense, but who becomes my friends, the cops, rival gang members?"

"If you plan to be successful, you must associate with other people who have the same drive and goals. It does not matter if it is a marriage, career, or religion, you must associate with winners if you plan to be one.

"As soon as you make that decision, your sand lot friends will not understand. They will accuse you of changing and even selling out to some mythical code of sand lot friends. If you succumb to this pressure, you will lose. If you let others dictate your goals, ambitions, standards, or level of success you will lose. Success takes sacrifice and change. If you will not sacrifice and are unwilling to change, you will always be the baby in the sand lot needing someone to change you.

"I am a Christian minister; I believe the Bible is the word of God. I can only tell you about that belief. I will not tell you that this is one belief equal to many others, just to make you feel good. When I made that decision I lost many friends, but the more strongly I stood on that decision, the stronger the friends I made. It is the same with you. When you decided to join the gang you lost many friends, but you and your gang members developed a closer bond the more you believed in the gangs. I am saying that as you mature you are more willing to change and lose those friends that will not change with you. You are not a child any longer, you are a man; you will have to do some leading with your following.

Jordan looked at the preacher for a moment before he spoke. "You are correct I am not a boy any longer. But why do men seem to have no respect for women? I noticed how hard we try to keep them down and seem to take pleasure in their misery. Why don't we protect the women in our families? Why don't we protect what is ours preacher?"

"Well Jordan, I am a preacher so let me preach a little. The work 'keep' in Hebrew is 'shamar'; it means to put a hedge about, to preserve, to keep from all intruders. God placed man in the Garden of Eden to protect it and to keep it from all intruders. Man's position in the garden was that of the ruler. It was his kingdom. God would not have given him a kingdom to protect against all intruders if man was not capable of defending it against all intruders, including Satan!

"God looked at man and determined that for our own good he would create Eve. It is not good for man to be alone; God has determined that. Today we can see that married men live longer and healthier lives than single men because God has said it is not good for man to be alone. We do not know if it is good for woman to be alone, but truly, man needs female companionship in his life.

"God's solution to man's problem was to take one rib, not two or three ribs to make us two or three women, but one rib. We can find all we could ever want in a female, in one woman. However, there is something else special about her creation that most men do not understand. Woman's creation was much different from the creation of Adam. With the creation of Adam, God put his hand into the dust, and formed man. Eve was not made from the dirt; she was created from the very part of a man that protects his heart. If modern man could understand this, perhaps he would treat his woman with more respect."

"One woman! I did not think that was possible. To have only one woman with all the fine honeys around seemed wasteful to me. But now I understand; that was selfish. Someone once told me that selfishness brings slavery. If I do not have one woman I cannot have one family, and subsequently I cannot have a strong community. The only one to benefit is Master."

"Jordan, it is time for men to stand up and fulfill our purpose to protect our kingdoms, and keep them from all intruders. It takes a real man to acknowledge his kingship. Real men should take control over what God has given them. What would happen if men decided there would be no more drugs sold illegally in their neighborhoods? What would happen if men decided that we would not allow our mothers, sisters, or daughters to be sold on the streets of our kingdom? What would happen if men decided to become examples to their sons, examples of true manhood, by being responsible for their children? We would show our sons how a real man treats a woman when he is in love with her; marriage and devotion. What would happen if men decided their daughters would be raised to know how to choose the father of their own children?

"Men are responsible for all of these problems. We direct and profit from the drug trade, not women. We bring it in, sell it on the streets, and protect it. Men place women to work on the streets and profit from them. If men decided it was over, then it would be over. It is time for the real men of God to stand up as David did and take God at his word. Gather up your stones and your slings real men; the problems are gigantic, and Goliath is laughing at us as he rampages over our kingdom.

"Men have to be determined to be what God created them to be. We must support each other in brotherhood and in honor. Men must realize that we cannot continue to have children we don't raise ourselves. It's not enough to just support financially; we have to be there in the home to assure proper protection and attention. For some of us, however, it is already too late for that. The problem begins when men fail to pick women qualified to be the mothers of their children and so then find it impossible to be in the home. Let us make better decisions.

"When we raise our children, we are not raising kids; we are raising someone's father, mother, boss, etc. We are raising adults, and it takes both parents. No more having women in our kingdoms that we aren't going to grow old with, protect, and cherish as God's gifts to us. No more blaming women for our unwillingness to do God's will.

"It is time we choose women that are worthy to become our queens and the mothers of our children. It is time we honor God by doing his will and accepting our role in his creation. The reason the earth is in the shape it is in can be put in very simple terms. Man left God, Man left his family, his family fell apart, and therefore Man's kingdom fell. If men stood up for God, God would provide the strength and we would conquer our enemies. If we stand up and act in faith, God will give us strength to carry the load, give us compassion to comfort our own. He will give us abundant love to cherish his gifts to us.

"I got to learn more about those people and I will," Jordan replied. "You are right; we must stand for honor or our women will be dishonored and we will be dishonored. I thought you Christians were weak men, but now I see how strong you really are. You have to live in a city with lost people, people who hate you because your very presence convicts them of sin. You have to maintain your standards in the face of a society wanting the opposite. I want to join your gang. I want your colors, and I want to stand with you. We left God and went into slavery; if we return to God we will leave slavery."

CHAPTER FOURTEEN
DIAMONDS OVERCOME!

Just as Jordan was about to speak, the door opened and his probation officer stepped in. Jordan used to hate this guy. This man was always on his case, placing restrictions on him. Looking at Mr. Douglass now, he seemed like a leader trying to keep things from getting worse for him. "Officer Douglass, I guess I am really in trouble, huh?"

"Yes, Jordan; you are really in trouble."

"Armed robbery with a gun and no telling what else. I believe it was part of a drug conspiracy that you and Jay-Low were setting up. You guys wanted to corner the market in the hood. That is racketeering, and that means hard time, even for someone your age."

"I understand officer, and I am ready for it. Just tell me how my mother and Iris are doing. Did they get hurt?"

"No, you were lucky; they did not. If anyone else had gotten hurt, that would have meant more charges against you. But you have another problem Jordan. Jay-Low is trying to turn state's witness against you. He says that the whole idea was dreamed up by you and your uncle. He is willing to testify against you and your uncle in court. He will say that your uncle strong armed him into it and forced him to help."

"But that is not true, officer." Jordan was disgusted that he ever trusted Jay-Low.

"He has witnesses saying they saw Thomas push his head through a car window when he refused to cooperate. He said the gun came from you, the cocaine came from you, and the protection came from Thomas. What do you say, Jordan?"

"There is nothing I can say, officer. The truth will come out, but there is nothing that you or I can do about it right now. Right now, I am free! Right now, I am glad to be alive. If that devil wants to blame me for his problems, let him. I am free, and so are my mother and my woman."

"Are you willing to talk to the police about the robbery? Are you willing to talk to us about the gangs in the neighborhood?" The probation officer was looking at Jordan with an intensive stare. Reverend Obedi spoke up.

"Officer, is it fair to question this young man right out of surgery? He is still under medication and not in his complete mind. Can we wait until he is out of the hospital?"

"Is that what you want, son? Do you want an attorney? Do you want protection from the system you have never joined? I can give you protection if that is what you want."

Jordan looked at both of them and said, "What I want is the truth. That is all care about. If I have learned anything, I have learned to follow leadership. Officer, I will help you with this case as much as I can, but this man here is my pastor. My pastor thinks I should not speak with you until I am well; I will take his advice."

"So, you do not have any comments on your partner spilling his guts on you and your uncle? If we get a case from him, we will not need you to talk. Your pastor may be right, and maybe you should not talk to us. You are only fourteen and your mother is not here. But understand that your uncle is not fourteen, and he is who we really want if he is involved."

"With or without a lawyer, you will get the truth from me. If you use my family to get me to cooperate, you still will get nothing more than the truth. If it is the truth you are looking for, then we will all find it. Let's go seek the truth wherever it leads."

Officer Douglass looked at Jordan for a long time. This young man was very confident, almost cocky. Did he have more information that they thought? Jordan was smart; everyone at the station knew that. They had tried for years to get into his head. However, this was a serious charge, and yet he seemed very calm. Douglass was wondering.

"You know, don't you?" Officer Douglass asked Jordan.

"Know what?"

"Don't get smart with me. You must know that we had a bug on Jay-Low for weeks. That is why you are so cocky."

"What do you mean, officer?" asked the preacher?

"I mean, Jordan here is claiming the truth will be good for him because he knows we have a recording of all the conversations they have had. We know it was Jay-Low and we know his uncle is not involved. We do have video of Thomas slamming the kid's head through a car window, and we probably should talk to him about it. However, since it was Jay-Low's car, we are not that interested. I was just trying to get more cooperation out of you by letting you know what kind of partner you had."

"I know nothing about your surveillance, officer, but I do know the truth will come out. I did not mean because of a video; I meant because it was right. It stops here; the lies, self-hatred, and the depression stops here. No more! Let us get this case over with so I can lead others to freedom!

Jordan used to really hate his probation officer. Here was another Black man working for the White man to keep him down. Now he understood that he was the problem to the Black community, and that the probation officer was trying to protect the community from Jordan and his friends. He was the real hero and Jordan was the villain. How could he change now? What steps could he take to explain to people what he had learned? Would they believe him? Would they say he was just dreaming?

He felt his arms to see if the chains left marks there. No, they had not! There were no marks on his body, but there were many on his mind. He needed to speak with someone that had already taken the journey. He looked at the probation officer and wondered if he had been where Jordan had been, and if he would teach him how to get to freedom.

"Officer, what happened to you to get your mind free?"

Officer Douglass did not understand what he was asking him. His confusion must have shown up on his face because Jordan clarified what he meant. "We live under a plantation mind set, officer. We are a product of our own thinking. If we do not change our way of thinking, then we cannot change the way we are. I know you grew up near the same place I live. You must have been under the pressure of the same plantation way of thinking that I now suffer from. How did you fight it?"

Whoa! What a question. This was not just some young punk trying to get an edge before court. This young man was thinking about something. He had never heard it put that way. 'The Plantation Mentality' was what he had fled. That was the reason he left the hood himself. That was the reason he became a cop; to lead people to freedom.

"As a young man, I began the journey off the plantation and I found the hardest thing was to begin. Just to think of myself as being on a plantation was insulting. I had to admit how wrong I was about myself and about my possibilities. I had to face the fact that so many people I had a great deal of respect for had misled me. That is the only way a con man can succeed; getting you to respect him. The journey was delayed as I took time trying to convince friends and associates they were going in the wrong direction.

"Whether the White man hated me or not, it did not matter. If he conspired against me, fine. What mattered was the question of what I could do with what I could control. I had schoolbooks in my hand and I could read. I controlled that. I could go to school and hear the lectures; I had control of that. The White man could not keep me from preparing myself to compete against him; I controlled that. I knew that leaving the plantation required studying the path to freedom. Therefore, I went to school, studied, read, and attended the lectures. I prepared myself for the competition ahead. I knew that my greatest weapon was the truth.

"We may have no control over drug smuggling from Columbia or gunrunning. However, can we control our children and community. Where are the militants of the 1960s marching against the gang members instead of the "White corporate structure?" Where is the call for "burn, baby burn" in front of the crack house? Where are the strong Black men confronting the pimp, demanding he free those women caught in his trap? The whole community will march on the police station the minute some Black person is slightly misused by the police; however, no one will shout disapproval when the system abuses your own child in school. Let them keep giving out condoms, graduating illiterate children, and teaching self-hate instead of self-motivation.

"To try to change others before they are willing to change themselves is a very frustrating and draining task. I had to stop arguing and debating with them because we were speaking two different languages and I was getting nowhere. I was analyzing with logic; they were reacting with emotions. I had to begin associating with people that would feed me knowledge and clarity.

"The results were amazing to watch. You find yourself turning from those you thought were your friends toward those you thought were your enemies. It will not take long to realize how wrong you had been and why you were led to think that way, however. In order for Master to keep control over the plantation, we must be full of fear and suspicion of others. The slaves use to say, 'We gone get dim damn Yankees' and go off to fight against their own freedom. All of this, 'Don't trust the White man, the rich, those capitalists and corporations' is the same as 'dim damn Yankees'; just a mirage to keep you out in the fields, working to maintain your own slavery.

"I did not change; I still had a passionate desire to help my community. America changed, and I wanted to participate and not be passed over. It takes courage to fight for one's freedom; it takes more than courage to take the advantage of that freedom. Once I understood the real obstacles of Black Americans to control the gangs, drugs, teen pregnancies, and other curses on our community, I began to speak out. My newspaper articles, public speeches, radio programs, and television appearances all came from a desire to sound an alarm.

"I could have stayed quiet and enjoyed my life and successful career. However, I was still a warrior, and the battle was not over. I was still a messenger, and the message had not been fully delivered. My message is clear; 'It's Okay To Leave the Plantation.'"

Jordan now understood, he was back and he had to go to freedom.

"Thanks, officer. See you in court, sir!"

CHAPTER FIFTEEN
JORDAN FINDS, "THE PASS!"

As Officer Douglass and Reverend Obedi left Jordan's room, his family arrived. Lynette had stopped by to pick up Iris, and they brought Uncle Thomas with them. They entered the room and no one spoke. They had a hard night and were still tired. They expected Jordan to be groggy and the doctor and asked them not to say long. However, Jordan was not at all groggy; he was excited.

He knew that no one else knew what he had gone through, but it was real. He could still feel the whip, and his back still hurt from pulling cotton. He could still see the fear on Iris' face; he could still hear her scream. He never wanted to see her or see them that way again. It was real for him, but only for him. He knew no one would believe where he had been, and he would not try to convince them. It had to be his memory and his reality.

"Hi, mama; hello, baby." Jordan tried to reassure them with a smile and a wave.

"You okay, baby?" Lynette came to his bedside and sat on the mattress. She wanted to know if he was all right and if his head hurt.

Jordan only wanted to know if they were okay and if they were worried. Iris told him how the police came and had taken him away. He was mumbling something in the back of the ambulance about calling 911 and other hysterical things. Even when he came out of surgery, he was talking to himself. Lynette thought he was reliving the shooting because he kept talking about escaping and getting away.

Jordan only laid there and smiled. He was so happy to see the women in his life. So happy that they were free. How could he had ever called Iris a Wench or a ho? There were no Black Wenches or hoes, only Black ladies. He would remember that; only Black ladies.

If he was going to be a Black man, he had to be raised by a Black lady. If he was going to be a man, he had to hang around men. If he was going to be a king in his household, he had to develop a relationship with a queen.

They were all in that room. His whole life and livelihood was there, in the room, together. They were all there, everyone who was important to him. His example of manhood, his example of a friend, and the mother of his children. He knew it was going to be a long time before marriage, but he knew who the mother of his child was.

He also knew who she was not. She was not a whore, wench, chicken head, nor community property. She would be a lady; his lady. That meant he had to become a man; a real one. But how? He had to follow a real man. Uncle Thomas was such a man, and he had been trying to direct his life for some time.

He looked up at his mother and wanted to tell her all of this, but he knew it was not the time. She was still getting over the fact that her son had been shot and had just come out of surgery. She could not be told that he had dreams of the past and all that. No, he would keep it to himself. If did not matter if anyone believed him anyway. He believed, and only he could act.

As they visited with him and as he and answered the normal questions about pain and discomfort, he remembered the baby Iris was carrying. He knew no one else knew yet. What a great time to announce the addition to the family. Right after nearly losing one, they now can gain one.

"Iris, sweetheart, can you come over here for a minute?" Jordan motioned to her.

"Yes, Jordan; how are you feeling?"

"Mama, Uncle Thomas, I've got something to say." He took Iris' hand and held it.

He looked her in the eyes as he told them. "Iris is having my baby. She is going to have a boy, and his name is James."

"What? Iris, is this true?" Lynette asked.

"Well most of it. I am pregnant, but how do you know it's a boy, and where did you get the name James?"

"It is a boy and you told me his name. It is a long story, sweetheart, but we will have a long time to talk about it. Iris, I am so sorry for treating you so bad. It wasn't fair, and you didn't deserve it. You deserve a real man that is going somewhere, and if I can't be him, I need to get out of his way.

"Mama, you have shown me what unconditional love is and I have shown you what hatred is. I will now try to out-love you. I want you to teach me love and affection so I can one day win a woman like Iris."

"Wait a minute son; this is just too much for me. First, you are shot, and then arrested, then surgery, all in the same day. Now you are telling me that I am going to be a grandmother before I am thirty years old? Oh, Lord, help me."

"Sorry, mama; you can only be grandparent if the boy has a father. His father cannot spend anymore time in jail; I have to spend time passing on the world to my son."

"Now back up Jordan; who told you his name was going to be James?" Iris said laughing. "James is my father's name, and you remember he died when I was three, so I have secretly wanted to name this child after him. But what if it's a girl, Jordan?"

"Iris, believe me, I have seen my son and I have held him in my arms. He is strong, and beautiful, and he looks like you. He has ten toes and ten fingers, and his name is James."

It was time for them to leave and let Jordan rest. As Uncle Thomas and Lynette left, Iris paused at the door. She told them to wait for her; she wanted to say goodbye to Jordan alone. Iris closed the door behind her and walked over to Jordan's bed.

"Babe, I am so grateful you made it. We have a lot ahead of us, but we can make it." Jordan was still excited about seeing her and could not believe what he had just gone through. "Iris, I wish I could tell you all I have just experienced, but no one will believe me and I don't want to scare you."

"I feel the same way, Jordan. I had a pretty interesting night last night myself. After seeing you shot and taken away to the hospital, and staying here with your mother while you went through surgery, I could not sleep last night, and had a terrible dream. Oh, by the way, before I forget, is this yours?" She held open her hand to show Jordan the rough white stone!

"What? Where did you get that? I thought I had lost it!" Jordan could not believe what he was seeing. Iris had the stone he had found and wanted to give to her.

"You don't remember, Jordan? You gave it to me while you lay in the field. You took my hand and squeezed it tight, and did not let go until you passed out. You were mumbling about some crazy things like escaping and freedom, but you never let go of my hand. When they lifted you up, your grip loosened, and you were pulled away from me. That is when I noticed the stone in my hand. It was the most beautiful thing I had ever seen. If you had not pulled through, I would have considered it the last thing you had given me. Now we can keep it together."

"Boy!" Jordan thought, that old rough stone had gone through a lot, and so had they.

Jordan went back to his mother's home to recover. His injuries were not life threatening and he was about ready to go to court. His uncle stopped by every day to check on him. With his mother working, he needed help fixing food and getting around. Jordan was glad his uncle came around. It gave them plenty of private time to discuss the "dream" everyone thought he had. He really needed some answers on what he was thinking. "Uncle, tell me about this 'society' that old Master talks about. How does it really work?"

"Have a seat and listen carefully. Society is concentrated on getting from the system, not changing the system. It is all good and it is all bad. It works for some and not for others. The power in society is only interested in keeping things the same. That is how they came to power. If things change, those in power may lose their power. This is why poor neighborhoods stay poor and rich neighborhoods stay rich. If the power elites in those societies came to power serving a certain type if people, they can only stay in power by continuing to serve that population. In other words, if a poor community becomes rich, do you think they will continue to vote for the same politicians? Do you think they will demand a change in the schools? How about street sweeping services and the attitudes of the police? These changes are changes no one at City Hall wants. It's not personal, it's just personal."

Jordan had seen that; no one would change unless the change produced a benefit to them. That is why all changes are called, "revolutionary" changes. Those in power will always seek to keep power. Boy, did he understand this. It is never personal; it is just personal; that meant they were just trying to take care of their own families. Why would Jordan or anybody else think someone would sacrifice their own family to benefit only your personal family? Life just was not like that.

"There is something else about success," Uncle Thomas continued. "It tends to be cultural. There is a culture of poverty and a culture of prosperity. If you identified it as a culture, it would be easier to recognize. However, if we identify this as a racial, economic, or religious culture, others that do not belong to the same groupings will find it harder to embrace the culture of success."

Jordan thought he understood what Uncle Thomas was saying. "You mean like the rap industry. It makes millions of dollars for its artists and producers. Most of the language is not Standard English, but slang. Within the industry, you can achieve some high level of success and still not master the English language. However, the rap stars speak perfect English when it comes time to sign record deals or negotiate with a tennis shoe company. They may speak in "Rap-ese" at the award ceremonies, but catch them talking to their lawyers. It becomes a frank, plain discourse in the strictest English language."

Jordan looked at his Uncle with pride; there was still time for a revolution or a civil war. There was still time for the slave to take control of his world and free himself. It was not too late, and for that, Jordan was grateful. "The train is leaving for freedom; only those who wish to be free are invited. Yes, Uncle; let's go tell them."

Jordan was still in contact with many members of the gang. They did not come by because too many cops were coming by to question him, Uncle Thomas was around the house far too much, and because Jordan and Jay-Low were fighting each other in court, and nobody wanted to get in the middle. The people who Jordan still spoke to saw a difference in him, however. One old friend walked up to him and said, "What's up, dog?" He received a thirty-minute lecture on not being a dog and his woman not being a wench. "Man," the friend thought, "what has happened to this guy?"

Jordan went to court two months after his robbery. He testified against Jay-Low, and it was powerful. What made Jordan's testimony so believable was that it was just as damming to his own case as it was to Jay-Low's. When word got out of what Jay-Low was trying to do, people started calling him, "Stay-Low." It became a nickname that stuck.

The trial lasted two weeks. The verdict came back 'guilty', and Jordan was sentenced to juvenile hall. He got two years imprisonment and five years probation. It did not phase him; he was thinking about his girl and the baby she would have by the time he got out. After sentencing, Jordan asked his lawyer if he could walk over to her before they took him away.

Jordan walked over and hugged her. He wiped away her tears and smiled at her. "It really will be okay," he promised her. "I will leave, but I promise to return to you. I kept that promise once, and I will keep it again." She did not remember such a promise; it was probably another one of Jordan's delusions that he suffered from the gunshot.

"I can do this time; I must! However, it will have no effect on me. I will survive because I have already survived. I will be back with you, and we will be together. The probation officer, judge, and police are not my enemies; I am my own enemy. From now on, I will be my best friend."

He gave her a note; it had ten things on it. She did not understand what they were. The probation officer came over looked at it. He smiled and looked up at Jordan, and then he turned the note over to Uncle Thomas. It read:

1. If you want to change your life, you must change your life-style. If you want a change in your life-style, you must change your life.

2. If Master is the problem, he cannot be the solution

3 No one should have more confidence in you than you.

4. Wisdom comes not from the journey, but from the experiences along the way.

5. Know belief, know action; no belief, no action.

6. If you do not know what you will sacrifice, you do not know what you want.

7. If you spend all of your time looking back into the past, you may stumble into your future.

8. You cannot correct the wrongs of the past...go forward and establish the future.

9. My position in life has nothing to do with my potential for life.

10. Pay attention! It is not "the system," it is your decision.

Jordan turned and walked away with the bailiff.

Lynette and Iris had become close during all of this. They rode back from the court every day, and talked a lot about Jordan. They had started going to church together because they felt someone should be praying over him. They began to listen to a Christian radio station because they wanted to hear more positive messages.

As they got into the car Lynette had borrowed from Uncle Thomas, they wanted to comfort one another, but it did not seem necessary. Lynette was feeling guilty because she was so calm. Her oldest son had just been sentenced to jail, and she was not upset or depressed. Iris felt the same way; there was a peace instead of the restlessness she expected. They had both seen a difference in Jordan, but did not know what it meant. They had both heard the strange things he was saying and the wisdom far beyond his years. However, what did it all mean?

As they sat quietly in the car, Lynette turned on the Christian radio station. A song was playing, and they listened to it as they moved along. As it lulled on in the background, both women were lost in their own thoughts. Both were looking forward to Jordan's return. The longer the song continued the more at ease they felt.

The song was called, "Swing Low, Sweet Chariot", and it had become one of Jordan's favorites. They both began to fight back tears. They remembered how emotional Jordan would get every time he heard this and certain other Old Negro Spirituals. When they would ask him to explain why certain songs brought on certain emotions to him, he would only have one response: "Know your past and control your future." No one understood what he meant.

As the car moved along, Iris toyed with the necklace she was wearing. It was the stone Jordan had given her. She had shown it to Uncle Thomas, and he had it mounted on a chain for her. When he took it to the jeweler, he was shocked at what he found. This little cloudy white stone was not some old piece of glass worn down by the creek. It was a raw diamond in the rough. Unpolished, uncut, and unmounted, it was a nine carat, raw diamond that Jordan had found. Its value was so great that the jeweler told Uncle Thomas he should insure it and keep it locked up in a safe. When he explained it to Iris, she was stunned. She and Jordan had the key to their future in their hands, and they were in charge of their future. She had the diamond insured and usually kept it safe. But today, she wanted Jordan to see it, so she had worn it to court. It would be placed back in the safety deposit box that afternoon. Now she was lost in her thoughts, listening to the music and thinking about her future.

However, it was nice to hear that song on the way home from the courthouse; it was very comforting. The song ended as they got off the freeway near Lynette's home. The radio announcer introduced the next song.

"We owe so much to those who came before us. For their struggles and sacrifices, we celebrate their victory. From the tears and misery they endured, we gain our strength. To all who struggled and died, to all who resisted and suffered, to those who lived a life not worth living to preserve life for us... I dedicate this song; our song."

> Lift every voice and sing
> Till earth and heaven ring,
> Ring with the harmonies of Liberty;
> Let our rejoicing rise
> High as the listening skies,
> Let it resound loud as the rolling sea.
>
> Sing a song full of the faith that the dark past has taught us,
> Sing a song full of the hope that the present has brought us,
> Facing the rising sun of our new day begun
> Let us march on till victory is won.
>
> Stony the road we trod,
> Bitter the chastening rod,
> Felt in the days when hope unborn had died;
> Yet with a steady beat,
> Have not our weary feet
> Come to the place for which our fathers sighed?
>
> We have come over a way that with tears have been watered,
> We have come, treading our path through the blood of the slaughtered,
> Out from the gloomy past,
> Till now we stand at last
> Where the white gleam of our bright star is cast.
>
> God of our weary years,
> God of our silent tears,

Thou who has brought us thus far on the way;
Thou who has by Thy might
Led us into the light,
Keep us forever in the path, we pray.

Lest our feet stray from the places, Our God, where we met Thee;
Lest, our hearts drunk with the wine of the world, we forget Thee;

Shadowed beneath Thy hand,
May we forever stand.
True to our GOD,
True to our native land

THE BEGINNING!

Mason Media Company

Made in the USA
San Bernardino, CA
14 May 2014